INDISPENSABLE PARTY

BY USA TODAY BESTSELLING AUTHOR

MELISSA F. MILLER

BROWN STREET BOOKS

This book is a work of fiction. Names, characters, places, and incidents either are the product of the author's imagination or are used fictitiously. Any resemblance to actual persons, living or dead, is entirely coincidental.

Published by Brown Street Books.

For more information about the author, please visit www.melissafmiller.com.

In memory of Max,
my constant office companion
and the sweetest mutt I ever met,
and
in memory of Gustave, an occasional thorn in Max's side,
but a friendly, fluffy cat who kept me company
through law school and a dozen years that followed.

1

FOR IMMEDIATE RELEASE
Contact: Office of Communications, CDC
KILLER FLU A REALITY, RESEARCHERS CLAIM

Modified H17N10 virus transmits efficiently from human to human.

The Center for Disease Control and Prevention today announced that an international team of researchers has successfully mutated the deadly Doomsday virus, the so-called "killer flu," such that person-to-person transmission can now occur easily. The mutated influenza virus is now known as H17N10.

The CDC reports that the naturally occurring

virus resulted from the combination of three highly virulent strains that, until now, have not posed a significant risk to humans. Lead researcher Jacques Bouchard, a virologist at the Pasteur Institute (Lyon), confirmed that the NIH-funded study, which included French and American research teams, was designed to determine whether the Doomsday virus could be genetically modified to allow for airborne transmission.

"Not only has the resultant mutation proven highly transmissible, the modifications have resulted in increased virulence. Our estimates are that a global pandemic of H17N10 could infect up to 50% of the global population, or up to 3.5 billion individuals, and could result in a 20% mortality rate, killing an estimated seven hundred million infected individuals," Mr. Bouchard stated.

In an unusual move, the U.S. National Science Advisory Board for Biosecurity has forbidden the researchers from publishing their results for reasons of national security. No further details have been released.

GOVERNMENT TO STOCKPILE KILLER FLU VACCINE

WASHINGTON, D.C. (Newswire) – The government released plans to stockpile more than twenty-five million doses of an experimental vaccine against the Doomsday virus in an effort to prepare for the possibility of a deadly pandemic. The pandemic, if it were to occur, would be capable of wiping out more than twenty percent of the world population.

A spokesperson for the Department of Health and Human Services said that the government has already contracted with Serumceutical International, Inc., a pharmaceutical company, to manufacture and deliver the stockpile as early as this month. And, with flu season already underway, the government has asked Congress to fast track a bill that would appropriate money for additional doses.

With the U.S. population now exceeding 300 million people, a killer flu pandemic would shut down the economy, quarantining hundreds of millions of unvaccinated people to their homes for as long as two to three months.

In laboratory tests, the vaccine, which is reported to contain a small amount of a live, but weakened, strain of virus very similar to H17N10, provided immunity much more quickly than traditional flu vaccines. Serumceutical documents indicate full immunity can be achieved within seventy-two hours, rather than two weeks.

In response to questions about the existence of an effective antiviral, scientists said that, while research is underway, to date, no antiviral medication has proven effective against the Doomsday virus, although ViraGene Corp. is slated to release results of trials of its experimental AviEx antiviral later this month.

ViraGene Shares Gain 38% on Rumor of Antiviral Approval

BETHESDA, MD (AP) – ViraGene Corp. (VGN) shares rose on heavy trading in response to reports that the company's AviEx antiviral NDA (New Drug Application) is being considered for accelerated approval in light of positive results from human trials. The company declined to comment on the status of its NDA, citing trade secret and national defense concerns, but CEO Colton Maxwell circulated an internal email message to officers and directors of the company congratulating his team "on this victory on the front lines of defense against the very real specter of a deadly killer flu pandemic."

To date, the federal government has not publicly committed to the purchase of AviEx and is staying the course with its plans to stockpile millions of doses of a new vaccine being manufactured by Serumceutical International, Inc. (SRM).

2

Friday evening

Celia Gerig's hands shook. She removed the keys from the ignition and took a long, slow breath. She watched the snow fall and stick to the windshield of the dirty Civic.

Once her heart rate slowed, she returned the keys and tried to start the car again. The first time, the engine had whined, coughed, and then gone dead. This time, nothing happened.

She pounded a fist on the steering wheel and blinked back hot, frustrated tears. This couldn't be happening. *Not now.* She searched the parking lot, looking for anyone, one of her coworkers, head bent against the wind, hurrying to get to his or her car and make it out to the bar at Chili's before the happy hour specials ended. She saw no one.

It was after five on a Friday. Everyone was long gone, which had been the plan, after all. She'd lingered after the shift had ended, taking her time in the locker room, so she could avoid questions—about her weekend, what was in her bag, whatever. Because no matter what else she was, Celia knew she was a terrible liar.

But, now what? She couldn't exactly call and say she couldn't make the meeting. She'd just get an earful of angry blather about being prepared for emergencies, and responsibility, and a lot of other disappointed scolding that she knew she deserved. She let her head drop down to the steering wheel and sat there, deflated and helpless.

A sharp rap on the driver's side window startled her. Outside, Ben Davenport's tanned faced filled the glass. His green eyes were wide with concern under the knitted cap he'd pulled down tight to cover his balding head.

"Everything okay?" he mouthed.

It figured. Just her luck that the only person still around was her boss. The last person she wanted anywhere near her car. But she needed help. The handoff was supposed to be at eight o'clock. Even if she left right now, she'd have to speed for at least part of the drive to make it in time.

She lowered the window.

"My car won't start."

"Why don't you hop out and let me take a look at her."

"That would be great."

He stepped back so she could open the door. As she slid out of the car, her eyes shifted to her oversized purse on the passenger seat to make sure it was still zippered shut. It was.

Ben got behind the wheel and placed his briefcase next to her purse. He turned the key in the ignition, but the only sound was the *click click* of the key itself. He reached up to switch on the dome light. Nothing.

"Battery's dead," he said through the open window. He reached for his briefcase and knocked her bag to the floor.

"Oops."

He bent to pick up the purse, and Celia felt the panic rising in her throat.

"No! Leave it!"

He turned and looked up at her, a curious, confused expression on his face.

"Uh, I mean, it's fine on the floor," she said. Despite the fact that she was standing outside in the snow, sweat beaded up on her hairline.

"Suit yourself."

He exited the car and said, "I can give you a jump. Do you have cables?"

"No, there's nothing in my trunk," she said quickly. She winced. *Stupid*. Why did she volunteer that her trunk was empty? He hadn't asked.

He squinted at her, puzzled.

"Are you sure you're okay?"

She was very sure that she was not okay. She was scared, and worried, and nervous. But she swallowed and said, "I'm fine. I'm just running late, that's all. But I don't have jumper cables. What am I going to do?"

Ben gave her a kindly look and patted her on the arm. He was such a friendly old guy that Celia felt a momentary pang for what she'd done, for what she was about to do. Then she remembered what was at stake, and the pang disappeared.

"Don't you worry. I should have a set in my car. Let me check, and I'll be right back."

He walked across the lot and around to the side of the building. Moments later, he returned, driving his Buick with the Florida plates, cautious, like an old guy, like a snowbird. He eased it into the spot next to hers. He popped his trunk and walked around to get the jumper cables. He raised his hood and motioned for Celia to do the same.

She fumbled with the little arm that held the hood up while he unwound the neatly coiled cables and hooked the red clip on one end of the cables to her positive battery terminal. He stretched the cable across the parking spots and clamped the other end onto his battery. Then he connected one black clip to his negative terminal and the other end to a bolt on the Civic's engine block to ground it. He stepped back and brushed his hands, satisfied.

He returned to the Buick and started the engine. After a few moments, he raised his head and gave Celia a thumb's up signal.

"All right. Start her up," he called.

Celia got behind the wheel and offered up a silent prayer. She turned the key, and the engine roared to life. She saw Ben smile.

She said, "Thank you so much. You don't even know."

"No worries," Ben said.

The snow clinging to his knit hat was starting to melt, and it dripped on to his face when he bent to remove the cables from the two batteries. He lowered her hood and then his, holding the cables in one hand. He wound the cables into a neat bundle and started back toward his trunk, and then he stopped like he'd thought the better of it.

"Why don't you keep these until Monday? There's a chance your battery's gonna drain itself again when you get wherever you're going. That way, you won't be stuck until you get that in to get it looked at," he said.

"No, please, it'll be fine," she insisted firmly. Mainly because she had no intention of opening her trunk for him. She figured the battery would die again, but she didn't anticipate driving herself anywhere for a while. After tonight, she'd need to hole up anyway.

He searched her face and then said, "Okay, but you really ought to be prepared for something like this to happen."

She couldn't help it. She burst into loud nervous laughter. She clamped her mouth shut as he turned around from his trunk and eased the lid closed. He cocked his head at her.

"Sorry," she said. "It's not funny. It's just ... I was thinking the exact same thing is all." She smiled broadly.

He stared at her for a few seconds, then he shrugged. "Okay, then. You have a good weekend. See you on Monday."

"Goodbye, Ben," she said. Her words conveyed a finality she hadn't meant to share.

She hurried into the car and slammed the door shut. She checked the time and cursed under her breath. Then she put the car in reverse, exited the parking spot, and raced out of the lot, giving Ben a short *beep* in thanks as she passed him.

In her rearview mirror, she could see him standing there, looking after her as she pulled away.

If she had looked back when she reached the end of the drive, she'd have seen him walk over to his Buick, kill the engine, and lock his car door, then head back into the building with a thoughtful, concerned expression.

Michel Joubert held his breath as he swiped his key card to gain entrance to the lab. There was never any way to know when he would encounter one of his coworkers. After all, what they did was part science and part art. When inspiration struck during dinner, the researchers had been known to tuck their children into bed and return to their work afterward. Not to mention, some experiments took hours to run. Some people left their experiments unattended or assigned a student to watch them, but others preferred to hover over their work in progress like anxious parents.

If there was ever a time to sneak into the lab unnoticed, though, it was twelve-thirty in the morning on a Saturday. As much as the researchers loved their work, they were, after all, French. A few bottles of wine and a leisurely meal were every Frenchman's due at the end of a long week. He expected that anyone still awake was in no condition to do anything but sit in front of a roaring fire and wax philosophical in the candlelight. He hoped so, at least.

He eased the door shut and crept down the darkened hallway. His rubber-soled, leather driving moccasins made virtually no noise on the tile floor. This pleased him because the safer move would have been to wear running shoes, but he'd dismissed that as an option. His views on appropriate attire for the laboratory were well known; if he did run into someone, sneakers on his feet would be a glaring announcement that something was out of place.

He reached the end of the hall and pressed his thumb against the reader. While the machine scanned his thumbprint, he stared at the biohazard sign that he'd seen a hundred times before without really looking at it and ran through the sequence again: get in; get what he needed; get out. It would be astonishingly easy.

To the public, he imagined the laboratory's designation as a biosafety level 4 facility—the institute was the first in Europe to attain the highest level—conjured up visions of multiple levels of impregnable security designed to prevent precisely what he was about to do. That was, of course, a fiction. The strict standards and precautions in place in a level 4 facility were designed to prevent an accidental release of a dangerous biological agent and to contain such a release if one were to occur. It was as if the drafters of the rigorous standards had never entertained the notion that a person might want to waltz out the door with the Ebola virus or some smallpox tucked into his pocket.

The machine finished digesting his swirls and beeped its approval. He passed through the double doors and walked into the outer change room. Here, he hesitated. The usual procedure before entering the lab when the biological agents were not secured would be to strip naked and suit up in the underpants, shirt, pants, shoes, gloves, and personal pressure protective suit, then enter through the shower room. He would reverse this sequence when leaving the lab: take off the lab clothes; shower; dress in his street clothes; and exit the laboratory.

But he didn't have that kind of time. And, currently, the virus was secured and the laboratory decontaminated. If he ran into anyone, he could explain away his appearance by saying he needed to check his station for some misplaced item. Besides, he thought, what difference did it make? Soon enough, he'd be toting the H17N10 virus around in a soft-sided cooler, for the love of the saints.

He shrugged and left the room, opting to enter the lab through the sealed airlock instead of the decontamination shower chamber. He pressed the pad on the wall to open the first airtight door to the passageway. Once inside, he pressed an identical pad to close the door. He felt the breeze from the HEPA filters blowing on him, something he never noticed while suited up. He stepped up to the second door. After the first door had sealed shut behind him, he pressed the pad to open the door leading to the laboratory.

Once inside, he breached protocol by leaving the door open. Then he ran across the gleaming, white tile floor to the glovebox that held the vials. Inside the box, a heavy, stainless steel container, shaped like a thermos, sat alone on a shelf. He reached for it, breathing hard, and twisted the top until the seal broke.

Michel had originally planned to take the entire container, but his buyer was interested in purchasing only a small amount of the virus. And he'd explicitly told Michel to leave the container behind as it would slow detection of the theft. Unless and until someone had a research need to open the container, no one would know the virus was missing. That was the buyer's belief, at least.

Michel knew the buyer was mistaken. When he didn't return to work on Monday, there would be concerns. By Tuesday morning—if not sooner—the supervisors would check the monitoring systems and see that he had swiped his card at twelve twenty-eight in the morning; pressed his thumb into the print reader at twelve thirty-four; and entered the airlock at twelve forty-five. And, then, they'd wonder what he'd been working on. They would open the glovebox and see that a sample of the H17N10 virus was missing. But, the Americans had a saying that the customer was always right, so he gingerly removed one sample and returned the thermos.

The tube was remarkably light considering the incredible weight its contents carried. In his hand, Michel held a weapon more powerful than any other yet made by man. A droplet or two sprinkled in a market could start a daisy chain of suffering, illness, and death that would stretch across the globe. A vision of moaning, dying children filled his eyes, and he blinked it away.

The buyer had promised he would not release the virus; he'd said he needed it for leverage, that was all. If the man had offered only money, Michel would have pressed for more details, better assurances. But, he hadn't offered only money—money *was* changing hands, and quite a bit of it. More than money, though, the American had offered him priceless information: the address where that tramp Angeline had taken his Malia. Four years old, a jumble of wild blonde curls and elbows and knees, singing her silly songs, oceans away from her *papa*.

He felt his grip tighten on the bottle and took a long, steadying breath. *Soon, Malia. Very soon your papa will come for you.* He slid the cold vial into the front right pocket of his trousers and hurried back to the airlock.

He retraced his path out of the laboratory. His anxiety began to recede with each step closer to the exit. The soft bump of the vial against his thigh with each quick stride thumped out a beat: He'd done it. He'd done it!

The hard part was almost over. Soon he'd be in his pristine Smart, with the cooler on the seat beside him, driving carefully through the countryside to the prearranged drop spot. He'd split the sample among the three smaller vials the American had provided and leave the cooler behind. And then he would begin his journey to retrieve his daughter and begin his new life.

3

Leo's cell phone came to life in his pocket, and he flushed with annoyance. He knew from the ring tone that the call was from Grace Roberts, his second in command. When he'd left the office at lunchtime to get an early start on the weekend, he'd instructed Grace not to bother him for anything short of a catastrophe.

Sasha's head rested against Leo's chest. She was reading some legal journal article about intellectual property rights in cyberspace. He tried to ignore the ringing in his pocket and continued stroking Sasha's hair. The warm, gingery scent of her shampoo rose and enveloped him like a cloud.

Leo watched through the window overlooking the lake as the outdoor spotlights illuminated the fat, wet snowflakes that floated past in the darkness. He was perfectly content—the happiest he'd been in months—if not entirely relaxed. The truth was he was on his best behavior. The lake house, situated in Deep Creek, Maryland—a resort town halfway between Washington, D.C., and Pittsburgh—was both a compromise and an experiment. In the two months since he'd left Pittsburgh and the Department of Homeland Security to take a private sector job as the chief security officer for Serumceutical International, headquartered outside D.C., the situation with Sasha had been delicate.

In his view, he had left her with an open invitation; but in her view, it had been an ultimatum. To her credit, though, she'd been the one to pick up the phone and call him.

She'd agreed to try out a long-distance relationship with some reluctance, and he didn't dare to revisit the issue of her moving to D.C. As an early Christmas gift to one another, they'd rented this lakefront vacation home for the season. The house was a place to spend time together on neutral territory while they figured out a long-term plan. Leo hoped that, by spring, she'd be willing to make a permanent move. But she was like a deer, liable to start at any moment and gallop away.

His cell phone rang a second time, and he felt Sasha stiffen. *Great.*

He caressed her arm and gently shifted her to the

couch, then fished the phone from his pocket and answered on the third ring.

"What is it, Grace?" Leo said, keeping his voice even on the off-chance that she was calling about an actual emergency.

"Not on the phone," Grace said immediately. Her voice was serious but calm.

Grace's tone conveyed urgency. And she hadn't apologized for interrupting him on a Friday evening, which meant she had no doubt that whatever was going on, it was important enough to merit his involvement.

He felt Sasha's eyes on him. Although Grace's judgment to date had been sound, he decided to probe her for some details, hoping to find a reason to let her handle the problem, whatever it might be, and return to lounging on the couch with Sasha in his arms.

"In general terms, then," he said.

Grace exhaled, a frustrated snort, and said, "Corporate espionage. That's all I can say."

Leo's stomach sank, but he nodded. As usual, Grace's instincts were spot on; if the issue was a spying competitor, they couldn't talk about it over the phone, especially not in light of the sensitive nature of their government contract.

He should have known she wouldn't have called him unless it was warranted. Grace was a former

National Security Agency analyst. She was blazingly smart. She was also something of an adrenaline junkie. Upon realizing that the NSA position entailed none of the glamour of a Jason Bourne movie but all of the paperwork of a position at the Department of Motor Vehicles, she'd put out feelers for a more exciting, not to mention more remunerative, gig.

Leo's friend Manny Ortiz, a special agent in the EPA's Criminal Investigation Division, had called him about Grace. Manny had known Leo wanted to bring in an outsider to work directly for him at Serumceutical. Someone who was smart and driven, and, most important, had no ties to Serumceutical. A lieutenant whom Leo could trust. Manny had promised that Grace fit the bill. He'd also mentioned that she was a knockout, a fact that shouldn't have mattered, but had ended up removing any objections the other corporate officers might otherwise have had to his first official act: hiring a well-paid assistant. To a man, they'd been utterly charmed by her. Women, by contrast, appeared to hate Grace.

"Leo? Are you there?" Grace asked.

He could tell from the tight way she spoke that she was tense and ready for action. And he realized he was going to have to leave the cocoon that he and Sasha had built.

"I'm here. I heard you. I'm leaving now. I'll be

there in about three hours," he said and ended the call.

He slid the phone into his pocket and looked at Sasha. Her head was still bent over the journal, but her eyes weren't moving.

"Hey," he said in a soft voice.

She twisted around to face him, her green eyes searching his.

"I have to go to the office. I'm sorry. I'll be back in time to start a fire before we turn in for the night," he said, nodding toward the hearth.

He glanced down at his watch. *No, he wouldn't.* It was after six. Even if the meeting with Grace only took an hour or two, it would be well after midnight by the time he returned.

Sasha cocked her head and looked at him for a moment. Then, she shrugged and said, "I see."

He knew what that look meant: she was really saying 'I see how it is. When my work comes first, you call me emotionally stunted, but, when it's your work, it's a different story.'

Leo took both of her hands in his. "Sasha, believe me, I don't want to go. I'd much rather have dinner by the fire and then beat you at Scrabble. But, it's an emergency."

She arched an eyebrow at him. "Did I say anything, Connelly? Go. Drive safely."

Before he could respond, she extricated her

hands from his, stood, and walked to the large window. She wrapped her arms around herself, hugging the oversize sweater—or dress or whatever she was wearing over leggings—tight against her body and stared out at the water shimmering in the dark.

She looked so small and vulnerable, even defenseless—although that was the last thing she was—that he suddenly felt a desperate need not to leave her there alone, isolated in a resort town off-season.

"Hey," he said, trying to sound casual, "why don't you tag along?"

She pivoted from the window. "Why?"

He knew better than to say he was worried about leaving her alone. If he did, she'd just pull herself up to her full four feet, eleven-and-three-quarter inches and glare at him. Might even remind him that the night they'd met, she'd disarmed him, breaking his nose and one of his fingers in the process—as if he could forget.

He couldn't lie to her, though. That was the down side of having a trial attorney as a girlfriend. She had an uncanny way of sniffing out untruths.

He decided to go with the partial truth and sell it well. "Because I'll be lonely on the road by myself for six hours. And six hours spent in a car with you beats six hours spent missing you."

Her eyes softened and her mouth curved up slightly at the corner.

He pressed on. "I'll drive both ways. You can read or take a nap."

She turned to face him full on, and he could see she was considering it.

"If it's still open, can we stop at The Perfect Cup on the way back?"

Leo was more than happy to agree to the detour to the coffee shop they'd found tucked away in a nearby town, but to save face he said, "As long as I control the radio."

Sasha broke into a real smile and said, "You have a deal, Connelly."

4

Colton Maxwell smiled reassuringly at the small Webcam sitting in the center of the highly polished conference room table. He resisted the urge to look at the image of himself projected on the wall-sized screen that hung on the other side of the room. It was critical to maintain eye contact with the camera so that the anxious board members who had called this unnecessary, last-minute board meeting would see how calm he was and realize how silly their panic has been.

"But how can you be so certain?" Molly Charles repeated, her worried face appearing on the screen in a small box superimposed in the lower corner, near Colton's shoulder.

When the IT team had first set up the Web conferencing equipment for him, they had programmed it so that Colton saw his own image until someone else spoke, at which point the screen would switch to a feed of the speaker. That had bothered him. He wanted to be able to see his own reactions to other people's comments and input in real time, just the way he appeared to them. The technical wizards had fiddled with the settings so that other people appeared in a small box, similar to picture-in-picture television screens.

Before answering, Colton studied Molly's forehead, furrowed with concern and noted the hint of a frown on her thin, pursed lips.

He nodded, still smiling, and said, "I understand your hesitation, Molly. I honestly do. It's frightening to take bold actions, to lead with confidence. You worry that others won't share our vision. And, I also realize that other board members have the same reservations. But, trust me, AviEx is going to propel this company, not just to the next level, but to the stratosphere of our industry. This is a medication that will treat a virus capable of killing hundreds of millions of people. We can't afford to think small now. The company is poised to make history."

He watched as Molly, who'd been nodding along with him while he spoke, relaxed her brow and softened her lips into a smile.

"We appreciate, and share, your enthusiasm, Colton," Tim Bailey interjected, his thin, rat-like face replacing Molly's on the screen, "but the government has flat out said they don't plan to stockpile AviEx. They've put their money on the vaccine. That's a reality."

Bailey narrowed his eyes and waited for Colton's response.

"I know what the press reported. So what?" Colton said. His tone was deliberately dismissive. His weak-willed board had overreacted to the press report, blowing it wildly out of proportion. The truth was that the report *was* a setback, but it was, at most, a manageable speed bump, not the insurmountable roadblock the board was making it out to be.

"So what?" Bailey repeated. His untied bowtie flapped against his neck.

He'd made sure they all knew he was going to be late for his black-tie holiday affair. As if any of them cared.

"Yeah. So what? Surely you aren't naive enough to believe the low-level press officer who handled that inquiry has a finger on the pulse of the decision makers? I'm telling you, Congress is going to appropriate a tidy sum to purchase tens of millions of doses of AviEx or more. I guarantee it."

"You guarantee it," Bailey said.

Colton reflected that, for a high-level banking professional, Bailey didn't add much to a conversation. In fact, they could have filled his seat with a parrot and gotten the same effect.

"Yes. I can't go into details as to amounts or timing, of course. The NDA is still pending approval, after all. But, the government *will* shift its focus from the vaccine to AviEx. You can take that to the bank," Colton said, ending with a hearty chuckle to highlight his pun for the bank officer.

Bailey chuckled, too, and shrugged, "Well, I don't much want to know the details of our lobbyists' efforts. They're the experts. And I think this call has gone a long way to assuage folks' concerns. You understand why we felt it necessary to talk, though, right?"

Colton could tell from his tone that the man was feeling sheepish about the board's decision to call the emergency meeting. *Good.*

"I do, Tim. Although I would have hoped that, by now, this board would have enough trust in me to lead the company forward without second guessing me."

He let the chorus of apologies and compliments about his leadership abilities wash over him, barely registering.

He didn't care at all, of course, what the board thought of him. But it was useful for them to *think* he did—to believe he had feelings that they could wound and to worry that if they overstepped he might move on to a competitor.

He suppressed a smile and considered his next steps. What he'd said to the board had been true: Congress would abandon its plans to stockpile Serumceutical's vaccine in favor of purchasing AviEx.

But, that decision would have nothing to do with ViraGene's cadre of unctuous, insincere K Street lobbyists. No, he would never leave such a critical issue in the hands of someone else. He'd make sure of it himself.

ANNA BRICKER SENSED her husband's presence behind her. The force of Jeffrey's personality was such that the air became electrified when he entered a room.

And, when he left a room, he took all the energy with him. It amazed her, how their home felt so quiet and still when he was gone—despite the noise and activity their six children generated.

She marked her spot in her notebook and placed her pen on the table. She stood from the table and turned toward him with a smile.

He smiled back at her, and she felt a tingle in her

stomach. After eighteen years of marriage, she still thrived on his attention.

"Leaving already?" she asked.

He shouldered his duffel bag and nodded. "I'll only be gone two days."

"I know."

She knew how long he'd be gone, just not where he'd be or what he'd be doing. He hadn't volunteered the information, and Anna had learned years ago that there was no point in asking. Jeffrey would simply tell her it wasn't her concern or, worse, he would lie—make up an innocuous story so that she wouldn't worry about him while he was out there doing ... whatever he did to protect their family.

He jerked his head to the tangle of Go Bags piled high on the scratched and worn wooden table. "Everything in order?"

"I'm making sure nothing's out of date," she said. "They'll be ready to go again by evening."

He clasped her shoulder. "That's good work, honey."

She flushed at the compliment and waved it off. "It's my job to make sure our family is prepared."

It was a job Anna took seriously. Every three months, she gathered the eight backpacks hanging on hooks in the mud room and the eight identical backpacks stored in the back of the family's aged but pristine Suburban and emptied their contents onto the dining room table. The Go Bags were to be grabbed if a disaster struck that required the family to evacuate in a hurry; they contained essential supplies to get the family through the first seventy-two hours after any emergency.

Each pack contained toiletries; a knife; a flash-light with spare batteries; a whistle; a face mask; two bottles of water and an assortment of energy bars; a small first aid kit; a change of clothes; and a pair of hiking shoes. Four times a year, Anna checked that the food hadn't expired and swapped out the clothes and shoes according to the season and her growing children's sizes.

In addition to the items in the kids' bags, each of her two bags contained a collection of antibiotics that needed to be checked for date; a small sealed packet of assorted seeds in case they never returned to their home and the garden she tended there; a water purification kit; and an emergency supply of games and activities intended to occupy bored, frightened children if the need arose. Jeffrey's bags each contained the basic items; a map; a journal; and a gun with ammunition.

She sorted through the rainbow of colored bags until she found the army green ones.

She held one out to him and said, "Your bags are done. Do you want to take one with you?"

"That's not a bad thought, Anna." Jeffrey reached

for it and slung it over his back, bumping it against the duffle bag he already wore.

He leaned in and kissed her forehead, pressing his lips against her skin for a long moment. Then he took her chin in his hand and tipped her head back so her eyes met his.

"I've already said goodbye to the kids. I'll call you when I can," he said.

She savored his touch, knowing she'd ache for it in his absence.

"Have a safe trip," she answered.

He turned to leave. When he reached the doorway, he turned back. "The rifle's in the closet in our bedroom, should you need it."

She searched his eyes but saw no sign of worry.

"Do you expect that I'll need it?"

"No." He shook his head.

A wave of relief flooded her. There was no clear danger, he just wanted her to be prepared for anything that might threaten their family while he was gone.

"Ammunition's in your sock drawer?" she confirmed.

He nodded, pulled open the door, and disappeared from view. The house immediately felt still and too quiet. She knew it would remain that way until Jeffrey returned.

She listened as the Jeep's engine roared to life

outside and waited until the sound faded at the end of the gravel driveway. Despite herself, she wondered where he was going, who he would be meeting, what important information he'd received during the middle-of-the-night phone call that had interrupted the silence two nights earlier. He thought she'd been sleeping, but she'd heard the undercurrent of excitement in his voice as he murmured into his satellite phone in the dark bedroom.

Stop it, she thought. Let Jeffrey handle his business; you handle yours.

She turned her attention back to her inventory of the bags. Clara's feet had grown. Anna removed the too-small hiking boots from her orange backpack and set them to the side. She shifted Lacey's boots to Clara's bag. Bethany's old pair should fit Lacey now, she thought. She scrawled a reminder in her notebook to check whether the same hand-me-down pattern would work for a Michael to Clay to Henry transfer, which would mean only the two oldest would need new boots.

Anna often lost herself in the mundane details of keeping her family organized, fed, and clothed on a strict budget with minimal waste. She approached the task seriously because she knew when the day came that the family had only itself to rely on, everyone would be counting on her most of all.

5

The SUV slid along the empty country road lined with dirty, gray snow banks. No one else was out, and the snow was falling harder now. Sasha watched as thick flakes bounced off the windshield and melted, leaving skinny wet tracks on the glass. She felt Connelly glance away from the road and look at her.

She turned. "What's up?"

Caught, he blinked, then grinned, "Nothing. Just looking at you."

She suddenly felt like an eight year old. She stuck out her tongue and said, "Take a picture. It'll last longer."

Connelly shook his head and turned his attention back to the road ahead. No snow plows had come through the small town, but Connelly guided the vehicle's tires into the ruts that had been packed down into grooves in the snow by cars that had passed by earlier.

"Take a nap," he suggested.

She wasn't tired. She'd brought along some reading material, but it had remained in the bag at her feet. The truth was, she'd agreed to come along on the drive because the point of renting the lake house was to spend time together, away from their respective jobs and other commitments. She figured she could spend time with Connelly in the front seat of his SUV as easily as she could curled up under a soft blanket in front of a fire.

So, here they were. Nearing the hour mark in their together time on the road.

It had been a quiet forty-five minutes. It was funny: they'd been so comfortable together for a year. But then, Connelly's move—and the way it had come about—had pried them apart, leaving an open space between them, where before there had been none.

The distance confused Sasha, and she wasn't sure how to bridge it.

"What's so important that they're dragging you into the office on a Friday night, anyway?" she asked.

As she heard the words aloud, she winced. It sounded accusatory, when she intended only to make conversation.

Connelly flicked his eyes toward her, then back to the road. "Corporate espionage, apparently. I don't have any details and couldn't share them if I did."

She understood. Of course, when *she* hadn't been able to share information with *him* because of attorney-client privilege or other confidentiality issues, he had never been quite so understanding. Water under the bridge.

She waited a moment then said, "I'm not trying to tell you what to do, but, if I were you, I would loop in your in-house counsel now."

Connelly bobbed his head. "That's probably a good idea."

He hit the Bluetooth connection and said, "Call general counsel."

"Dialing general counsel," the tinny, computer voice reported.

While the phone rang, Sasha stage whispered, "Make sure you tell him I'm in the car, so he knows the conversation's not protected by privilege."

Connelly rolled his eyes.

"Oliver Tate," a rich, tenor voice boomed through the SUV's speakers.

"Hi, Oliver, it's Leo."

"What can I do for you, Leo?" the man responded immediately, his voice betraying a hint of impatience.

Connelly cleared his throat and said, "Before I

get to that, I want to let you know I'm in the car, so I have you on speakerphone. I also have my … friend in the car, and she tells me that means this conversation isn't privileged."

Tate's voice took on a note of amusement. "Would this be your lady friend, the lawyer from Pittsburgh?"

Lady friend? Sasha swallowed a giggle.

Connelly flushed pink and said, "That's right. Sasha McCandless."

"Hello, counselor," Tate said.

"Hi," Sasha responded.

"With Ms. McCandless's admonition firmly in mind, let's get down to business," Tate said.

"Sure thing, and I'm sorry to bother you on a Friday evening, but Grace called me to report a possible corporate espionage issue," Connelly said.

As they neared the town of Frostburg and began their climb up the mountains, the temperature dropped, and the wind howled. Sasha hit the button to activate her seat warmer. Connelly must have seen her from the corner of his eye because he raised the temperature on the dashboard control.

Tate was silent for a long moment. Then he repeated, "Corporate espionage?"

"Yes, sir," Connelly responded.

Tate exhaled loudly.

Connelly waited.

"That's not good, Leo."

"No, it's not," Connelly agreed.

He looked at Sasha, as though she might have something to add.

She shrugged at him.

"ViraGene is behind this."

"We don't know that, Oliver."

Tate snorted. "*I* know it."

"I understand where you're coming from, but we shouldn't jump to conclusions until we have all the details," Connelly cautioned.

"Nonetheless, I think the facts will bear me out. Keeping in mind that Ms. McCandless is listening; do you have any details you can share?" Tate asked.

"I really don't. Even if Sasha weren't here, I don't know anything beyond what I've said. Grace didn't want to discuss it on the phone, which was the right decision. I'm on my way back to town from Deep Creek now. I can meet you in the office in two, two-and-a-half, hours," Leo offered.

"That won't work. I'm in Jackson Hole. I've got a little place in the mountains," Tate said.

Little place in the mountains. Sasha was fairly sure that was inside the Beltway code for 'luxurious ski chalet.'

Leo and Tate fell silent, considering their next steps.

Tate spoke first.

"I'd really rather not interrupt my vacation,

particularly since this isn't the sort of issue I'd handle personally." His tone was equal parts sheepish and defensive.

Sasha twisted her mouth into a smile. That was the upside of being an in-house lawyer: instead of ruining Tate's ski vacation, this little emergency would end up ruining the weekend for some unsuspecting associate at whichever outside firm Tate retained to handle it.

As if he were reading her mind, Tate went on, "Unfortunately, over my objection, our new legal budget froze rates for all of our legal services providers. The unintended consequence of that brilliant cost-saving measure is that all of our work gets pushed down to some baby lawyer who can't find his bar card with both hands and a flashlight." Tate guffawed.

Sasha rolled her eyes.

Leo's hands tightened on the wheel, making his knuckles go white. He was getting agitated.

"So, how do you propose we handle this, then?" he asked in a neutral voice, masking his annoyance.

Tate thought for a moment. Then he said, "Ms. McCandless, you handle complex commercial litigation, don't you?"

Sasha's stomach dropped as she realized where Tate was going with this.

"Excuse me?" she managed.

"Your firm handles trade secret, breach of contract, unfair competition—those sorts of matters —does it not?" Tate answered.

Sasha shook her head as if he could somehow see her through the phone.

"No. Well, yes. But, I absolutely do not handle criminal matters. And corporate espionage has the potential to veer into the white collar crime area," she said.

Leo frowned at her.

She hurried to add, "I'm flattered to be considered, of course. It's just a firm policy that I really cannot bend."

Will not bend, she thought. *Not ever again*.

Tate was undeterred. "That practice limitation shouldn't matter. If any crime has been committed here, we'd be the victim, not the actor. You'd simply have to interface with the authorities."

He was right, of course. But, still. Sasha had vowed not to leave her comfort zone again. She was a civil litigator, not a comic book superhero. Corporate espionage sounded exciting, and she'd had too much excitement in the past eighteen months. She wanted to focus on the mundane aspects of practicing law: responding to discovery requests; taking depositions; putting together doorstop-sized briefs in support of motions for summary judgment. No intrigue. No adrenaline. No nightmares.

"That's true," she said, "but, I'm not a member of the Maryland bar." It sounded like a weak excuse, even to her.

"Oh, that's no problem," Tate assured her.

She looked at Connelly. He was looking back at her, a pleading expression on his face.

She couldn't.

"Mr. Tate, as much as I appreciate the offer, I don't think it would be a good idea," she said.

Tate exhaled audibly.

"Listen. I don't care that you and Leo are involved, okay? That doesn't bother me. What *will* bother me is having to tell my thirteen-year-old twins—who I've pulled out of school for the week—that we have to cut our trip short. And what will *really* bother me is dealing with their horrible mother when she finds out I am going to want to rejigger our visitation schedule yet again. I don't have any litigators in our legal department—they're all regulatory lawyers and patent folks—but they'll give you whatever support you need." He spoke in a firm tone that made clear he would brook no argument on the subject.

Sasha was prepared to argue anyway, but Connelly put his hand over hers. He caught her eye and mouthed the word 'please.'

She stopped.

Connelly rarely asked her for a big favor. Or

anything, really. The last request he'd made of her was that she marry him (maybe, that part still wasn't entirely clear) and move to D.C. to be with him. She'd fumbled that question pretty badly. Couldn't she just take the stupid case, appease Tate, and show Connelly that she was willing to put his needs first every now and again?

"Great," she mumbled. "I look forward to working with your people on this."

Leo blew a kiss her direction and turned his attention back to the road, all smiles now.

She looked out the passenger window while he said his goodbyes with Tate. Her mouth went dry, a hard lump lodged itself in her throat, and a knot took up residence in the pit of her stomach. All signs that she had made a mistake. A bad mistake.

As Sasha hurried alongside Connelly through the hushed corridors of the sprawling Serumceutical complex, she tried to shake off her conviction that getting herself involved in her boyfriend's company's corporate espionage problem had been a mistake. She told herself this matter was in her wheelhouse: complex commercial litigation—a business dispute between competitors, by the sounds of it. She'd cut her teeth on unfair competition and interference with contractual relations cases as a baby lawyer at Prescott. And yet, she couldn't deny the very real queasiness that she'd been fighting ever since she'd agreed to do it.

Connelly stopped in front of a frosted glass door. A nameplate on the wall announced this was his office. He waved his company ID card in front of a card reader mounted on the wall beneath his name. A red light flickered and a *beep* followed by a mechanical *click* indicated the door had unlocked. As he pushed it open, he turned and looked at her closely.

"You okay?"

She nodded and swallowed. "Yep. My stomach's a little upset, that's all. Your driving being what it is." She threw him a grin.

He narrowed his eyes as though he didn't buy her story, but then he smiled back at her and waved her into the office ahead of him. "After you, Counselor."

Sasha stepped past him and into the office. The motion-sensing lights came to life, and Sasha looked around. The room fit Connelly. It was understated and warm. The furniture was Mission style: solid, sturdy, yet attractive. A brick red carpet anchored a seating arrangement, and a large photograph of the Sedona Red Rock Mountains, mimicking the red of the carpet, hung over the sofa.

"Nice office," she said.

"Thanks." Connelly moved over to the desk and pushed a button on his phone. "Grace helped me decorate it," he said as the ringing of a telephone sounded through the speaker of the phone on his desk.

Grace was the woman who had called Connelly's cell phone earlier in the day. She'd also helped him pick out his office furniture?

"Grace?" Sasha asked.

"You'll meet her in a moment; she's my deputy," Connelly said, holding up a finger to forestall further conversation as a woman picked up the ringing phone on the other end.

"Roberts," said the woman in a crisp, no-nonsense voice.

Connelly had often mentioned someone named Roberts when he'd talked about his new job. For some reason, Sasha had assumed Roberts would be a man.

She conjured up an image of the female Roberts. Late middle-aged, with cropped gray hair and a firm handshake. She probably wore pantsuits to work four days a week. But today was Friday, so, in the time-honored faux informality of casual day, she would be dressed in pressed khakis and a cotton button-down shirt—possibly light pink in a concession to femininity.

"I'm here," Connelly said. "Come down to my office when you can."

"Be right there, boss," the woman replied and ended the call.

Connelly walked around his desk and joined Sasha near the seating area.

"Sit wherever you want," he said. "Do you want anything to drink? Grace can make some coffee."

Sasha raised an eyebrow. Connelly had his female underling fetching coffee? How 1960s of him.

"No, thanks," she said, although she would have loved a cup. Poor Roberts.

There was a light rap on the door, and Connelly walked over to open it.

"We take security very seriously around here," he told her over his shoulder. "No one else's key card will open my door. Not even Grace's."

"How's everyone else's work?" she asked. Surely, the company didn't program each individual employee's card so precisely.

"Good question," Connelly said. "We can get into the procedures after Grace gives us her report."

He pulled the door inward, and a tall, shapely redhead with bright blue eyes strode into the room. The woman's hair tumbled past her shoulders in big waves. Instead of the Brooks Brothers business casual uniform Sasha had imagined, Grace wore a fitted wrap dress that highlighted her curves and knee-high black boots with a heel that put her about even with Connelly's six feet in height.

Sasha suddenly felt even smaller than usual—at a hair under five feet and shy of one hundred pounds soaking wet, she was used to being the tiniest adult in a room. But this woman was a giantess. A gorgeous giantess.

"How was the drive?" she asked Connelly.

"Easy. I had company. Grace Roberts, this is Sasha McCandless," Connelly said, gesturing toward Sasha.

Sasha stood and tugged down the hem of the oversized sweater she wore as a dress.

Grace followed Connelly's arm and met Sasha's eyes with a surprised look.

"Oh. Hello, there," she said, crossing the room with a long, loping stride. She smiled broadly and stuck out her hand.

Sasha stepped forward to shake her hand and found herself eye-level with Grace's breasts. A hint of smoke-gray lace peeked out from the neckline of her dress.

"Nice to meet you," Sasha managed, ignoring the clutch of emotion in her stomach.

Grace turned back to Connelly and lowered her voice as if Sasha couldn't hear her. "Um, I don't think this is a conversation that your girlfriend should sit in on. Do you want me to set her up in one of the lounges with a magazine or something?"

Connelly laughed. "It's okay. Sasha's going to represent the company on this issue if it ends up in court. She can stay."

Grace's eyebrows shot up her forehead. "Really? Tate approved that?"

"It was his idea, actually," Connelly said, giving her a confused look.

Grace was silent for a moment. Sasha could see her calculating what this news might mean.

Finally, the other woman said, "Oh, great. In that case, let's get started. Welcome to the team, Sasha."

Sasha smiled and hoped it looked more sincere than it felt. "Thanks."

It suddenly seemed perfectly appropriate for Grace to be a coffee-fetcher.

She turned to Connelly, "Before we start, I think I would like that coffee, after all."

Connelly shut his almond eyes for an instant, then exhaled slowly, and said, "I could probably use a cup, too. I'll get it. Grace, can I bring you anything?"

"No, thanks," the other woman said in a bright voice, "I'm all set. I did just make some, though. I thought you might need something to pick you up after your drive. The fresh stuff is in the kitchenette near the library."

"Thanks," Connelly said. He shot Sasha an unreadable look before he left his office.

Sasha and Grace sat in silence. Sasha on the leather couch; Grace draped across a chair, her legs crossed, the top leg swinging back and forth.

They looked at each other.

"So," Grace said, "what do you think of the building?"

"It's impressive," Sasha said. "I haven't seen much of it, but I was surprised by how spread out it is."

Grace nodded. "We have more than one hundred employees working on-site, as well as a gym, a child care center, and a cafeteria. But, the majority of our employees are stationed at our various research and development centers, located throughout the world." She spoke with the soothing, practiced tone of a tour guide.

"How many R & D centers are there?" Sasha asked.

Grace ticked them off on her fingers. "Four state side, and three foreign centers in England, France, and Switzerland. We also have manufacturing plants in Asia and South America."

"Can you give me an overview of how security is handled at each facility?" Sasha asked.

"That's a complicated question. I'm not sure where to start," Grace said.

"Okay, for instance, I noticed Connelly's ID card

is keyed to his office door. That seems like a piece of a pretty sophisticated, multi-layered system. I just wondered how it fit into the bigger picture."

"Well, as you recognized, it is a multi-layered system; and security is tailored to the needs and weaknesses of each part of the corporation. Here at headquarters each employee has an ID card that provides access to the building, the common areas, and the employee's department. Accounting personnel cannot access human resources; HR can't access security; and so on. But, with the exception of Leo's office, the individual offices within a department are not secured."

"Why is his?" Sasha asked. She spotted a fresh legal pad on Connelly's desk and grabbed it to jot down some notes.

"The decision predates us. The system was in place when he was hired. Apparently, the Board of Directors thought it was important that the Chief Security Officer's office be unbreachable." Grace leaned in and said in a conspiratorial tone, "He thinks it's overkill."

Sasha was sure he did. Connelly despised security theater—dramatic displays intended to create the impression of security without actually improving safety or security.

"What about the research centers and the manufacturing plants?"

"It depends. The R & D buildings are locked down pretty tightly; that's where the patented information resides, after all. The manufacturing plants probably *should* be, to prevent theft, but the focus there is more on sterility and cleanliness," Grace said.

Sasha thought for a moment, then she asked, "What about your computer systems? Are they centralized?"

"Yes." Grace nodded and was about to continue, when they heard a bump against the door.

Sasha looked up to see Connelly's silhouette through the frosted glass door. He was turned to his side, juggling two mugs and his key card. She stood and started for the door, but Grace strode past her and pulled it open for him.

"That freaking card reader . . ." he trailed off, shaking his head at the unnecessary security, and smiled his thanks to Grace.

Sasha stood halfway between the door and the couch, feeling about as useful as the card reader.

"Here you go. Strong and dark, like you like it," Connelly said with a grin as he handed off one of the mugs to her.

"Thanks." She trailed him back to the couch and sat next to him.

Grace waited for them to get situated with their

mugs. Sasha took a long sip of coffee. Hot, and, as promised, strong and dark.

She took another swallow then placed the mug on the side table to her right and picked up the notepad she'd stolen from Connelly's desk.

Grace looked at Connelly. "So, I was filling Sasha in on the security at the various locations. She had just asked about the computer systems. Should I continue or do you want to hear what happened?"

Connelly combed a hand through his thick, ink-black hair, making it stand up in short spikes. "I'm awfully curious, but walk Sasha through the computer security first. She might need the background."

Sasha could tell Grace was bursting to tell them about the espionage, but she nodded and turned to Sasha.

"So, all of our data is centralized on one intranet, which we run out of this building. All the various programs and databases for orders, purchases, shipments, everything resides on the intranet. We can tell who's accessed what and when. An individual employee's password only enables him or her to open or view documents that are required to perform the functions of his or her job. So, for instance, a billing clerk couldn't open the marketing plan for one of our drugs."

"What about remote access to the systems? Can employees log in from home?" Sasha asked.

"They can, but it's discouraged. In addition, in order to do it, an employee would need to use a secure fob to log in, which provides a series of random, frequently changing numbers. Once logged in, access is terminated after four minutes of inactivity. So, if you log in, start working, then step away to go to the bathroom or get a snack, you would likely need to go through the sign in process again. It's designed to keep the data secure and to disincentivize people from accessing files remotely."

Sasha nodded. It made sense. Protecting the company's sensitive data probably outweighed efficiency concerns.

Connelly and Grace shared a look.

"What?" Sasha asked.

Grace continued to stare at Connelly but didn't speak.

Connelly turned toward Sasha. "Grace has strong feelings about the security of our electronic data. Despite all these safeguards, we are, in many ways, leaving our information wide open."

"How so?" Sasha asked.

Grace piped up. "Many of our research scientists —most of them, in fact—have come to us from academia. They are in the habit of collaborating with colleagues all over the world by loading information to the cloud. They seem to think no one other than their fellow researchers would be interested enough to try to access it." She shook her head at the naivety.

"You mean they use Dropbox or something?" Sasha asked.

"Dropbox, Boxy, Google Drive," Connelly confirmed. "We've tried to explain to them that those sites are not sufficiently secure to house proprietary research and development material, but they don't seem to believe us. They argue that at their universities, they were working in level four secure facilities and throwing this stuff up in the cloud, and no one objected."

Grace's eyes took on a glint of steel. "And they continue to do it, even though it's against corporate policy. I monitor those uploads myself. They just do whatever they want."

Sasha addressed Connelly. "That's fairly serious. To claim that information is trade secret and entitled to legal protection, you guys have to take steps to actually protect it."

"I know," he said. "Tate and I have argued with the head of R & D until our voices are hoarse. Those scientists are the company's bread and butter. No one is going to make them do *anything*. So, right now, the best we can do is have Grace monitor their activity and hope none of their accounts get hacked." He shrugged, helpless and frustrated, then said to Grace, "Please tell me that's not what happened?"

"No, it's not. There's a problem at the Pennsylvania DC." Grace said.

"DC, as in distribution center?" Sasha asked.

"Right. I guess I didn't mention it, did I?" Grace answered. "In addition to research and development centers and manufacturing facilities, we used to have regional distribution centers—one on the West Coast, one in the South, one in the upper Midwest, and one in New Kensington, Pennsylvania, just outside Pittsburgh, which served the Northeast and Mid-Atlantic. They were nothing more than warehouses. In recent years, the company moved to just in time production and closed the DCs."

"Just in time production?" Sasha asked again, scribbling as fast as she could.

The learning curve for a new client's business was always steep. But she'd found it was important to gather as much information at this stage as she could. Once litigation was underway, clients tended to assume their lawyers understood their business operations. Sasha had seen more than one instance of a case going south because an attorney misunderstood or never fully knew how a client ran its business. It hadn't yet happened to her. And she wasn't about to let Connelly's company be the first.

"Right. Instead of housing inventory, which gets

costly, we've honed our systems so that we manufacture just enough of each of our drugs to fill the immediate demand. And as soon as they're produced, we send them directly to the customer. It's more efficient and less expensive than having pallets of drugs sitting around, potentially going out of date, while we wait for someone to place an order," Connelly explained.

"Okay, so if you closed all the distribution centers, how is there a problem at the Pennsylvania DC?" Sasha said, asking the obvious question.

"We just reopened it for a special project. We have a government contract for a minimum of twenty-five million doses of a vaccine. Obviously, we can't produce that amount instantly. And the government, being the government, can't pay for it all at once either. So, as doses are manufactured, we're going to ship them to the Pennsylvania DC and hold them. Each time we reach a million doses, we're to invoice the feds, then they'll send reservists from Fort Meade in Maryland to come pick up the vaccines," Connelly explained.

"The government's going to stockpile vaccines at Fort Meade?" Sasha asked.

"It's a national security issue. We're not talking about just any vaccine; this one provides immunity to the killer flu," Grace explained.

Sasha had reached the awkward part of an initial

client meeting, where she had to admit she had no idea what the business people were talking about. Usually, the confession was well received, and the business people tripped all over themselves to be helpful and educate her. This time, she had a vague suspicion that Connelly might have told her all of this during one of their telephone conversations and she simply hadn't focused on the details.

She'd been busy the past several weeks. In her efforts to adjust to living alone again and to block out her disastrous foray into criminal defense work, she had taken on four complicated new cases and had been working hours that were long, even by her standards. On top of that, she'd been trying to fit everything into a four-day workweek so she could spend long weekends at the lake with Connelly. On the weekends that they hadn't met up, she'd made it a point to get together with friends or spend time with her extended family. All that activity, on top of her workout routine, had kept her mind off Connelly's absence and the outcome of her Lady Lawyer Killer case, but it left her somewhat absentminded. Now she was going to have to explain she had no idea what Connelly and Grace were talking about.

"Let's step back. The federal government has decided the flu is a matter of national security?" she said.

Another look passed between Connelly and Grace.

"It's not just the flu, it's the Doomsday virus—the killer flu. I know I told you about this," Connelly said.

"You did," Sasha agreed quickly. "I just need a better understanding as your corporate attorney than I had as your girlfriend. Tell me everything you know about the Doomsday virus, okay? Pretend I don't know anything."

"Okay," he conceded. "After the bird and swine flu scares, researchers realized that a flu pandemic would be, for lack of a better word, devastating. The death toll would make historic plagues look like a joke, and the quarantines and panic that would result could cripple the global economy."

Sasha tried not to let her skepticism show on her face. It sounded like Y2K hysteria all over again.

But Connelly knew her too well. "It's a very real threat, Sasha. So real, in fact, that the government became concerned about bioterrorism."

"We're worried someone will use the flu as a weapon?" she asked.

"Right," Grace confirmed. "So, we decided to develop it first."

"What?" Sasha cocked her head.

"The National Institutes of Health funded a study to combine the three most severe naturally occurring flu strains into a mutant superflu," Grace said, her tone neutral.

Sasha gasped despite herself. "We made it? On purpose?"

"We did. But, the resultant flu wasn't highly contagious. It was difficult to transmit," Connelly explained.

"Oh, that's good," Sasha said.

Connelly continued, "So, the NIH funded another study to see whether the new flu virus could be genetically modified to make it more contagious."

"What? Why?"

Connelly put down his coffee mug and threw up his hands. "I don't know why, Sasha. I guess it seemed like a good idea at the time."

"Did it work?" Sasha asked. She was almost numb with disbelief.

"Oh, it worked all right. The new strain, which is what the press is talking about when they refer to the killer flu, is not only capable of airborne transmission, making it very easy to pass among humans, it's more virulent. Researchers have created an extremely contagious, deadly flu virus," Connelly said, reaching across the couch and taking her free hand in his. "I guess I downplayed all this when I talked to you about the vaccine, but it's been all over the news."

Sasha had been avoiding the news in the aftermath of her own infamy but was too stunned to form a response for a moment. Then, she said, "But you guys have a vaccine that will work against it?"

Grace smiled reassuringly at her. "We do. It was quite a challenge, because after the researchers announced they'd concocted the killer flu, the National Science Advisory Board for Biosecurity forbid them from publishing their results, citing national security. That made it virtually impossible to work on an effective vaccine until we hired away some members of the research team. And, we had to take the unusual step of using a small amount of a live virus that's as close to the Doomsday virus as we could manage instead of a killed virus to make the vaccine."

"But it works?" Sasha asked.

"It works in ferrets," Connelly said, rubbing the skin between her right thumb and index finger with his. "Ferrets, apparently, are close to humans in germ transmission."

"Okay." Sasha figured that fact was no less believable than anything else she'd heard. "So, the government wants to buy millions of doses of a vaccine that works in ferrets to protect us from a deadly flu that it created."

"Basically," Connelly said.

"And you're making it as fast as you can and sending it to this distribution center in Pennsylvania to await pick up by army reservists," she continued, grateful for Connelly's warm hand in hers. She gave it a squeeze.

"You're all caught up," Grace said. "Now, do you want to hear the problem?"

"Yes," Connelly and Sasha said in unison.

"ViraGene has a mole in the DC," Grace said. She leaned forward, and Sasha recognized excitement shining in the woman's brilliant blue eyes.

Connelly's hand tightened over Sasha's as he said, "You're sure?"

"I'm sure."

"Ben Davenport called me shortly after six o'clock this evening. He said he'd had an unsettling encounter with one of the clerks—a woman named Celia Gerig, who started working for us the Monday before last. Her job responsibility is to check in the pallets when they arrive at the warehouse, count them, and shrink wrap them to await pick up."

"Ben is the distribution center manager. He seems like a good guy and a straight shooter," Connelly interjected for Sasha's benefit.

"Anyway, Ben ran into Celia in the parking lot. Her car battery was dead, so he gave her a jump. As he explained it, she seemed edgy or nervous. He didn't go into detail except to say that the conversation left him with the strong feeling that something was wrong."

Grace seemed apologetic about the amorphous nature of Ben's report, but Sasha just nodded. Intuition was real, as far as Sasha was concerned, and had saved her life on more than one occasion. Whenever her gut told her something was off, she listened. Her Krav Maga instructor had a saying that the human brain has the remarkable ability to know things it doesn't know it knows.

"Tell me you didn't drag me all the way in here because Ben had a bad feeling," Connelly said.

Grace briefly twisted her mouth into the expression disbelieving underlings reserved for mildly insulting questions from their neurotic bosses. Sasha recognized it well from her years at Prescott & Talbott. She had given it to her share of partners in response to questions confirming that she'd cite checked the cases in a brief or served all the parties of record.

After a moment, she answered. "No, Leo. Ben was concerned enough to go back into the office and pull her personnel file. It looks like Human Resources confirmed her social security number against the government database, and it checked out, but they hadn't yet gotten around to checking her references."

Sasha saw Connelly's eyes flash, but his expression remained impassive.

Grace must have picked up on the flicker of anger, too.

"I know. I called Jessica at home to find out why. She said they're backlogged with all the new hires to get the warehouse open. They're running the socials as they get them, but they can only check so many references a day, and Gerig was a low priority."

"She should have told us. We'd have authorized overtime," Connelly said in a flat tone.

"I told her that. I also told her to get in here tomorrow and start doing them herself. I reminded her that the government doesn't play around with security on its contracts and that she doesn't want to be the one who loses this one for us. Trust me, she got it," Grace said.

Connelly nodded his approval.

Grace continued. "So, Ben picked up the phone and started calling around. None of her references check out. Either the telephone number is bad, no one answers, or the person who picks up the phone has never heard of Celia Gerig."

Connelly considered this news. "That's not good."

"It gets worse. Ben called her number she'd listed as her home phone and got a recorded message that the number had been disconnected. Then he got really worried, so he drove over to the address she'd provided as her residence. He said if she ever lived there, she's cleared out. It looks abandoned. He peeked in the front window, and there's no furniture. There's a realtor's sign stuck in the lawn saying the place is for rent or sale. He called the realtor, but she hasn't gotten back to him yet. Celia Gerig's gone."

"Is anything missing?"

"Nothing obvious, according to Ben. He's still at the office, going through all the files, looking for something out of place, but, so far, he hasn't found anything. He had a weekend shift scheduled to come in tomorrow anyway, so he's going to go back in the morning and take another look with fresh eyes." Grace's grim voice matched her expression.

Connelly and Grace fell silent.

"And you're convinced a competitor is behind this? ViraGene?" Sasha asked.

"Yes," they said in unison.

"How can you be so sure?"

"It's them. Who else would it be?" Grace said, echoing what Tate had said.

Connelly nodded. "Almost certainly. Okay, call Ben and tell him Sasha and I will be there first thing in the morning."

"You don't want me to come?" Grace's disappointment was splashed across her face.

"I need you here to ride herd over the Human Resources folks."

Connelly gave Grace one of his most heartwarming smiles. It started at the right corner of his mouth and tugged his lips into a grin. It seemed to ease the sting, and Grace smiled back.

6

Michel was dying. He could tell by the foamy, red bubbles of blood that escaped from his lips with each breath he managed. The stranger had punctured his left lung.

The stabbing had been swift and impersonal. A heavy knock at the thick, wooden door. Then, when Michel had opened the door, in a flash, the man had forced him backward and into the kitchen of the old stone farmhouse. Once inside, the attacker had produced from his pocket a curved hunting knife and plunged it into Michel's chest with no comment, no fuss. Then he'd wiped his knife on the checkered tea towel hanging near the sink and had walked out, pulling the door closed behind him.

Sweating and gasping, as pain seared through his

chest, Michel collapsed into a chair at the table where he'd eaten breakfast just hours ago and considered his options. He was hours from the nearest modern medical facility. He would die before he reached care.

He supposed he could stumble down the hill to the village below and either die on the rocky path or, if he was very lucky, on the couch in Docteur Bonnet's parlor.

Mais non, Michel decided, exhaling and spraying blood across the table, he would die here, in the farmhouse where his grandfather had been born.

His breaths were coming faster now and with greater effort. He wished he had time to uncork a bottle of Cabernet from Monsieur Girard's vineyard, but he would have to settle for turning his chair slightly, so he could see the cold, white sky through the window. He paused to fix in his mind an image of the fields as they looked during the summer, when the rows of sunflowers turned their faces upward to the golden sun like a class full of schoolchildren watching their teacher at the chalkboard.

As his pulse thudded toward the finish line, Michel shivered. He stared out the window and considered the actions that had brought him to this point. Although he didn't know the man who had stabbed him, he knew for a certainty why he'd been attacked and left for dead: the Doomsday virus.

But, he had known from the beginning that he was taking a risk by selling the virus to the American. The potential rewards had made the risk worth taking. He could no sooner undo what he'd done than will the sunflowers up from the frozen ground.

And now he would die without bouncing his Malia on his knee one last time. Without feeling her warm arms wrapped around his neck as she snuggled in for a hug, smelling of crayons, and milk, and sunshine.

Regret is just wasted energy, he told himself, drawing a last, shaky breath as the sun and the dormant fields faded, first to gray, then to black.

7

Saturday

Leo glanced across the front seat of the Passat at Sasha. Her hands gripped the steering wheel tightly, and her eyes were fixed on the stretch of Route 28 that unrolled in front of them. She wore sunglasses to combat the early morning glare of the sun off the snow banked along the sides of the highway. But he knew that, behind the lenses, her eyes would be dull and tired.

He was worried about her. After their meeting with Grace, they'd driven back to the lake house just long enough to pack up, shut off the water, and pick up her car. Then, they'd caravanned to Pittsburgh, gliding into the city on quiet streets in the dead of night.

By the time they fell into bed it was nearly three o'clock.

Leo hadn't spent the night at Sasha's condo in over a month, and he'd been surprised how out of place he'd felt there.

He'd had trouble falling asleep, and Sasha's restlessness hadn't helped. For most of the night, she'd flailed, tossing and turning, and mumbled about killers and killer flus in her sleep.

If he hadn't been worried she'd misinterpret his action, he'd have gone out and slept on the couch. But, he didn't want to introduce any more distance between them.

I shouldn't have convinced her to take the case, he chastised himself.

But it was too late now.

Earlier, over bowls of baked oatmeal with dried fruit, he'd tried to suggest they find a labor and employment lawyer to handle the investigation into Celia Gerig's background. She'd waved him off and changed the subject to the recipe for her oatmeal, proudly gesturing to the slow cooker where the steel-cut oats had cooked while they'd slept—or tried to, at any rate.

Leo knew one thing for sure: if Sasha was changing the subject *to* her cooking, she was uncomfortable with the topic at hand.

He'd been selfish to ask her to take the case. So

what if Tate was inconvenienced? Shouldn't Sasha's happiness come before some random corporate big shot's?

He cleared his throat. "So, what's in this town? Old boyfriend?"

Sasha had insisted on driving to their meeting in New Kensington, saying she was familiar with the town.

She took her eyes from the road to look at him, and he smiled to let her know he was kidding.

"Hardly," she said, smiling back at him for a moment.

Her smile stirred a feeling of tenderness, a lump in his throat.

"Then what's the connection?"

She turned her attention back to the road and said, "During law school, I did a clinical placement with a community economic development organization, helping small businesses incorporate in depressed former steel towns. I had clients in New Ken, Oil City, Montour, all over. I spent a lot of time driving this stretch of road a decade ago."

"New Kensington's depressed?"

"It was back then, but there were lots of local micro-businesses getting off the ground," she said.

"And now?"

"I'm not sure, to be honest." She signaled a turn and took the exit ramp. "I guess we'll find out. So, tell me about ViraGene. Why is Grace so sure they're spying on you?"

Leo took in the homes on the edge of town. Tired-looking brick ranchers sat next to small aluminum cottages with metal awnings that had once been white but were now streaked with black grime. A lopsided chain link fence ran along a cracked sidewalk. Someone had strung a row of large Christmas lights across the top in a halfhearted attempt at making it festive for the holiday. Tall weeds poked up between the cracks.

"Your economic development project doesn't look like it stuck," he commented.

Sasha glanced out the window herself then repeated her question.

"ViraGene, Leo?"

"Right, sorry. We have a history with ViraGene. Well, let me back up. The pharmaceutical industry as a whole is highly competitive and secretive. If you can find out what another company's working on, you might be able to beat them to market with a drug. If you can hire away their sales reps, you can gain access to their client lists, price lists, all that stuff. So, it's not unusual for companies to try hard to hire away one another's employees. Most employees have to sign noncompetes, but I don't have to tell you that those are often ignored."

"Sure," Sasha agreed.

"So, we've had multiple instances, even just in the short time I've been here, of ViraGene hiring our employees, and those employees trying to walk out the door with client lists, price lists, you name it. Mainly, they were hiring sales representatives, but we heard rumblings that they were talking to the scientists, which made the board nervous."

"Did you go after them?"

"Oh, yeah. Tate got fed up with the nonsense and started firing off temporary restraining orders left and right. That's one of the reasons the legal budget is frozen."

"Yeah, I imagine litigating a bunch of TROs got expensive pretty quickly," Sasha commented.

"Apparently. So, after Tate's legal offensive, ViraGene got creative. One of our security guards noticed a guy on the cleaning crew walking out of the building at one in the morning with papers stuffed inside his shirt. He detained the guy and called me. Grace and I interviewed him. He said he'd been approached by a man outside the building who called him over and said he'd pay five hundred dollars for any paperwork he found in the wastebaskets. He was supposed to meet the guy at a deli in Takoma Park, right across the border in the District. We took him down to the deli to identify the guy, but he said he didn't see him. The guy probably got spooked." Leo shrugged.

"But, that wasn't necessarily ViraGene," Sasha said.

Ever the lawyer, Leo thought, suppressing a chuckle. She was right that they couldn't prove ViraGene had been behind it, but he knew in his bones that they had been—just as Oliver and Grace were likely right that they were behind Celia Gerig and her fake references. The pharmaceutical industry was cutthroat, and no one played dirtier than ViraGene.

"That's true, but the timing suggests it probably was. We had just signed the contract to supply the government with the vaccine. The cleaning guy incident happened the day after the deal was made public," he explained.

"What happened to the cleaning guy?"

"He was probably fired, but I can't say for sure. We terminated the contract with the company and hired a new outfit," Leo answered.

A green traffic light marked the first major intersection they'd encountered since leaving the highway. Sasha accelerated, and they entered a commercial strip that showed no signs of commerce: an abandoned car dealership; a hair salon that sat in a small Cape Cod building, its sign hanging askew and several letters missing; and a Chinese restaurant with a "For Sale" sign hanging in the front window.

"Let's assume it was ViraGene. What could they

possibly have expected to find in the trash—a copy of the signed contract?" Sasha said, turning right just past an appliance repair shop that had an "Open" sign hanging in the door but no cars in the snow-covered parking lot.

"It's a desperate move," he agreed.

As they left the town's pitiful business section behind, the road grew increasingly uneven and bumpy.

"Do they have a competing vaccine?"

Sasha crossed a set of railroad tracks, and the paved surface ended entirely, replaced by snow-covered gravel.

Leo grabbed the dashboard with his right hand to brace himself as they jostled along.

"No, that's one reason they were trying to hire away our researchers—they lack the knowledge base to create a vaccine. We've been very good at recruiting away junior academic researchers, and they have had less success with that. They do claim to have created an effective antiviral, though," he said.

"An antiviral treats flu symptoms and a vaccine prevents you from catching it in the first place, right? I mean, basically?"

"Basically. A scientist would cringe, but, yeah, that's pretty much it. But we're careful to always say a vaccination will either provide immunity to a specific strain of the flu *or* lessen the severity and duration of the flu if the immunized person is infected. It depends on the individual," he said.

"Yeah. My brothers had all their kids vaccinated for chicken pox, but Siobhan managed to catch it at preschool, anyway. Ryan said she was mildly itchy on one thigh and ran a low fever for a day, but that was it," Sasha said.

"That's actually pretty amazing, if you think about it. I mean, I had the chickenpox when I was a kid. I was a miserable, itchy mess. It was a rotten week stuck at home and taking baths in that pink stuff," Leo said. He had to resist the urge to scratch just remembering it.

"Oh, definitely," she agreed, glancing over and giving him a quick smile, then she was all business again. "If ViraGene has an antiviral now, why would they still care so much about your vaccine? The stockpile won't have anywhere near enough doses to immunize everyone if the flu does hit. Won't everyone else be begging for the antiviral?"

"Sure, people probably would, but that's not how ViraGene views it. We have a guaranteed contract for millions of doses. They have nothing, unless the virus actually hits. And the government has already come out and said they aren't going to stockpile the antiviral. Meanwhile, ViraGene has just spent *a lot* of money developing this drug. I'm sure they'd love to find out that our vaccine doesn't work as well as we claim, or has some sort of horrible side effect, or that our production schedule is backed up—anything they could take to the government to try to convince them to switch horses."

ViraGene's increasing desperation made perfect sense to Leo. In the short time he'd worked in the private sector, he'd come to realize that shareholder confidence and the markets were the altars at which corporations worshipped. They'd do just about anything to appease those twin gods.

"I suppose," Sasha murmured.

The gravel ended. A heavy metal gate marked the beginning of Serumceutical's property. The gate hung open, and the parking lot had been cleared of snow. Sasha bumped the car up onto the paved lot and headed across it to the nondescript, low-slung rectangular building that sat at the far end.

As they neared the gunmetal gray building, Leo spotted Ben Davenport, the collar of his coat turned up against the cold, pacing back and forth in front of the glass-doored entrance. Ben raised a hand in greeting, and Leo saw the worry etched on his face even from a distance. Leo tensed.

"Something's wrong," he said more to himself than to Sasha as she eased the car into a parking spot and killed the engine.

She looked at him with bemusement in her glittering green eyes. "What?"

"Never mind," he said. They'd find out soon enough if his feeling was right.

Ben walked over to the car to greet them.

"Leo, Ms. McCandless. Hope the drive wasn't too bad," he said with a smile and an extended hand.

Leo shook the warehouse manager's hand and searched his eyes. "Piece of cake; the roads are dry. How are you, Ben?"

"Good. Not used to the cold anymore, though," he said, barking out a laugh. "Let's get inside."

Ben turned to Sasha and explained, "After Serumceutical shuttered this place when it 'right-sized' operations back in the 90s, I took advantage of the early retirement package and moved down to Clearwater with the Missus. She was none too happy when they dragged me back from Florida to reopen this place as a consultant."

Sasha laughed and shook his outstretched hand. "If I were her, I think I would have held down the fort in Florida," she said with a laugh.

Leo had to smile as he watched her utterly charm the anxious older man.

"Don't you give her any ideas if you run into her, Ms. McCandless," Ben said, guiding Sasha toward the door with a hand on her back. "Watch your step now. I shoveled the walk, but I might have missed a patch or two."

"I'll be careful. And, please, call me Sasha," she said.

Leo trailed behind them, wondering why Ben hadn't had someone else do the shoveling. He knew that the distribution center was staffed by a skeleton crew, but surely Ben could have found an extra pair of hands to wield a shovel.

A blast of hot air hit the trio as they entered the foyer, a small square that sat between the outer door and the inner, locked door. Ben fumbled with a key card that hung around his neck on a lanyard and held it up to the reader.

"How many people are there on the weekend shift now?" Leo asked as the card reader beeped its approval and the door unlocked.

"Well, we've got an even dozen scheduled," Ben said, holding the door and ushering them in ahead of him. "But, we're kind of scrambling this morning. We've got a situation. I was just getting ready to call you, actually. It's all hands on deck over in the storage area. Including my secretary, who doubles as the receptionist. So, I'll apologize in advance for the quality of the coffee and the lack of pastries. Maggie would be spitting nails if she knew what a bad host I'm being."

He led them past an empty reception desk to a

small, square office. Faint Christmas carols were just audible through the static on an old black radio. The back wall was lined with metal filing cabinets. In front of it, sat a small metal desk that housed a computer, a metal in-box, and three Styrofoam coffee cups. Two fabric-covered metal chairs were jammed between the desk and the open door.

Ben squeezed past them and sat behind the desk.

"Make yourselves comfortable," he said. "There's a coat rack behind the door."

Leo took off his overcoat and waited for Sasha to wriggle out of her red wool coat, then hung them both on the rack behind the door and eased it shut.

"Are those your grandkids?" Sasha asked, leaning in to see the only personal touch in the musty room —a wood-framed picture of a group of towheaded kids, arms linked, standing on a beach, squinting in the sun and laughing.

Ben's tanned face lit up. "Yep, all five of them."

"They're beautiful," Sasha said.

Ben laughed. "Well, I think so. Might be biased, though."

Then he nodded toward the cups. "Help yourselves. It might not be good, but it should still be hot. That gal of yours said you'd both appreciate a cup of joe when you got here."

"That sounds like Grace, all right. Thanks, Ben," Leo said.

Leo sipped at the muddy coffee out of politeness. Grace's request had been for Sasha's benefit, not his. Although he liked the stuff, he didn't need it. Sasha seemed to be fueled entirely by coffee; despite being a fraction of his size, she consumed it in quantities that would have rendered him jerky, shaking, and frenetic.

He looked over the cup at the man on the other side of the desk.

He'd met Ben once before, when the older man had visited headquarters to work out the details of his contract and discuss with the operations team the logistics of filling the government's orders. The face-to-face meetings had been unnecessary—the details could have been worked out over email or by arranging a web conference. But Ben was old school, a man who believed in handling things personally.

"Thank you for meeting with us, especially on short notice and while you're scrambling to meet your schedule," Leo said, a gentle nudge toward getting down to business.

Ben's smile faded, and his skin drained white under his tan. "Well, as a matter of fact, I'm scrambling on this Celia Gerig thing."

Leo found himself leaning forward at Ben's ominous tone. Beside him, Sasha put down her cup and mirrored his posture.

"Oh?" Leo asked.

"I know Grace told you about my run-in with Celia and how her references were bogus. That realtor lady called me back this morning: Celia never lived in that house. And I asked everyone on the warehouse floor today. She never shared any personal information with any of them. We have no idea where to start looking for her."

"Don't beat yourself up. This was a human resources error, not yours. You've done us a favor by ferreting it out. We're grateful," Leo told him.

Ben shook his head. "Don't be. It's about to get ugly."

"Ugly?" Sasha echoed.

Ben nodded and pushed himself up from his desk.

"Come see for yourselves," he said as he headed for the door.

Sasha and Connelly followed Ben along a long hallway lined with metal filing cabinets. Sasha took in the worn, thin carpet and peeling paint with one part of her brain while another processed the information Ben had shared so far: the woman Grace and Connelly suspected of being a ViraGene plant was in the wind, leaving behind a fake address, fake references, and a non-working telephone number.

She considered the company's options. If she were Tate, she wouldn't let this one go. She'd hire a private investigator to track down Celia Gerig and fire a shot across ViraGene's bow. But, what? She didn't have the evidence to connect the missing employee with a competitor.

Not yet. She wondered if whatever Ben was going to show them would help build a case against ViraGene.

Leo glanced back at her, his face tense as he waited to see what Ben had in store.

Ben pushed open one side of a set of large metal doors and held it while they passed through and entered a brightly lit, cavernous room with a concrete floor and a high ceiling. The temperature dropped a good twenty degrees as Sasha crossed the threshold, and she shivered involuntarily.

"Sorry," Ben said, "I should have told you to bring your coat. The vaccines are supposed to be refrigerated. We get them into the walk-in as quickly as we can, but have to check them in first, so we keep it cool in here."

The room was three-quarters empty. The final quarter was filled with rows of wooden pallets. The pallets were stacked high with cardboard boxes. Each pallet was wrapped in a giant sheet of what looked to be industrial-grade cellophane.

Men and women wearing fingerless wool gloves

hurried back and forth between an open loading dock bay and the columns of pallets, wheeling dollies piled high with more cardboard boxes.

"Another truck full of vaccines came in this morning," Ben explained. "So, we have to check them in, make sure nothing's been damaged in transit and that the shipment quantity matches the manifest. Then, we restack them and wrap them up for pickup by the Army."

"You open every box?" Sasha asked.

Ben nodded. "It's a pain in the rear, but the contract requires a manual check of each box of vials. That's the government for you. And that's the other problem we've got."

He crossed the room and walked past the tall rows of pallets and headed for the far corner where one lonely, wooden pallet had been shoved up against the wall, its clear wrap torn open.

"What's wrong with that one?" Leo asked.

"Well, Jason over there got his keys caught on the wrap as he was walking by this morning," Ben said, pointing to a tall, muscular man whose keys dangled from his belt.

Jason kept his head down and moved in the self-conscious way of someone who knows he's being watched, every motion exaggerated.

"And, thank God he did. Because as he was rewrapping the pallet, he noticed that a box lid was open. So, he went to close it and, sure enough, two vials were missing."

"Missing?" Sasha asked, her stomach dropping with dread.

"Yup. That box was two vials short. So, Jason called me. I came down here and went through the rest of the boxes myself. Each pallet holds 144 boxes. Every box on this pallet is missing two vials. That's 288 missing doses that we know of." Ben flung his arm wide, gesturing toward the stacks of pallets. "Who knows how many more there are? I'm going to have to have these guys work mandatory overtime and recount six pallets."

"Why just six?" Leo asked. "Why not all of them."

Ben removed his glasses with one hand and pinched the bridge of his nose. "Because Celia Gerig checked in a total of ten pallets, according to our records. One is right there, with the missing doses. Six more are somewhere in the stacks."

"And the other three?" Sasha asked, afraid she knew the answer.

"The other three were picked up on Friday and taken to Fort Meade," Ben said.

8

Colton pushed the brown, wilted lettuce around on his plate with the side of his fork. He realized it was the dead of winter, but for the amount of money he was paying for a salad he expected fresh greens.

He snapped his head up and scanned the room. When he caught the waiter's eye, he gestured with a finger. The young man gulped visibly and trotted over to the table, walking as quickly as he could without breaking into a run.

"Is everything okay, Mr. Maxwell, sir?" he said, the crisp white napkin draped over his arm, still fluttering from his rushed approach.

"No, everything is not okay, Manuel," Colton said, reading the waiter's name from the small gold bar pinned to his starched shirt. "I ordered the fresh grilled salmon salad, did I not?"

Manuel's eyes darted to the salad plate to confirm that he'd brought the right dish. Then, they clouded with confusion, and he answered slowly, "Yes, sir."

Colton speared one soggy leaf of arugula with the tines of the fork and held it up for Manuel to inspect. "Does that look fresh to you?"

"No, sir," he said immediately.

"That's right. It does not. Take it back and bring me a new one," Colton said. He released the fork, and it clattered to the plate. He congratulated himself on resisting his initial urge, which had been to fling the lettuce at Manuel's face.

Relief flooded the waiter's face, and he ducked his head and scooped up the plate. Colton realized Manuel had been expecting to be pelted with greens. It appeared the story of how he'd returned cold chowder at his last visit had made the rounds of the Club's wait staff.

He didn't need to draw attention to his temper. He indulged in a small measure of regret for his decision to dump the crab chowder over Marta's head.

"Thank you," he called to Manuel's retreating form in a belated effort at damage control. Then he turned to his lunch companion and smiled. "How's your sandwich?"

"Fine," he said, mumbling the words around

bites of his Reuben. Then he returned the sandwich to his plate and dabbed his mouth with his napkin.

Colton's guest took a long drink of water and then said, "So, I have what you want."

Colton flicked his eyes to the nearest occupied table. Two trophy wives were babbling about their tennis lesson and paying no attention to anyone else.

"Are you sure?" he asked.

The man—who'd told Colton to call him Andre, even though they both knew he wouldn't be using his real name—shrugged. "I think so. You're the expert, not me."

Andre reached into his jacket pocket and pulled out a small glass vial. He handed it across the table, "The rest of it's in my trunk. You can inspect it there. Either way, payment's due in full."

Colton stared at the ampule in his hand. The man was insane to just pull it out in the middle of the dining room.

He scanned the room to ensure no one was watching them, then hissed, "Don't worry, Andre, your money's in my trunk."

Colton slipped the vial into his briefcase as adrenaline coursed through his body.

"Forget the salad. Let's go."

He stood and waited for Andre to gulp down the last bite of his sandwich, eager to get on with his plan.

9

Sasha let Connelly drive her car back to Pittsburgh so she could work the phone. Her representation of Serumceutical had taken on a new urgency. The familiar sense of all-consuming drive filled her.

Connelly glanced over at her. "You look jazzed," he commented.

She was sure she did. The stakes had been raised, awaking her love for competition. ViraGene was going to pay for what they'd done to her newest client.

She just smiled at Connelly and held up a finger to silence him as she waited for Naya, her legal assistant to answer the ringing phone.

"The Law Offices of Sasha McCandless," Naya's

voice rang out through the speakerphone, clear, formal, and businesslike, especially for a Saturday.

Sasha felt a smidgeon of guilt for asking Naya to come in, especially with all the holiday preparations she had going on with her church's pageant, but Naya had assured her it was fine, as long as she didn't miss the pageant rehearsal Sunday afternoon.

"Naya, it's me," she said.

"I know, Mac, just messing with you." Naya laughed. "How'd the meeting go?"

"It was interesting. Oh, you're on speaker," Sasha said, giving Naya an unspoken warning not to ask about her relationship with Connelly.

"Hi, fly boy," Naya cracked.

"Hello, Naya," Connelly said, unable to hide his smile at Naya's ribbing. "Have you missed me?"

Before Naya could respond, Sasha jumped in. "You two will have plenty of time to play your games when we get back to the office. Naya, I need you to get started on something."

"Got it," Naya said, the playfulness gone from her voice. "Hit me."

"Okay, first, Celia Gerig is gone. As far as we know, all of the information on her application was false, except for her social security number and her name. I need you to run her down."

"Will do. Do we know what she looks like?" Naya asked.

"Ben's secretary is going to email you a copy of her personnel file, which includes a digital photo they took at the distribution center for her employee ID. That's all we're going to have, I think. A name, a social, and a picture," Sasha said.

"I've done more with less," Naya told her.

It was true. Naya had what Sasha considered good people skills. She wasn't always great at dealing with people, but she was an ace at two more important things: finding them and reading them. Naya could track a person down. She could also look at a person and know if he was lying. Those two valuable traits more than made up for her occasional lack of tact in her personal interactions.

"Great. There's more, but start there, because we have to find this woman. And fast."

"I hear you. Hey, should I order you guys some food from Jake's?"

Sasha checked the time. It was past lunchtime. After Ben had dropped his bombshell, the three of them had returned to his office and hammered out their next steps. None of them had been in any mood to eat at that point.

Now, she felt too wired to eat. She looked over at Connelly, who was nodding vigorously. His stomach rumbled loudly, driving home his view.

"Connelly's stomach says 'yes,'" she told Naya. "We'll be there in about forty minutes."

"See you later," Naya said and ended the call.

Sasha cleared her throat. She had more calls to make, but first she wanted to take one more run at Connelly.

"Connelly?"

"Yeah?" he said in a tone that suggested he knew what was coming.

"You have to call Tate," she said in a soft voice.

"I know, Sasha. Not yet."

She watched his knuckles turn white as he gripped the steering wheel tighter and waited a moment to see if he would say anything further. He did not.

"Waiting's only going to make it worse," she said.

She'd tried to explain as much back in Ben's office. But Connelly and Ben had refused to budge. Ben wanted to finish checking in the new shipment of drugs, then have his employees open the six pallets that Celia had handled and recount all the boxes to determine the extent of the problem before they told anyone.

Connelly had agreed with Ben's suggestion because he wanted Grace to coordinate with human resources to finish all of the distribution center employees' reference checks to ensure there were no other Gerig-type problems lurking in the files.

She understood their instinct to get a full picture of the damage done. But the board of directors had to be informed and soon. They needed to authorize a move against ViraGene and, perhaps more critically, they needed to tell the government.

Sasha knew from past experience representing companies in antitrust, accounting, and bribery investigations conducted by the various arms of the federal government that self-reporting always resulted in cooperation and leniency from the governmental alphabet soup. If, however, a government agency suspected a corporation of stonewalling or covering up a problem, there would be consequences—usually to the tune of several hundred million dollars, but occasionally jail time for corporate management. Sasha was fairly certain her relationship with Connelly could not withstand distance *and* an orange jumpsuit.

"The board has important decisions to make, and I want them to do that with full information. Surely you understand," Connelly said in a firm voice.

Sasha shook her head. "I do understand. But it's really not your call to make. You need to talk to Tate," she repeated.

"Later. We'll get Oliver on the phone as soon as Ben and Grace finish," Connelly promised.

Connelly had instructed Ben and Grace to work around the clock if necessary to get him all the information he needed.

"Connelly, if ViraGene is behind this, nothing's

stopping them from anonymously tipping off the government that the shipment was short. In fact, they probably will. You have to get out in front of this."

"We will," Connelly said, setting his mouth in a firm line.

Sasha exhaled loudly. She knew him well enough to know he felt responsible for the theft. And he wouldn't drop a problem in the decision makers' laps without also presenting them a solution. He was right that they needed to know the full extent of the issue in order to address it. She just hoped it wouldn't be too late by then.

"You're the client."

She opened the Amazon shopping app on her phone.

Connelly glanced over at her. "What are you doing now?"

Sasha answered without looking up. "Some Christmas shopping."

"Really?"

"Yes, really. I have to do it some time, don't I? And until you're ready to talk to Tate, there isn't much I can do for you."

She was working her way through her list methodically. She started with her nieces and nephews because shopping for kids was easy and fun and saved the harder people for the end. Connelly was, not surprisingly, dead last on her list.

"Who are you shopping for?"

"I'm finishing off Jordan now. I'm just getting her a box of ginger cookies and some preggie pops."

Both of her brothers' wives were pregnant. Again. But, this time Jordan was carrying twins and having a difficult time of it. Sasha'd gotten both Jordan and Riley gift certificates for pregnancy massages at their favorite day spa, but she wanted to add something small for Jordan's stocking.

"Preggie pops?"

"I don't know, Connelly. They're these special lollipops that are supposed to help with nausea."

"Oh. Could you imagine having twins?" Connelly asked.

The undercurrent in his voice made her look up. "I can't imagine having a cat, Connelly, let alone two human beings who are utterly dependent on me."

"Don't you ever see yourself having kids?"

Sasha wasn't sure how to answer. "Maybe, I guess. Sometimes. When I'm reading a book with Daniella or helping Liam work on a science project, I think about how amazing it must be to have that relationship. But, right now? How would that work?"

Connelly didn't answer.

"What about you? Do you want kids?" As she

asked the question, she realized she had no idea what his answer would be. They'd never discussed it.

"Yes." He said it immediately and decisively.

"Oh."

She returned to filling her order and turned this new information over in her head.

"What are you thinking?" he pressed.

"I'm trying to decide whether to get Naya a cashmere sweater or a boxed set of Law & Order DVDs," she lied.

She felt his eyes on her but didn't look up.

"Watch the road, Connelly."

WHEN THEY REACHED THE OFFICE, Naya was waiting for them with a tray of wraps from the coffee shop downstairs. And, more importantly, a carafe of fresh coffee. Connelly beelined for the food; Sasha went straight to the caffeine source.

Naya shook her head. "How about some lunch, Mac? Jake had the kitchen make you a brie and green apple sandwich."

"Brie and apple?" Connelly said around a mouthful of roast beef.

Naya shrugged. "She claims it's good. I haven't tried it." She plucked a turkey and Swiss wrap from the tray.

"I'll eat later," Sasha said. She couldn't eat now—she'd never been able to eat when stress hormones were flooding her body. It had made her first year of law school a bit of a challenge.

"Suit yourself," Naya said. She handed Sasha a manila folder. "Here. This is what I've managed to find on your girl. Well, maybe your girl."

Sasha flipped the folder open. A copy of the personnel file records were clipped to the front of the folder along with a picture of an unsmiling Celia Gerig. Naya had crossed through the information they knew to be inaccurate with a thick black marker. The social security number was highlighted, along with the woman's educational background.

"What's the rest of this?" Sasha asked, leafing through printouts of what appeared to be threads from an Internet chatroom. "This Preppers Pennsylvania stuff?"

"I couldn't find any property records or other public records in her name or social, but I ran some Google searches. She's not on Facebook, Twitter, or Google+, unless she uses a pseudonym, but I found a 'cgerig' on a prepper forum, posting on a Pennsylvania-specific sub-forum—Preppers PA. This 'cgerig' uses an avatar of the American flag, not a profile picture, so I can't say for sure it's your girl, but if it is..." Naya trailed off, shaking her head at the thought.

Sasha looked up at her. "What's a prepper?"

Connelly abandoned his sandwich and came to peer over Sasha's shoulder at the papers.

Naya's voice lacked its usual confidence when she answered. "I haven't had a lot of time to dig into it, but I think preppers are survivalists. They're all about preparing for catastrophe and being self-reliant if—or, I guess they think, when—the government collapses."

Connelly nodded his agreement.

Sasha remained confused. "So, I have a case of bottled water and a flashlight in my hall closet. Am I a prepper?"

Connelly shook his head. "These people are a bit more enthusiastic about it than that. They have secure locations set up in remote areas; they stockpile nonperishable food, clothes, antibiotics, gasoline, ammunition and weapons, you name it."

Naya chimed in, "Yeah, this cgerig was posting looking for a good source for vacuum-packed heirloom seeds in case she has to bug out and leave her vegetable garden behind."

"Bug out?"

Naya laughed. "I picked up some of the lingo. When SHTF—uh, that'd be when the shit hits the fan—a prepper needs to decide whether to bug out or bug in. Bugging out is what Leo was talking about. Grab your go bag, your family, and a container of extra fuel and jump in your car, headed for your secure outpost, away from society and all the chaos."

"And bugging in, I assume, that's sheltering in place?" Sasha asked.

Naya nodded. "Bar the doors and windows, fire up your generator, keep your weapon handy, and hunker down until everyone else dies or whatever."

Sasha considered this information. "So, Celia Gerig may be affiliated with a group of preppers. Do we think she's dangerous?"

Naya shrugged. "It looks like any other group, Mac. Some people really seem to be throwing themselves into it: they're organizing meet ups, making up secret passwords, and sending coded messages. They talk about converting their currency into gold bars or silver ingots and learning how to field dress deer. Some people are dabbling—they want to plant a garden, can some vegetables, maybe learn how to purify water. I'd say based on what I've seen, Celia Gerig, if this is even her, was in the second group. But, I don't know for sure. She could be skinning a rabbit somewhere as we speak."

Sasha grimaced.

Connelly cleared his throat. "There's nothing inherently bad in preparing for a disaster. That's a good thing, actually. But we need to find out, fast, if Celia Gerig was actually a member of a fringe group." The muscles under his cheeks twitched.

Sasha cocked her head and took in his grim expression. "These preppers are on some kind of list, aren't they?"

When Connelly had still been working for the Department of Homeland Security, she and he had engaged in several heated, ultimately unproductive, debates about whether it was appropriate, or even useful, for the government to surreptitiously gather information about private citizens based on, say, their membership in an environmental group or their ethnic-sounding surname.

Sasha's defense of the First Amendment had repeatedly bumped up against Connelly's commitment to national security, and, finally, the subject became one of those topics that couples just avoid. Only, in their case, it kept popping back up at really inopportune times—like when a rogue employee disappeared with an indeterminate number of government vaccines needed to prevent a pandemic.

Connelly exhaled and glanced down at her. "Can I use Naya's office? I have to make some calls," he said, by way of answer.

That was fine with Sasha. She had some calls of her own to make. She nodded, and he walked across the hall, stopping only to kiss the top of her head as he passed her.

As the door shut behind him, Naya pounced.

"What's going on, Mac? This is obviously more than an employee helping a competitor."

Sasha flung herself into her desk chair. "That's for sure, but, to tell you the truth, I have no idea what's going on. We think ViraGene's behind it. But if Gerig is a prepper, who knows? All we know is she's missing, along with a bunch of vaccines."

Naya pulled out the chair across from her. "She stole vaccines?"

"We think so. Not just any vaccines, though. The vaccine for the Doomsday flu. The government's stockpiling it at Fort Meade."

Naya narrowed her eyes. "Well, ViraGene makes an antiviral, right? It makes sense that they'd want to screw up the contract for the vaccine. And having the shipment show up short would go a long way toward doing that, don't you think?"

"I do. At least that's what I *did* think. But, this prepper stuff adds a wrinkle."

"First of all, we don't even know if Gerig is a prepper. And, say she is, it could just be a hobby, unrelated to her corporate espionage career." Naya cracked a smile.

Sasha's return smile was weak. "Or it could be the beginning of another Ruby Ridge. You know that's what Connelly's thinking."

"What are you thinking?"

The question stirred up all the anxiety and worry

Sasha had spent the weekend tamping down. Sasha looked at Naya for a long moment then said, "I'm thinking this is getting too ugly, too fast. And I'm not up for anything other than a civil lawsuit between two corporations."

Naya's voice was softer and had a note of concern when she asked, "So, what are you gonna do, Mac?"

"The first thing I'm going to do is call Gavin Russell. We have to find out whether we even have a problem."

Gavin Russell, formerly of the Clear Brook County Sheriff's Office, had struck out for greener pastures and better coffee after the dust settled in Springport. He'd refused the promotion from deputy to sheriff, taken an early retirement package, and opened a private investigator's office across the street from the courthouse in the space recently vacated by the town doctor.

He answered Sasha's call on the second ring.

"Russell Investigations."

"First of all, it's Saturday, why are you in the office? Second of all, you still don't have a secretary?" Sasha asked.

"Hey, Sasha," he laughed. "As to your first question, you're one to talk—I see you're calling me from your office. And, as to the second, I can't convince Gloria that I'll pay her better than the new judge. I'm still working on her, though."

Sasha smiled, surprised at the fondness she felt for the former deputy and the judge's secretary. "You'll wear her down," she said. "So, how's business?"

Russell's voice rumbled across the line, and Sasha could picture him, his chair tipped back on two legs and his feet propped on his desk. A cup of shade-grown Cubano at his elbow.

"Good. It's a piece of cake, actually. Mainly, I'm doing what I used to do for the sheriff's office—serving subpoenas, tracking down witnesses, that sort of thing. But, I can charge less and still make more than I was earning. And the oil and gas people are like an untapped market." He chuckled at his own pun.

"How so?"

"Well, the riggers aren't local, most of them, anyway. And they've been up here a long time, months on end. Some girlfriends and wives are starting to get worried. One of them found my website and hired me to follow her guy around for a few weekends. Took a bunch of pictures of him playing cards and watching football at The Hole in the Wall, and she was delighted. She told all her friends, and now everybody wants me to follow their guy."

Sasha wasn't sure that was a great idea. Her last messy case had involved broken marriages and photographic evidence of bad behavior. "That sounds kind of dangerous, Gavin."

"Naw, I tried to explain to these ladies—there's not a huge single woman population up this way. Trust me, I know. Their guys aren't going to get into that kind of trouble, not in Springport. But, they just want the peace of mind and are willing to pay top dollar for it. Speaking of long-distance relationships, how are things with Leo?"

"We're working on it," she said simply.

"Good. He's a good man," Gavin proclaimed. Then, his tone changed, and he said, "But, I know you didn't call me just to shoot the breeze. What's up?"

"I might need to hire you. Can you still access state databases?"

Gavin answered slowly. "Do I still have personal access to the state databases? No."

"That's not what I asked."

"To answer your question, then, yes. But, what exactly do you need?"

"I'm not sure. I have a corporate client that's trying to find an employee. She used fake references and a phony address but her social checks out. Her last whereabouts were in New Kensington, outside of Pittsburgh. Naya's going to run down all the publicly available information, but we have a bit of a time crunch. Are there any databases you know of that would help?"

"Does she have any known prior arrests or convictions?" Gavin said.

"None that I know of, but to check the criminal dockets on our end would be a nightmare."

Each of the sixty-seven counties within the Commonwealth of Pennsylvania maintained its own criminal docket sheets, which were theoretically searchable on-line, but it would be tedious and time-consuming for Naya to run the searches one at a time, and there was always the risk that some county clerk had mistyped a letter when entering the data or that a county wasn't completely up to date with its dockets. No, Naya's time was better spent running down other leads. Especially if Gavin could go straight to the source.

"Okay. Give me the name and social. I'll call you back with anything that pops."

"The name is Celia Anne Gerig. That's G-E-R-I-G and her social is—"

"Celia Gerig?"Gavin repeated, cutting her off. Surprise registered in his voice.

"Don't tell me you know her."

"I know *a* Celia Gerig. She's local. If it's the same woman, I took her to my prom."

10

Celia woke up late and bone tired on Saturday afternoon. She checked her watch. She'd slept past noon. She couldn't remember the last time she'd done that. She didn't feel refreshed, though. She felt wrung out and flat.

She pushed herself up on her elbows and blinked the sand out of her eyes, trying to figure out where she was. As the fog lifted over her brain, the events of the previous evening returned: the dead car battery and the run-in with Ben; the drive north to the rendezvous point; the meeting; the vaccination. It all came back, and she realized she was in Lydia's guest room.

After Ben had jumped her battery, she'd had to drive way up north to the rendezvous point to deliver the vaccines to George and Lydia. With Ben's warning in her ears, she hadn't stopped to get a bite or even use the restroom for fear the Civic wouldn't start again if she did. By the time she reached the old union hall, she was exhausted, hungry, and sore from sitting hunched over the wheel.

She didn't recognize any of the cars in the crowded parking lot, but she was tired, and it was dark, so she just slung her purse over her shoulder, hauled the larger bag from the trunk of her car, and headed across the uneven lot for the side door to the basement, hoping George and Lydia would be there as promised.

When she walked through the door, she nearly fell over. Not only were George and Lydia there, but there must have been somewhere between thirty and forty other people milling around in the brightly lit room. Her heart started to race, and she felt the heat rise on her face.

Who were all these people? What had she just walked into? She gripped the straps of both bags, hugging them tight to her body, and stood in the doorway wavering.

She swayed from side to side and tried to decide whether to plunge into the crowd or back her way out the door.

George and Lydia pushed through the sea of milling bodies and appeared at her elbow.

"What is this?" Celia asked. Her voice shook.

George smiled and patted her arm.

"A good thing. We told Captain Bricker about your success in acquiring the vaccines. He's privy to some news that led him to move up the timetable on the inoculations. That's why all the bigwigs are here," he said, easing the strap of the larger bag off her shoulder.

His explanation cleared up exactly nothing. She'd always been a bit player in the organization—a dabbler, really. Not because she wasn't interested, because she was, but because she lacked any special skill or background that would enable her to take a leadership role. George was former military. Lydia, his girlfriend and second-in-command, was a nurse. Celia was just a nobody who wanted to learn how to take care of herself.

So when George had asked her to stay behind to talk after their November troop meeting, she'd been more than surprised—she'd been shocked that her troop leader was interested in talking to her personally. Flustered, but excited at the prospect of *doing* something, she'd agreed to apply for the job at the distribution center and acquire the vaccines.

Throughout the mission, George and Lydia had always been careful to say 'acquire' or 'obtain,' never 'steal.' And, although Celia knew darned well that what she'd done was stealing, she'd adopted their usage, too. Still, she hadn't felt overly bad about her actions, because George and Lydia had repeatedly told her how important it was to the organization that they get the vaccines.

Now, looking out at the room full of troop leaders that were here because of her, and what she'd done, she didn't feel bad at all. She felt puffed up with pride.

"*He's* here," Lydia whispered in a conspiratorial, awed voice.

"Who?" Celia asked.

"Captain Bricker."

A jolt of excitement coursed through Celia's body, and she felt her eyes go wide. Captain Jeffrey Bricker was the head of Preppers PA, but in the nearly eighteen months that she'd been a member, Celia'd never shared the same air as him. She'd seen videotaped talks that he posted on the members portal of the website, and she'd read his weekly newsletter, but she'd never personally met him. Judging by the shimmer in Lydia's eyes, she wasn't the only one.

"He's here? Really?" Celia asked.

"Really. And he wants to meet you," George said. He laughed at her star-struck expression and steered her down the two steps that led to the floor and through the crowd.

They approached a tall, handsome older man. Even from behind, Celia recognized his close-cropped blond hair shot through with silver and broad shoulders from the videotaped speeches he'd posted on the website.

George tapped the captain on the arm, and he turned toward them. In person, his bright blue eyes were even more arresting.

"Sir, this is Celia Gerig," George said, gesturing toward her.

As the captain searched her face, Celia felt her cheeks flush.

"Celia, your mission is going to save untold lives. To say thank you seems entirely inadequate, but you have my personal thanks," he finally said, taking her hand and shaking it in the two-handed manner of a politician.

Celia stammered, "You're welcome."

He swept his gaze wider to include George and Lydia. "All three of you are to be commended for your service. We'll be moving into the next phase this weekend. As a show of my gratitude, I've decided you may each designate one civilian to bring to the camp with you if you choose. Do you have any non-preppers you'd like to save?"

George and Lydia were holding hands. They looked at each other and then shook their heads no in unison.

"Save?" Celia managed to squeak.

Captain Bricker nodded gravely. "Our intel is

solid. The virus is on its way. The American way of life as you know it is about to end."

Celia's stomach lurched, and her mind spun. Finally, she said, "My mother. Please."

He nodded again and patted her shoulder. "Of course. Tomorrow we'll be running vaccination clinics, but you can get her on Sunday and bring her to the compound. I expect anyone who wishes to save themselves will be convening at the compound by Monday at the latest. Now, if you'll excuse me, I need to explain the plan to our gathered brethren."

She nodded, mute and grateful, and stepped back to stand beside George and Lydia, who released each other's hands and straightened to attention.

Captain Bricker called for silence, and the din of laughter and conversation ceased immediately. It was as if someone had pressed a mute button. Forty-odd faces turned toward the leader, expectant and eager.

With a solemn expression, he delivered the news, "Friends, thank you for gathering on such short notice. As some of you know, two weeks ago some disconcerting news came to my attention. Without going into details, I became convinced that the pandemic was imminent, and the government is ill-prepared to deal with it."

He paused and allowed a muted murmur to make its way around the room. To Celia, it sounded disapproving, but unsurprised. As if those assembled already knew this information.

"Now," he said, "let me forestall the obvious questions. Hasn't the government contracted with a pharmaceutical company to stockpile an effective vaccine? Doesn't that mean we'll all be safe? The answers are that they have, indeed, and it means the exact opposite."

He squared his shoulders and jutted his chin forward and thundered, "Our government, ladies and gentlemen has bought all the available doses of the vaccine. All of them. That means when the day comes—and it's coming soon—that the first American citizen is stricken with a flu unlike anything we've ever seen, you won't be able to protect yourself. Stay inside and wash your hands, that'll be the government's advice to you."

"That's right!" a voice from the crowd shouted.

Several people nodded. A woman near the front raised her fist and shook it.

Celia felt the outrage rising. The room grew close, hot.

"What else can they do? They don't have enough for everyone. So, they'll decide whether they deem you worthy of protection or whether you'll be left to suffer and die. Do you trust them to make the right choices?" Captain Bricker asked the crowd.

"Noooo!"

The call and response reminded Celia of church. To her left, Lydia was bouncing on the balls of her feet, raring to go.

"No, indeed. Which is why I'm pleased to tell you that George Rollins, with the assistance of two members of the D Unit, has secured us our own supply of the vaccine," Captain Bricker said.

He spread his arms wide and raised his palms toward the roof. The room reacted with hoots and applause. George, red-faced and awkward, shuffled his feet and waved. Lydia ducked her head. And Celia felt frozen in place as all eyes turned her way.

He continued, "So this evening, each of us will be vaccinated, and Nurse Markham will train us in administering the vaccine. Then, you need to return to your communities and reach out to your troops. Anyone who intends to weather the pandemic with us at the camp needs to be vaccinated, make final arrangements, and be ready to bug out ASAP. The vaccine takes seventy-two hours to reach full effectiveness, so you will each leave here tonight with a supply of doses sufficient to vaccinate your troop."

He paused and surveyed the room. "This is it, people."

His excitement bubbled to the surface for a moment, but he tamped it down so quickly Celia thought she imagined it.

Lydia organized them into teams and presented a

crash course in how to give vaccines. She demonstrated on George, who, in turn, gave Celia her shot. Celia vaccinated Captain Bricker with shaking hands, and he vaccinated the next person in line. On and on it went, one leader vaccinating the next. More than an hour passed in a blur of alcohol swabs and syringes.

It was nearly midnight when they finished, and when Celia trudged out to the icy parking lot, she wasn't surprised to find that her car battery had died again.

After a failed attempt to jump the car, Lydia grudgingly offered Celia her guest room.

Now, Celia shifted in the bed and winced. The injection site where George had administered her vaccine was sore. She gently rubbed the spot, then she rolled onto her side and out of the bed, with its stiff plaid comforter and matching bed skirt.

She moaned as her feet hit the floor. Her entire body ached. Lydia must have opted for the cheapest mattress available for her spare bedroom, she thought as she shuffled to the door and out to the kitchen.

The ranch house was quiet, but Lydia had left a note propped up against a still-warm coffee pot. She plucked it from the counter.

Celia,

Make yourself at home. George will drop off your car

with a new battery this afternoon. When my shift's over, we'll do a shot clinic for the unit.

Lydia

CELIA YAWNED. She really needed to perk up. She poured a cup of coffee and helped herself to a muffin from the tray next to the coffee maker.

She carried her breakfast into the living room and lowered herself onto the couch. She picked at the muffin with her fingers and considered calling her mom. She knew she should prepare her, warn her for what was about to happen, and give her time to pack and close up the house. But she was so tired. She'd just rest a while and call her later.

She placed the mug on a coaster and set the muffin beside it. Her eyes were closed before her head hit the couch's backrest.

She was still asleep when Lydia returned home four hours later.

11

Leo sat at Naya's desk, staring at the phone in his hands, swallowing the acid that rose in his throat, and focusing on not vomiting. He didn't know how long he'd been sitting there like that, but he felt like he would never move. Judging by the growing darkness, the sun had set some time ago. Still, he sat.

Then Sasha banged through the door, no doubt ready to bring him up to date on her search for Celia Gerig.

He swung his head around to face her.

"I just talked to Gavin—" she started, then stopped abruptly. "What's wrong?"

He imagined he looked the way he felt: Scared. It wasn't an emotion he had a lot of experience with, but fear had seized him in a physical way. He was cold. Frozen.

He looked up at Sasha and forced the words out. "It's worse than we thought. It's really, really bad."

She came to him immediately and placed a warm hand on his rigid arm. "Talk to me, Leo."

Sasha had just called him *Leo*. He must look bad. Even in the throes of pleasure, the woman called him Connelly.

He swallowed. "I just got off the phone with a friend who's assigned to Shield America."

She gave him a blank look.

"It's one of the ICE projects. Immigration and Customs Enforcement runs all the Homeland Security investigations, right?" he said, ignoring the quaver in his own voice.

"Sure." She nodded, encouraging him to go on.

"So, there's a bunch of task forces—drug trafficking, human smuggling, transnational gangs, money laundering. Shield America is part of the strategy to stop counter-proliferation. Basically, its charge is to prevent the export of components of weapons to our state enemies."

"Okay."

"Equipment that could be used to assemble weapons of mass destruction or agents that could be used to make biological or chemical weapons, in theory, would be stopped by Customs officials before ever making it to the Middle East or Asia, or wherever."

Leo could tell he was over-explaining, trying to put off the inevitable delivery of the news he'd learned.

Sasha nodded again.

"They focus on the export side. And, while there are lots of task forces that would work to prevent the import of those materials, there's no one project dedicated to it. I guess that's why France called Shield America."

"France called?"

Leo dropped his phone on the desk and took both of Sasha's hands in his. The contact slowed his heart rate. He allowed himself a moment to just connect with her warm skin before he answered.

"Yes, the French government wanted to alert Homeland Security about a situation, and they had a working relationship with Shield America."

"Is someone trying to export the vaccines?" Sasha asked, her eyes wide.

"No. Someone's trying to import the live virus." The words stuck in his throat.

"What live virus?"

"The killer flu. A man named Michel Joubert, a French researcher on the Pasteur Institute team that mutated the virus, was murdered in a village in the Loire Valley."

Her eyes grew wider still at the mention of murder, and her hands tensed in his.

Leo continued, "When the local authorities found his body, they contacted the Pasteur Institute. The news threw the institution into an uproar, and they quickly discovered the Doomsday virus was missing. The working theory is this researcher sold the virus to person or persons unknown. After the purchaser had the virus in hand, he or they dispatched someone to kill Joubert."

Leo felt her hands go cold. He rubbed them in what he hoped was a reassuring manner.

The room was silent, save for the soft ticking of Naya's wall clock and their breathing.

"And the French authorities think the virus is on its way here, to the United States?" Sasha finally asked.

"Yes. Actually, they suspect it's probably already within the borders. Joubert's body was found early this morning, but he'd been dead for several hours—possibly a day. Joubert signed into the building very late Friday evening, his time and didn't stay long. So, the time line goes like this: assuming he was involved, on Friday, he stole the virus and handed it off to the purchaser—"

She interrupted him. "Why do they think he sold it?"

"There was a large wire transfer into his account

from an off-shore bank on Saturday morning. It fits the theory."

"Okay, sorry I interrupted. Go on."

"No, stop me if you need to," Leo said.

Laying it all out for her, step by step, was enabling him to step back from the crisis and view it analytically. It was helping to loosen the fear that gripped him.

He went on, "After the money hit Joubert's account, he stopped at a bank machine and withdrew his daily limit. He did the same thing again, a few hours later. Judging by the locations of the banks, he was making his way to the Loire Valley, where his family has an old farmhouse they use for getaways. Apparently, he was going to hole up there. A neighbor reports seeing him in the village market Saturday afternoon buying groceries. That evening, he was found stabbed to death in the home by a friend who'd heard he was in the village and stopped by for a glass of wine."

"But, Homeland Security thinks the virus is already here?"

Leo realized it likely wasn't appropriate to pull one's outside counsel onto one's lap while discussing a possible national crisis, but he did it anyway. He noted that she didn't resist.

"It's just a theory. But, the theft and the murder were both well-planned and organized. The smart way to do it, if you were going to steal the virus and then kill the only person who could link you to the theft would be to get the virus out of the country immediately and then have a second, unrelated person kill Joubert. A cleaner. The CIA has a team on the ground now, combing through the Pasteur Institute and the Marshal's Office is pulling all the flight manifests that left France today to look for anyone that pops out as even remotely suspicious. The French authorities are working the murder scene. The first priority, of course, is to determine if the virus is stateside and to find it. Given the time difference, the scene is already cold. Don't forget, it's already Sunday there."

Sasha nodded. It was very early Sunday morning in France, but Connelly was right: time was not on their side.

"Just out of curiosity, assuming this theory's correct, what's the going rate for stealing a deadly virus?"

"The equivalent of four million U.S. dollars was transferred into Joubert's account," Leo said.

"Oh."

"Yeah, oh."

Sasha twisted around and pressed her hands against his chest. She searched his face then said, "I don't understand how this all fits together, but it can't possibly be a coincidence that you're missing vaccines."

Leo nodded. "I know. I called Tate and told him to schedule a videoconference board meeting for this afternoon. He complained about it, but I told him he's just going to have to come in from the slopes for half an hour."

Sasha bit down on her lip for a moment before asking her next question. Leo steeled himself, knowing what it would be.

"What's our worst case scenario? If the virus is here and it gets released, how bad is it going to be?" she asked.

Really bad, Leo thought. During his years at the Department of Homeland Security, he'd participated in more national security disaster war game scenarios than he could count: terrorists taking hostages; unhinged militia groups storming the Federal Reserve; jihadists seizing control of nuclear power plants; the list went on. The scenarios that had worried him the most were the natural disasters—hurricanes, meteor strikes, and, most worrisome of all to him was the pandemic. A government could stop a madman, or a dozen madmen, but one vial of death slipped into a pocket and released on a New York subway car would have unstoppable consequences that rippled across the country and, eventually, the globe. In addition to the painful deaths those who were infected would suffer (which he could now imagine in Technicolor detail, thanks to his time working at Serumceutical), the infrastructure would break down quickly. The rule of thumb was that it could take up to seventy-two hours for the government to respond to an affected area. But in three days, the public would be hit with food and medicine shortages, followed by rioting and looting, freeways clogged with desperate residents fleeing urban areas, overcrowded hospitals, emptied banks, corpses stacked like firewood on the roadside—the list of horribles was virtually endless. And, human nature being what it was, Leo expected the citizenry to turn on one another in a violent struggle pitting the strong against the weak, the wealthy against the poor.

"Worse than you can imagine. End of the world bad," he said.

Sasha was silent. Her green eyes narrowed as she considered the implications of what he'd said. Then she straightened herself, squared her narrow shoulders, and nodded. As if she'd imagined the end of the world and was now ready to move on to prevent it.

"So, what's our first step?" she asked. Her voice was clear and firm, without a hint of fear or hesitation.

"Well, the first step is to get the board up to speed and see what Tate wants to do. Then tomorrow, you and I should head to D.C. and try to set up a meeting with the task force for Monday."

"There's a task force?"

A chuckle surprised Leo by bubbling up from his throat in the midst of his dread. "There's always a task force, Sasha."

12

Colton did not appreciate being kept waiting. Not by a pretend military officer, not by anyone. He checked the time and stifled a sigh. It would be a weakness to show his irritation, so he merely returned to his book.

The bartender must have sensed his impatience, though, because he came over and swabbed the scarred bar in front of Colton with a filthy rag. Without looking up, he said in a low voice, "The captain's on his way, sir. It shouldn't be long now. Can I get you a refill?"

Colton marked his page with a finger and declined the offer of a second glass of watered-down no-name whiskey.

"I'm fine," he said with a tight smile.

The bartender nodded and returned to staring

vacantly at the football game on the television screen mounted above the bar.

Colton tuned out his surroundings and focused on Steve Jobs' biography. He believed he could learn something from any successful leader, although he had yet to find anything in Jobs' story that was new to him.

The door swung open and a tall man with a crew-cut bustled in, bringing a burst of cold air with him. Colton would have pegged the man for Bricker based on how he carried himself, but the bartender's posture confirmed it: he went from slouching against the bar to ramrod straight in a flash.

"Sir," the bartender said to Bricker.

Bricker favored him with a flash of white teeth. "Charlie."

The bartender inclined his head toward Colton, as if Bricker couldn't figure it out himself. Colton wondered which of the flannel-shirted roughnecks trading oil rigging stories over bottles of beer the bartender thought Bricker might mistake for the CEO of a publicly traded, international pharmaceutical corporation.

Colton closed his book and stood, folding his tan cashmere overcoat with precision over his left arm. He approached Bricker and extended his right hand.

"Captain Bricker?" he said, managing to keep the

sarcasm out of his voice while he used the ridiculous military honorific.

Bricker pumped his hand with a too-firm grip. Typical.

"Mr. Maxwell. It's a pleasure."

Bricker caught the bartender's eye. "Is the back room free, Charlie?"

"Yes, sir."

Bricker gestured with his hand for Colton to follow him along the length of the dimly lit, narrow barroom. Colton observed that The Hole in the Wall was an apt name for the establishment. At the far end of the room, a windowless, steel door was set in the wall next to a door that appeared to lead to the john.

Bricker opened the steel door and flipped a light switch on the wall. He ushered Colton inside as the fluorescent bar overhead buzzed and blinked to life.

Colton surveyed the dismal room and selected an ugly green armchair whose stuffing was exposed in several spots. Bricker sat across from him in an even uglier chair, with battered and scratched brown leather worn almost white in spots.

Bricker unbuttoned his wool peacoat and tugged the knot out of his scarf, then leaned back in the chair. He got right to business, a trait Colton shared and appreciated.

"Do you have it?" Bricker asked.

"Yes."

"How much?"

Colton also appreciated the other man's economy with words. Although Bricker had insisted the dive bar was a safe spot, Colton saw no reason to run any unnecessary risks: he'd seen "Casino."

"The price we previously agreed to," Colton said, cocking his head to the side and narrowing his eyes.

Bricker threw his hands up in a gesture that said he meant no harm. "Of course. I just wanted to confirm you aren't interested in the trade I proposed."

Colton snickered. The trade. This pseudo-officer idiot had actually proposed bartering him doses of Serumceutical's vaccine for a vial of the virus. It had amused him at the time, but he wasn't interested in going over this again. He shook his head no.

"Suit yourself." Bricker stood and crossed the small room. He opened a cheap plywood closet to reveal a large fireproof floor safe. He crouched and shielded the keypad from Colton's view while he keyed in the combination. He swung the door open and removed a stack of silver bricks. He hefted them and dropped them heavily at Colton's feet.

"Do you have a bag or something? They're heavy," he said.

Colton reached into his pocket and unfolded a reusable cloth shopping tote. He shook the creases out of the fabric and piled the silver inside. Bricker watched him, his mouth curled in mild amusement.

Colton didn't care. He would look out of place trudging around his luxury building with a duffle bag or rucksack. He'd blend right in with a Trader Joe's bag. Even a heavy one. He lifted the bag by the handles, testing the bottom. It would hold. He let the bag fall to the floor with a thud and reached into his breast pocket.

He removed one vial, which he'd wrapped in a small rectangle of bubble wrap, and held it out to Bricker.

"You remember the terms of our deal, I trust?"

Bricker took the vial gingerly and unwrapped it. He turned it over in his hand, watching the thick liquid roll around inside. Colton suspected he was marveling that something so small could hold so much death.

Bricker met his eyes. "Yes. I told you, your timetable isn't a problem. Our people are getting vaccinated now. We won't have full immunity until Tuesday, at the earliest. And the families, probably not until Wednesday or Thursday—"

Colton cut him off. "I don't care about the details. Just remember. Don't release it any earlier than Thursday morning. Beyond that, do what you like."

Bricker pressed his lips together in a white line

but said nothing. Colton imagined he wasn't used to taking orders. Tough.

Colton put on his coat. He hefted his Trader Joe's bag and nodded to Bricker. Then he opened the door and walked straight through the bar and out into the night without looking back.

13

Sasha ignored Connelly's grumbling and pulled on her winter running tights. As she stuck her head through the opening of her SmartWool base layer, she saw him dig his own running clothes out of his duffle bag, despite the steady stream of mumbling he kept up.

She turned away so he wouldn't see her smile. Yes, it was nearly midnight. Yes, they'd had an emotionally draining, mentally exhausting day. Yes, Tate had more or less jumped through the phone and demanded that she file a temporary restraining order against ViraGene immediately. All true.

But she knew what they needed. A long, fast run in the raw December wind would take their breath away and clear their minds. And, afterward she'd promised him an equally long, hot steamy shower for two.

He glared at her and jammed his wool cap down over his ears.

She pulled up her hood and flashed him a smile.

"Let's do it," she said and headed for the door. He trailed her down the corridor to the stairwell, down the stairs, and through the lobby. She waved a gloved hand at the security guard lazing near the Christmas tree and pushed the vestibule door open into the gale.

"Jeez," Connelly complained, the minute they hit the pavement.

It *was* cold. But Sasha had a destination in mind that would silence all his complaints.

She headed toward Penn Avenue. He fell into step beside her, and they ran in silence. Their shoes slapped out a rhythm in the quiet night.

The storefronts were dark, and traffic was light. Sasha let her mind wander as they passed the Bloomfield Bridge, ran through the burgeoning arts district and entered the Strip District, headed toward downtown.

The call with the board of directors had gone as well as they could have expected. The board had been of the unanimous opinion that Connelly should share all the information they had with the task force and that Sasha should file an emergency temporary restraining order against ViraGene. Tate—who, Sasha was certain, had been cozily sitting in front of a roaring après-ski fire—had, without consulting his outside counsel, promised the papers would be filed electronically within twenty-four hours.

Sasha and Naya had flown into action after the call, leaving Connelly to set up the meeting with the task force and then wander around Shadyside brooding. But the temporary restraining order was in good shape, if Sasha said so herself.

She and Naya were like an old married couple, anticipating what the other needed and balancing each other's strengths and weaknesses. Sasha had concentrated on telling a compelling story through the brief, confident that Naya was lining up the factual support she'd need for each legal point.

By eleven that night, they'd had a work product they were happy with, and Sasha had emailed it to Oliver Tate for his review and comments. She was tired, but it was a satisfied sort of tired that came from pulling out all the stops to meet a deadline. She could tell from the faint smile on Naya's face that she shared the same feeling.

They'd walked Naya to her car and extracted a promise that she'd call to let them know she made it home safely. Then, they'd headed back to Sasha's place. Connelly had been preoccupied, quiet. His forehead was furrowed with anxiety, and his eyes were distant and worried.

She knew he was picturing a hellscape caused by the release of the Doomsday virus. So she'd decided to do something to drive the images of death and despair from his mind. The run was only the first part of her plan.

When they reached the end of Smallman Street, they hung a left. They jogged past the dark, utilitarian Greyhound station that sat hunched in the shadow of Union Station. Sasha slowed her pace to take in the sight of the grand old train station with its spectacular rotunda and sweeping arches. Beside her, Connelly slowed as well.

She jogged across the busway to Grant Street and stopped short at the US Steel Plaza. The second part of her plan loomed in front of them. Long stairs led to a sixty-four-foot wide, forty-two-foot high stable: the Pittsburgh Crèche.

The crèche filled her heart with a sense of wonder and faith in humanity every time she saw it. Judging by the amazement splashed across Connelly's face it had the same effect on him.

"What in the world?" he asked.

"It's the only authorized replica of the Vatican's crèche. The original is on display at St. Peter's Square in Rome. You're looking at an exact duplicate."

The crèche filled a good portion of the plaza in

front of the USX Tower. The two dozen figures were larger than life-sized and intricately crafted. At a glance, the people and the animals inside the house-sized stable seemed to breathe and move. Soft lighting bathed the nativity in an ethereal glow.

"Wow," he managed.

She just nodded. It was impossible to feel overwhelmed or defeated in the face of such painstaking artistry. She loved to come to the plaza late at night, when the choral groups and lunchtime visitors were long gone, and soak in the manger scene's quiet beauty.

Connelly finally turned to her and said, "Thank you. For bringing me here. For this."

She let a slow smile spread across her lips. "You're welcome. It's going to be okay, Connelly. It really is."

He looked back at the crèche before answering. "I hope so."

She rubbed her gloved hands together and bounced on her heels. "It is. You'll see. Now, what do you say to a race home?"

She took off, sprinting down Grant Street before he could answer.

14

Sunday

Sasha was stretching in the living room, when her Blackberry buzzed to let her know Tate had sent along his comments to the brief. She hurried to silence the phone before it woke Connelly, and then grabbed a travel mug of coffee and headed to the office to finalize the temporary restraining order and papers in support.

Naya, not a morning person under any circumstances, growled a greeting when Sasha walked past her open door.

"Morning, sunshine," Sasha said in response to what she believed was a muttered expletive.

"If you say so, Mac."

"What's wrong?"

Sasha's mood was light and optimistic. She'd paged through Tate's changes on the Blackberry; they were minor. There was no reason they wouldn't be able to make the revisions and get the papers filed electronically well before Naya's pageant rehearsal.

Naya exhaled, frustrated. "Nothing. Sorry. I've just been wrestling with this PDF/A thingy that the federal district court in D.C. requires for e-filing the exhibits. It's a pain in the rear."

Sasha walked into the small, neat office and came around to peer over Naya's shoulder at the monitor.

"Are we screwed?"

Naya twisted in her seat to glare at her boss.

"Not if you back off and leave me alone. Go make Tate's changes to the brief. I'll figure this out."

Sasha raised her hands in surrender and backed out of Naya's space. In her own office, she booted up her laptop and cranked the Christmas carols at top volume.

She had to admit Tate's changes strengthened the papers. Reading through the arguments, she was convinced the court would grant the temporary restraining order. She found herself whistling "Walking in a Winter Wonderland" while her fingers flew over the keys. In fact, it was so strong that she decided to file it under Rule 65(b).

The federal rules governing civil procedure allowed a court to grant a ten-day temporary restraining order without first providing notice to the defendant under certain circumstances. In practice, the circumstances that justified issuance of an *ex parte* order were rare. The plaintiff had to show that it would suffer an immediate and irreparable loss before the court could hear the defendant's side of the story. Ordinarily, Sasha would have counseled her client to provide notice, but given the importance of the vaccine contract to national security concerns, she'd agreed with Connelly and Tate that if they could put together compelling papers, they should seek the *ex parte* order.

She nodded, satisfied that they had the goods to justify it. All she'd need was for Connelly to verify the complaint. After their run and the crèche visit the previous night, they'd agreed he'd stop by the office before lunchtime.

She checked the time. She was done—with time for a beverage and some chitchat. She e-mailed the file to Naya and shut down her laptop, then wandered across the hall to harass her legal assistant into grabbing a cup of coffee at the corner table at Jake's on the first floor of the building.

Naya put up a halfhearted fight, but the truth was, all they really needed was Connelly's signature, and then they could file the temporary restraining order. The tidy stacks of papers lining their desks and unread emails filling their inboxes could wait until Monday.

There was no reason they couldn't while away half an hour or so with conversation and Jake's winter blend—a dark, spicy full-bodied roast. Naya closed her browser and followed Sasha down the stairs to the coffee shop. Instrumental jazz versions of Christmas songs played to the mostly empty room.

At the counter, Sasha tried to wave off the dark chocolate caramel brownie that Kathryn forced on her.

"Jake's orders," Kathryn insisted. "He said you're getting too skinny again now that Leo's not cooking for you."

Sasha rolled her eyes and grabbed two forks from the silverware bin.

"You're sharing this with me," she informed Naya as they wove their way into the table they favored, jammed in between the bookcase and the window.

"Oh, yeah, twist my arm, Mac," Naya deadpanned.

They settled into their table and dug their forks into the dense treat while their steaming mugs of coffee cooled to a drinkable temperature. Sasha watched through the window as shoppers hurried through the cold to get from one boutique storefront to the next in the faint late morning light.

She turned to Naya, about to ask about her church's pageant, when Naya kicked her under the table and turned to nod meaningfully toward the table to their right.

Sasha smiled. She and Naya both loved to people watch. When they'd worked at Prescott & Talbott, they had both traveled extensively, working on cases that were pending in jurisdictions scattered throughout the country. Whenever they were assigned to a trial team together, they'd passed countless hours sitting in mediocre restaurants and swinging night spots watching the natives.

And, now—right under their noses, in the coffee shop in their building—they'd been given the gift of a couple having an awkward blind date just one table away. Sasha leaned back and picked up her coffee as she appraised the pair. Naya, whose back was to the couple, scooted her chair over next to Sasha's under the guise of sharing the brownie, so she, too, could have an unimpeded view of the date unfolding at the next table.

Both the man and the woman were probably in their early forties. The woman was tall and thin with thick, copper-colored hair that sprang back from her face in a tangle of curls. She sat facing Sasha. When she spoke, she gestured broadly with her hands. She had an eager, hopeful smile pasted on her face. The man looked kind. From what Sasha could see, he had a boyish face and most of his hair.

The blind nature of their date was obvious from the halting, biographical questions the two lobbed back and forth. Sasha learned that she was a labor and employment attorney employed by the City of Pittsburgh. He was an architect. They were both divorced. He had a seven-year-old daughter. She had two sons, four and two years of age. She was a Pittsburgher, born and raised; he'd moved to the city with his ex-wife and didn't seem to be impressed by its many hidden treasures.

For the first few moments, Sasha thought the two might be a good match, but then Naya's right eyebrow flew up her forehead as if it had wings.

"What?" Sasha asked. Her mind had wandered to Connelly briefly, and she must have missed something.

"Just listen to this jagoff," Naya muttered, stabbing at the brownie.

Sasha leaned forward to hear what he was saying.

"So, you have no hobbies, no outside interests? Nothing at all?" he said in a disbelieving, disapproving voice.

The woman smiled even more broadly and tried to explain, speaking quickly and gesturing all over the place, nearly tipping over her mocha. "I work really long hours, and that keeps me away from the boys a lot. When I have free time, I want to spend it with Henry and Charlie. I feel like I miss so much as it is."

He shook his head, dissatisfied with her answer. "But what about the weekends when they're with your ex-husband? Why don't you take a pottery class or take up a sport or something to fill that time?" he demanded.

Sure, Sasha thought, and the laundry, cleaning, grocery shopping, and all the other attendant tasks involved in raising two small children would just magically take care of themselves.

The woman flicked her eyes away from him and caught Sasha's gaze. Sasha saw a hint of exasperation before she looked away, so she was hopeful the woman would put him in his place.

Instead, she murmured, "I guess I could use that time differently."

He straightened in his chair and launched into a speech about his horseback riding class, his card club, and his judo class.

Sasha rolled her eyes at Naya, who whispered, "Bet you could whip his judo-loving hiney."

Sasha swallowed a giggle and took a quick sip of coffee to hide the laughter. She bet Naya was right.

The Renaissance man hit the woman with his

follow up question, "Don't you worry that by having your identity so wrapped up in being a lawyer, you run the risk of being combative and unpleasant?"

Sasha and Naya waited for the woman to unload on him, but she took her time answering. Finally, she said, "Well, I don't just identify as a lawyer; in fact, I think I principally see myself as a mother." The wide smile stayed fixed in place.

But that, apparently, was no better an answer. "Please, don't tell me you're one of those adults who claims to enjoy crawling around on the floor stacking blocks and racing toy cars around. My ex always maintained she enjoyed that stuff. Let's be honest, here. Child's play is fun for children, not grownups. I mean, children are inherently selfish. Take Emma, my daughter. She always wants me to do things she's interested in, never what I want to do. She'll ask me if I want to play with Legos. Of course, I don't want to play with Legos. But I will occasionally do it so that she can get the interaction that she seems to want. I have a clock running in my head, though, so that I do it for the minimum amount of time that I have to in order to check that box."

Naya snorted, and the woman looked at their table. Sasha saw a sadness and a resignation in her eyes, as if she knew the architect lacked a soul, but her options were sufficiently limited that she was willing to settle for this loser.

Sasha wanted to shout at her. Presumably, he was on his very best behavior, trying to make a good impression. This display was as good as it was going to get. What was this woman thinking? How could she ignore the red flags that were popping up over his head?

"Are you done with your coffee? I can't bear to watch any more of this horror show," Naya said.

Sasha drained her mug and gave herself a moment to reconsider what she was about to do.

Then she stood and squared her shoulders. She strode toward the couple. When she reached their table, she stopped beside the man's chair.

He twisted in his seat to look up at her with a mixture of annoyance, confusion, and interest, "Can we help you?"

Sasha smiled at him and then turned to the city attorney, who was discreetly checking her watch. She waited until the woman glanced up and met her eyes, "I realize I don't know you, but my friend and I couldn't help overhearing your conversation. I'm a lawyer, too, and I know the hours can be brutal on a social life. And, I'm not lucky enough to have children, but I have to tell you this: there are worse things than being alone."

She tilted her head toward the guy, just in case her message wasn't clear.

The woman gave her a half-smile and a nod. Naya choked back a laugh.

Sasha walked away with Naya trailing her.

"Lesbians," the architect muttered behind her.

LEO WAS SURPRISED to hear peals of laughter floating down the hall from Sasha's office. In light of the stress and time constraints they were under, he expected Sasha and Naya to be intent and subdued.

"Hey," Sasha managed, wiping tears from her eyes with her finger.

"Hey, yourself. What's so funny?" he asked.

Naya shook her head. "Long story."

She pulled a sheet of paper from the printer and handed it to him. "Here, sign this verification."

Leo skimmed the document, which required him to verify the factual truth of the motion for a temporary restraining order.

"Shouldn't I read the motion first?" he asked.

Naya shrugged. "Good point."

Sasha printed the document, and they watched in silence as Leo read it carefully.

When he got to the end, he looked up. "Okay. Looks good to me. Can I have a pen?"

Sasha tossed him a blue ballpoint from the

Prescott & Talbott mug that sat on her desk. He scrawled his signature and passed the paper to Naya.

Naya gathered a stack of printed pages and disappeared into her office.

"Now what?" Leo said.

"Now we file. This part's done," Sasha said, standing and stretching.

She bent at the waist then turned, with her head resting on her ankle, and peered up at him. "Did you get a meeting with the task force?"

"Tomorrow morning. Are you stiff?" he asked.

"A little bit. I haven't been to class in nearly a week," she said. She stretched her other side and then stood up straight and rolled her neck.

Leo felt himself frowning. "That's not good. You need to stay sharp."

Sasha was a danger magnet. He already worried about her nearly constantly. The only saving grace was that she was a skilled Krav Maga student and could take care of herself capably. But, it wouldn't do for her to get rusty or soft. Not with the country teetering as it was on the edge of crisis. If there were a societal breakdown, a small woman like her would be viewed as easy prey for any number of evil acts.

She wrinkled her brow at him. "I know. I've just been busy, and I guess I'm going to miss class tomorrow morning, too, if we're heading to D.C. You want to spar?"

She dropped into a defensive posture, legs shoulder-distance apart, arms raised in a block.

Leo laughed. "No. I'm not crazy. Just ... don't get complacent."

She smiled up at him, and his heart squeezed.

"Get your stuff together. We need to make a stop before we get on the road," he said.

15

Gavin rapped on the bowed aluminum screen door, hitched his thumbs through his belt loops, and waited. He stood on the small porch, more of a covered step, really, of a small rancher. Its aluminum siding had once been white but was now a dingy gray, scratched and dented. An old broom rested against the exterior wall, right next to the door. The concrete space where he stood had been swept clean. Was probably swept clean each day as part of a morning routine.

He was about to knock again when the interior door swung open, causing the wilted, red-bowed wreath that hung on the door to bounce against the glass. A woman in her late sixties stood in the doorway, blinking up at him from behind streaked glasses. She clutched a housecoat around herself, defensive, but once she realized who he was, her face relaxed into a smile.

"Gavin," she cried, joy and surprise coming through in equal measures in her tone. Her hand continued to grip the robe closed, but he sensed it was now out of modesty, although he could see she was wearing pajamas beneath it.

"Afternoon, Mrs. Gerig," he said. He gave her a reassuring smile.

"Where are my manners?" she asked, moving aside. "Come in, come in."

Gavin shuffled his feet on the rubberized welcome mat and ducked his head.

"I can't stay, Mrs. Gerig. I just wanted to stop by real quick and ask if everything's okay with Celia. I tried to call her, but her number's been disconnected."

Mrs. Gerig's rheumy eyes flickered with hope. "You're trying to get in touch with Celia? After all these years?"

Gavin cleared his throat. "I just wanted to see if she's okay."

He didn't see any upside in explaining to his high school girlfriend's aging mother that, after several sessions of sweaty fumbling beneath the stadium bleachers after football games, they'd both realized she was more interested in what was under her fellow cheerleaders' skirts than what he had to offer.

Celia had stayed the course until graduation, attending prom on his arm and then drifting away gracefully, instead of exposing herself to the special brand of cruelty practiced by small-town high school kids. He'd always been surprised that she stuck around town after graduation, given her preferences. But she was an only child, whose father had died when she was twelve. She was close to her mom. Although apparently the two weren't close enough for Celia to share the truth about her sexual orientation—the romantic reunion dancing in Mrs. Gerig's imagination would require a serious lifestyle change on her daughter's part.

Mrs. Gerig's smile faded. "I'm not sure if she's okay, Gavin. She was supposed to come up and take me to church this morning, but she didn't. I haven't heard from her, and that's not like my Celia. She would never miss church during Advent. And to not call..." her voice trailed off, wobbly and soft.

"Come up from where? She's not living in town anymore?"

Gavin hadn't made any effort to stay in touch with Celia, but he'd seen her around town from time to time—at the post office or the diner, pumping gas at the Shell station, or when he was shopping for groceries at the supermarket where she'd worked. They'd always been cordial. Now, he tried to recall the last time he'd seen her, and he couldn't. Her vehicle registration still listed her mother's address, so he'd started here.

"Oh, heavens, no. She moved down toward Pittsburgh just last month. She was staying with a friend and looking for a job. You know, she felt this town didn't have much to offer her. Wanted a change, she said."

That didn't sound like the Celia he remembered.

"What kind of change?" he pressed.

Mrs. Gerig sighed heavily. Gavin watched her struggle with herself. Her desire to keep up a brave front and pretend that all was well with her only child was colliding with her niggling concern that Celia was in trouble. The internal debate played out across the old woman's face. Gavin waited.

Finally, she exhaled and shook her head, "I told her not to get mixed up with those Doomsdayers, but she didn't listen."

"Doomsdayers?" Gavin repeated.

"They call themselves preppers, but it's just another cult if you ask me." Mrs. Gerig crossed herself hastily.

"Preppers," Gavin said. "You mean, like those folks who have the compound up past Firetown?"

"Those very same folks, as a matter of fact," she answered with a short nod. "She fell in with them a while back. At first, it seemed harmless. She did ordinary things—kept her gas tank full, batteries in the flashlight, an extra gallon of water. But, then she started worrying about the collapse of the government and the monetary system. Next, it was poisons in the water supply. Or a meteor strike. She was obsessed with the fall of civilization, I guess. She bought a gun—Celia!—and learned to shoot it."

Gavin stared at her.

"It's true. She was spending all her free time up at that compound, doing exercises and drills. So, when she said she was moving to New Kensington, I was thrilled. Relieved that she'd be getting away from those nutjobs, to tell you the truth. And, now she's disappeared." The old woman's face crumpled, and her chest heaved, but she held back her tears.

"When did you last see her or speak to her, Mrs. Gerig?" Gavin was careful to keep his tone neutral; he didn't want to get her any more worked up than she already was.

She thought back.

"Two Sundays ago, she came up, and we went to church. Then, last week, she called and said she was very busy and couldn't make it, but she'd see me this week."

"Did she say what she was busy with?"

"A new job. She said she'd found a job, something seasonal. She didn't go into details because Betty Caponata was here, waiting to take me to get my hair done. But she said she'd tell me all about it when she saw me on Sunday." Mrs. Gerig huffed out a ragged breath as she finished.

"Do you have a telephone number for her? Or an address?"

She shook her head, a little bit sad and a little bit embarrassed. "I had the long-distance service shut off years ago. I never used it, why pay for it? And she was bouncing around, staying with this friend, that friend ... and she always called me."

"These friends, were they preppers?"

Her eyes met his, and he saw fear and realization as it dawned on her how little she knew about her daughter's life.

"I have no idea," she admitted.

And then, the tears she'd been fighting back poured from her eyes and her frail frame shook. Gavin crossed the threshold and stepped inside to comfort the woman, and she burrowed her face into his chest and cried.

After Gavin had calmed Mrs. Gerig with a promise to help her find Celia, he hurried to his car and pulled up Sasha's cell phone number while his engine came to life.

His call rolled straight into voicemail and Sasha's businesslike, but pleasant, voice urged him to leave a message. He ended the call and drummed on the steering wheel, thinking. He could try her office number. Then he glanced down at the clock on his dashboard. It was not quite two o'clock. He didn't have anything scheduled for the rest of the afternoon. He might as well drive out to the compound and see if any of those blasted preppers were around, on the off chance one of them knew how to get in touch with Celia. Once he talked to Sasha, she'd probably ask him to check that box. Might as well do it now, before it got any darker and the promised snow started to fall.

His mind made up, Gavin turned on the car's heater and cued up *The Nutcracker* in the CD player. Next to the perfect cup of coffee, there was nothing Gavin liked better than big, sweeping orchestral scores, especially this one, especially during the holidays. Well, that and Sunday Ticket. He checked his rearview mirror and pulled out, leaving Mrs. Gerig and her worry behind.

The compound was way up in the far northeast corner of the county. Bordered on two sides by state game lands and more than thirty minutes from its nearest neighbor, the site was a perfect place for the preppers to hole up, practice their idiotic war games, and avoid complaints. They were in their own little world up there, which Gavin presumed was the point. In fact, he only knew they existed because he'd stumbled across their compound a few years back during a hunting trip.

Tracking a deer through the woods, he'd come out into a clearing and bumped into an armed sentry, for lack of a better word. The man wore some sort of makeshift uniform—army green cargo pants and a tan flak jacket with a desert camouflage pattern. He sported a graying buzz cut and a Ruger. It was evident that he was as startled as Gavin was, but he recovered quickly, pointed his rifle at Gavin's chest, and announced that Gavin was on private property.

Over the guard's shoulder, Gavin glimpsed a large garden, several sheds, and an enormous stack of firewood. Beyond that, in the distance, he could make out several log structures. In light of the gun pointed at his center mass, he chose not to move in for a closer look.

At the time, he had still been with the Sheriff's Office, but his jurisdiction was limited. He'd apologized and backed away, back into the wooded game lands, his heart thudding and the buck long gone. He'd tromped back through the woods, almost running, until he found his hunting buddy—a state trooper—crouched in a thicket. When Gavin described the man and the compound, Phil had nodded.

"Sounds like those dang preppers," Phil said.

"Who?"

Phil shook his head. "Some numbnuts who think the world's gonna end. So, they started a survivalist group—'cuse me, preparedness group."

"Are they violent?" Gavin asked.

Phil spat on the frozen ground and considered the question.

"No," he finally said. "They seem to keep to themselves. But, if the crap ever does hit the fan, I expect they'll be plenty trigger-happy."

Just to satisfy his curiosity, one afternoon, he'd stopped by the Recorder of Deeds Office and sweet-talked a clerk into pulling the property records on the parcel. She'd leaned against the counter to give him a good look down her fuzzy, low-cut sweater and explained that the land, and the cabins on it, had been transferred from the Commonwealth Department of Natural Resources to a husband and wife, Jeffrey and Anna Bricker in 2000. She told him the state had used the property as a campground in the 1940s and 50s, but it was one of dozens of campsites that had fallen into disuse and were being auctioned off for whatever sums the state could get for them.

Gavin had tucked their existence away in the back of his mind.

And now, according to her mother, Celia had fallen in with the preppers. The thought sent an unpleasant chill up Gavin's spine. He pressed his foot down on the gas pedal. It'd be better to get up to the compound and back to town before nightfall.

The sun hung low in the gray sky when Gavin pulled up in front of the gated drive leading from the state road to the gravel approach to the compound. He sat and peered through the metal arms into the distance but couldn't make out whether any smoke rose toward the horizon.

He chewed his lip, then pulled out and drove past the private drive. He continued down the road another fifty yards and parked along the shoulder on a patch of frozen ground that was at least partially hidden from view by some naked brush. He killed the engine and opened the glove compartment.

Gavin took out his gun, weighed it in his hand, and thought. Anyone he ran into on the preppers' land was guaranteed to be armed. He was licensed to carry a concealed weapon, of course. But, as a civilian, he sometimes felt carrying the gun was more of a drawback than an advantage. When he'd been a deputy, he'd had a clear mandate and defined guidelines for when to draw and use his weapon. As a citizen, the lines were grayer, the risks greater, and the chance for mistakes seemed higher. He'd taken to leaving the thing in the glove compartment more and more.

He moved to return it to the space now and stopped, his hand hovering near the box, undecided.

Finally, he closed the glove compartment. He confirmed the gun was loaded, and the safety was engaged, then slipped the weapon into his shoulder holster and smoothed his jacket flat over it.

Better safe than sorry.

He put his cell phone in his pocket and emerged from the car's warm interior into the frosty late afternoon air. The car gave an electronic beep as he locked the doors and jogged toward the compound, his head down against the wind.

As he rounded the bend in the road and neared the compound, he slowed to a quick walk to lessen the noise from the crunch of frozen snow beneath his boots. The only other noise was the sound of his breathing. Traffic would be light up here. Deer season was over for the year, so the only hunters would be the hardcore types who hunted rabbits and squirrel in the off-season. Aside from hunting, there wasn't much to draw anyone up to these parts. Gavin reasoned that was part of the location's appeal to the preppers.

He stopped twenty feet away from the gate and stared hard at the cabins off in the distance. He saw no signs of activity, and no recent tire tracks on the driveway. The place felt empty. He approached the gate and vaulted over it. He felt exposed as he walked up the driveway toward the cluster of cabins. He quickened his pace.

The first grouping of cabins sat off to the right of the driveway, off behind the woodpile. A tarp covered the firewood. The crusted snow showed no recent footprints. No noise hummed from the nearby cabins. The land was quiet under its blanket of snow; it felt deserted. Nobody home. He turned to leave.

Gavin exhaled, and the tension drained from his shoulders. He realized he'd been prepared for a confrontation if he'd run into anyone. His time away from the sheriff's office had brought into stark relief just how much stress had been involved in serving bench warrants and bringing in defendants on contempt charges. Always wondering, as he raised his fist to knock on a door, whether the residents had weapons, kept vicious dogs, or were under the influence of booze, meth, or both. His private work was considerably less dangerous. And, to his surprise, he'd become somewhat risk adverse.

The notion that he was scared forced him to turn back to the cabins and check them out more thoroughly.

He neared the first cabin and pressed himself flush against the cold log wall to peer in through a bare window. He could make out the shapes of four single beds in the dark room. All four beds were made with gray wool blankets pulled taut across their tops. He crept past the window to the second cabin. A quick peek inside revealed an identical setup: four neatly made beds, no light, nobody inside.

He moved quickly from cabin to cabin, glancing inside each and finding nothing but empty beds until he reached the last cabin in the back row. It was set apart slightly from the others. As he had with the others, he ran to it in a low crouch. He raised himself to look through the window so he could confirm there were four empty beds and get on with his day, having proved to himself he wasn't a coward.

Inside, three beds sat empty, but the fourth was occupied. Its occupant had kicked the wool blanket partially off the bed; it hung over the edge, trailing onto the floor. The sheets were twisted around a pair of legs. Gavin jammed his face against the frosty glass and stared hard into the gloomy interior, trying to make out the details of the person who lay face down in the bed. One pale arm was flung out over the edge of the bed. Gavin stared hard. He thought he saw a shape of a tattoo on the inner wrist. His pulse sped up.

Celia had a flower tattoo on her right wrist.

The shape in the bed reared up and rolled to the side.

He saw a flash of a ghostly white, sweat-slicked face as the woman leaned over the side of the bed and vomited into a metal bucket that sat on the floor. Her head hung over the side for a moment. Gavin studied the knot of red curls that flopped over her face.

It was definitely Celia.

Gavin let out a long breath and watched as Celia wiped her mouth with a shaking hand and lowered herself back onto her pillow.

There were no vehicles in sight. Someone had dropped her off and would probably be back to check on her. He told himself he'd just confirm Celia was here of her own free will and not in distress, then he'd drive back to town and let Sasha know he'd found her.

He walked around to the front of the cabin, raised his hand to knock on the door, and stopped. Affixed to the door was a glowing yellow triangle, about the size of a stop sign, outlined in black. The international symbol for biological hazard filled the triangle.

He rapped on the door and ignored his suddenly dry mouth. No answer.

He knocked again, louder, and cleared his throat.

"Celia, it's Gavin Russell. Are you okay?" he called. His voice echoed then died in the wind.

He pressed his ear against the oak door. No sounds from the other side.

He ran around to the window and pressed his forehead against the glass. Celia was looking toward the door and struggling to push herself up from the bed. He raced back to the door and shouted again, "Celia?"

Minutes passed. He heard a muffled moan and the shuffling of feet, then, the sound of a deadbolt sliding back.

The door swung inward several inches, and Celia's face appeared. Dark circles ringed her eyes. Her face was as white as a sheet of paper except for two bright red spots on her cheeks. Her lips were cracked and bleeding. She clung to the door frame, shaking from the effort of crossing the room.

"Gavin? What are you doing here?" she croaked in a hoarse whisper. Confusion flooded her dull, cloudy eyes.

Gavin glanced over his shoulder once then turned back to Celia.

"I'm looking for you. May I come in?"

She didn't answer but shuffled to the side to make room for him. Her footing was unsteady, and her knees buckled. Gavin caught her under her armpits as she collapsed toward the floor.

He pushed the door closed with one foot.

"What's wrong, Celia? Are you sick?"

It was a stupid question. She was obviously sick. Her skin burned hot through the flannel pajamas she wore, and she smelled of sweat and vomit. Her body shook in his arms.

She gave a weak nod in answer and leaned into

him. He led her back to the bed and helped her into it. She curled herself into a ball, hugged her arms around her knees, and shivered. Gavin retrieved the blanket from the floor and covered her.

He crouched by her bedside.

"How did you know I was here?" she asked. Her eyelids fluttered closed, then open.

"Your mom's worried about you," he said.

"Oh no, Mom," Celia said. "I missed church."

Gavin looked around the room. Aside from the beds and the puke bucket, it held a rough-hewn wooden table at the head of each bed and a metal footlocker at each foot. An unlit pot-bellied stove sat off to the side of the room with a small stack of wood beside it. The room was chilly and damp. There was no bathroom, no kitchen. It was not a place he'd have chosen for convalescing.

Celia barked out a wet, phlegmy cough that racked her thin body. She opened her eyes, and they rolled back into her head as she coughed again.

Gavin grabbed Celia's fleece jacket from the footlocker. "Come on, we're getting out of here."

Celia opened her eyes wide, and terror filled her slack face. She struggled to her elbows. "No!" she shouted, triggering another coughing fit. She moaned and leaned over the side of the bed, heaving dark yellow bile into the bucket.

Gavin ignored the irritation that flared in his

chest and kept his voice soft. "Celia, you need to see a doctor."

Celia clamped her hand around his wrist, like a claw. "You don't understand. I need to lay low."

The realization that he didn't know why Sasha was looking for Celia hit Gavin. "Are you hiding from someone? Are you in trouble?"

Celia stared up at him with watery eyes. "Gavin, please, go. You can't get involved in this."

"Are the preppers keeping you here?"

"They're letting me stay here, is all. And they'll be back soon to check on me. Please, you have to leave."

Celia sank back into the bed, out of breath from talking.

"Well, they aren't taking care of you. And I didn't see your car anywhere. I'm not leaving you here as sick as you are with no way to get to a hospital, Celia."

"It's just the flu," she protested. Her hairline was slick with sweat.

"Whatever it is, you're too sick to be here. What are you doing for food? Water? Heat? This is insane. I'm going to get my car and come back for you."

Gavin placed her jacket beside her on the bed.

"I'll be back in less than five minutes. Put your coat on. I'll pull as close as I can to the gate and come in and help you to the car."

Celia shook her head but didn't answer. Her eyes were closed again.

He headed for the door. If he had to carry her out against her will, then that's what he'd do. She was in no shape to stop him.

He looked back at her before he closed the door. She had turned on to her side and appeared to be asleep already. He stepped out of the cabin, sucked in a lungful of cold air, and jogged down the path.

16

Anna heard the old Jeep's rattling engine off in the distance and hurried to finish her thought. Then she capped her pen, closed her journal, and rose from the table. She hurried through the kitchen to the powder room and flicked on the light to assess herself in the mirror. She patted her hair, whisking a stray strand behind her ear, and smiled at the natural flush that stained her cheeks. Joy stirred in her chest: her husband was home.

She was in the kitchen putting on the water for tea when Jeffrey eased open the door.

"Welcome home," she said, turning from the stove to greet him with a smile.

He returned her smile and dropped the duffel

bag on the old oak table then crossed the room to kiss her.

"It's quiet around here. Did you sell the kids while I was gone?" she heard him say, his voice muffled by her hair and their embrace.

"No such luck. They had lunch then fed the chickens and did their chores in record time, so I told them they could run around for a bit outside before we tackle math. How was your trip?" she laughed, pulling back to look up at him.

He was tired. She could tell by the deep lines that creased his upper cheeks under his eyes.

"Productive. How were things here?"

"Productive," she answered. "We wrapped all the gifts for the toy drive and the kids finished their science projects. I think Clay has a chance to take the home school division this year."

He nodded, proud but not surprised. They'd raised their children to work hard, set goals, and achieve those goals. She knew Jeffrey expected nothing less.

The kettle steamed out a whistle, and she removed it from the heat. She was eager to sit quietly with her husband for a spell before the kids realized their father had returned and came bounding into the house to greet him.

She stretched on her toes to bring down two of her grandmother's china teacups and saucers from the cupboard. She shook the loose herbal tea, made from dried herbs picked from the garden, into two metal balls and poured hot water over them. Then she carried the sugar bowl and spoons over to the table. Jeffrey followed with the teacups.

Anna considered him as she stirred a lump of sugar with her spoon, dissolving it in the water. He wasn't just tired; there was something else shadowed in his face. Tension, maybe? If she didn't know better, she might have thought it was fear. But, to her knowledge, Jeffrey had never felt fear. He'd certainly never shown it. Not even when she had hemorrhaged during Clara's birth, nearly dying. He had remained calm, implacable.

She placed a hand on his arm. "Is everything okay?"

He met her gaze and smiled. "It is now." He raised the cup to his mouth and sipped the hot tea.

Anna pretended not to notice the way his hand shook.

They drank their tea in companionable silence, then Jeffrey said he needed to tend to some business and disappeared into the basement.

Anna busied herself with washing the dishes and wiping down the counters. She spotted the duffle bag on the table.

Might as well get Jeffrey's laundry started now, she thought. She could put his dirty clothes in the washer and then switch them to the dryer while she guided the kids through their weekend math lessons.

Anna lifted the bag and was surprised by its weight. She hefted it over her shoulder and carried it into the laundry room. Something inside made a clanking sound. When she unzipped the bag to toss the clothes into the washer, she stared down at its contents, unsure what she was seeing: jammed in among her husband's dirty socks and undershirts were dozens and dozens of tiny glass bottles.

Anna picked one up and squinted at the tiny writing. The clear liquid rolled like syrup inside the vial. She shoved it back into the bag and zippered it closed. Then she hurried across the kitchen to return the bag to the table, dread settling in the pit of her stomach with the knowledge that she had just seen something she wasn't supposed to see.

17

Colton ate an early dinner alone with one eye on the flat-screen television mounted under a bank of kitchen cabinets, the other on his iPad.

Nothing. He had flipped among all the cable news channels and searched the newspaper homepages, and *nothing*. Not a single reputable mention of the incredible danger currently facing the American people.

It seemed impossible. And, yet, it was true. No one knew that death waited around the corner for most of the country—aside from some fringe lunatics and conspiracy theorists babbling amongst themselves in the darkest corners of the Internet and the inbred preppers down in Pennsylvania, of course.

He pushed his grilled salmon from one side of his square black plate to the other, then let his fork clatter to the table, his appetite deadened by disappointment. He took a long swallow of the crisp Chenin blanc and pulled up a web browser. Another cycle through the homepages of the major Western newspapers, magazines, and television stations yielded no information about the situation in France or the potential for destruction stateside.

Colton envisioned himself smashing his Riedel Vinum glass against the fireplace on the other side of the room. Then he inhaled, deeply and slowly. To what end? Thirty dollars' worth of pulverized glass he'd have to either sweep up or step around until the cleaning service came at the end of the week?

"No," he said aloud and loosened his grip on the wineglass's stem. He'd devise a way around this blasted news blackout. Or force them to lift it by creating a story they dare not fail to report on.

He drained his glass and slammed it down onto the table, then pushed his chair back. He stalked across the open floor plan to the foyer, where his briefcase sat on the gleaming marble entryway floor. He crouched and retrieved his cell phone and one of the vials that he'd wrapped in his cloth sunglasses pouch to protect and hide it.

He turned the vial in his hand, watching the

viscous liquid inside catch the light from the chandelier. *Take control of the situation*, he told himself. He slipped the tube into his pocket and punched a number into the phone.

18

Connelly paced around Sasha's condo while she tossed some clothes in a bag. Finally, he went downstairs and made a phone call. She could hear his low voice, mumbled words, and urgent tone. A few moments later, he came back into her bedroom and hustled her out the door.

Instead of driving toward Edgewood and the Monroeville entrance to the Turnpike, Connelly meandered through the Oakland traffic and parked in a faculty lot behind one of the research buildings for the University of Pittsburgh Medical School.

Before Sasha could ask what was going on, a slight Asian woman emerged from behind a pillar and trotted across the lot to the SUV.

Connelly popped the lock, and she hopped in the back seat.

He turned and shook her hand. "Thanks for doing this, Dr. Yu."

She nodded, her eyes serious behind her square glasses. She leaned forward over the center console and extended a hand to Sasha.

"Hi. I'm Ashleigh Yu."

"Sasha McCandless."

"Dr. Yu is a researcher at the Infectious Disease Division. And a friend," Connelly said. "So, I called in a favor."

Dr. Yu patted the seat next to her and smiled at Sasha. "Why don't you step into my office?"

She unzipped the bag and started removing medical supplies. She laid out a syringe, a vial, and a bandage in a neat line on the seat using quick, efficient motions.

Sasha turned to search Connelly's face. She watched him take a deep breath before he launched into an explanation.

"Dr. Yu was on the team that tested the vaccine. She happens to have a few doses from the trials. I was vaccinated as part of the study. And, in light of—everything—you really need to be, too. Please don't argue with me, okay?" His voice contained the barest hint of pleading.

Sasha realized that her instinct was, in fact, to

protest. For a number of reasons. Some legitimate, some less so. But the stress was showing around Connelly's eyes, so she simply nodded.

She slid out of the passenger seat and joined Dr. Yu in the backseat.

The other woman rolled the vial between her hands, gently reconstituting the liquid inside.

"Okay. I'm going to assume you are currently healthy and not feeling any flu-like symptoms," she said.

"That's true," Sasha confirmed, shrugging out of her coat and placing it beside her on the leather seat.

"Roll up your sleeve, please. Use your non-dominant arm. It might be sore for a while," Dr. Yu told her.

Sasha paused. She was left-handed. She wrote, threw, and used utensils and tools with her left hand. But, her power was in her right. She considered writing with a sore arm versus trying to land a jaw-breaking punch with a sore arm, and rolled up her left sleeve.

Dr. Yu inserted the syringe into the vial and took Sasha's forearm in her own warm hand. As she drew the syringe full of vaccine, she said, "So, in case you don't know, you should achieve full immunity within seventy-two hours. In the interim, you will be protected, but there is a chance you could—if you were to somehow encounter the H17N10 virus that is locked away in a Level Four facility—contract the Doomsday flu."

The researcher's voice dripped with curiosity, but it wasn't Sasha's place to fill her in. She met Connelly's eyes in the rearview mirror.

He twisted in the seat and said, "Ashleigh. Trust me. It's better if you don't know."

Dr. Yu shrugged and plunged the syringe into Sasha's arm. "Okay. Here are the side effects you need to look out for: fever, chills, a very sore red welt at the injection site, and general flu-type symptoms."

Sasha stared at her as she removed the syringe and plastered a small bandage on Sasha's arm.

"Wait. The side effect of this flu vaccine is getting the flu?"

Dr. Yu pursed her lips. "Sort of. Because the vaccine uses a weakened live virus similar, though not identical, to the H17N10 virus, there is a chance you could come down with a very mild case of the flu. That's fairly typical when a live virus is used. The problem in this case is that a very mild case of something that approximates the killer flu—well, it could kill you."

"What?!" Sasha couldn't keep the outrage out of her voice. She stared at the back of Connelly's head, drilling a hole in his skull with her red-hot fury.

"It's a remote possibility," Dr. Yu continued in a mild voice as she reached into her medical bag. "And the Doomsday virus itself is sufficiently horrible that the government weighed the risk of side effects against the benefits of preventing a pandemic and decided it was worth it. Honestly, you're unlikely to die."

"How comforting," Sasha said in a dry, tight voice.

Dr. Yu pressed several small, square packets into the palm of Sasha's hand. "Here. This is AviEx, Vira-Gene's antiviral. I don't know how well it works against the true H17N10 virus, but I can tell you that if you do start to experience flu symptoms, this will help. It will lessen the severity and duration of your illness. You'll still be contagious, though."

Sasha stared down at the foil packages. "Thanks."

Dr. Yu patted her arm. "You're welcome. And try not to worry. Leo was vaccinated, along with the entire board of directors and the officers of his company. No one died, and, as far as I know, no one experienced any side effects at all."

She zippered her bag and leaned forward. "Whatever you're involved in, Leo, take care."

He smiled at her and said, "We will. Thanks again. I know you put yourself on the line to do this, and I won't forget it."

She waved off his gratitude and hopped out of the SUV. Sasha watched her run across the parking lot and disappear into the boxy, white building across the way.

Sasha returned to the front seat and placed the antiviral medicine in the inside zippered pocket of her bag. She exhaled slowly and reminded herself that Connelly was under a considerable amount of pressure and stress. She cleared her mind of her irritation and smiled at him.

"Do you have any other surprises in store or can we hit the road now?"

He reached out and caressed her jaw. "Thank you. No more surprises," he said in a soft voice. Then the engine roared to life, and he backed out of the spot.

BY THE TIME Connelly barreled through the Easy-Pass toll lane and merged onto the Eastbound Turnpike daylight was fading behind the mountains.

He stared down the miles of patched and uneven road that unfolded in front of them, his hands gripping the steering wheel tight enough to turn his knuckles white.

Sasha sat in silence for a while, letting him work through his worries on his own. Finally, she cleared her throat and tried to decide how to phrase the suggestion that they stop for a bite. A green and white mermaid flashed past as Connelly sped by a sign advertising the amenities at the upcoming service plaza.

"Can we stop at Somerset? I think it's the last clear shot for Starbucks until Breezewood. I could really use a cup of coffee," she said. *And you could use to decompress and eat a snack or something*, she added silently to herself.

"You don't like Starbucks," he answered, accelerating.

"Come on, Connelly. I'm in the mood for a gingerbread latte," she lied.

He raised an eyebrow at her but sighed, and eased the car into the right lane.

He followed a minivan into the rest area. The parking lot was nearly deserted. He took a spot close to the entrance, and they hurried out of the car and jogged toward the doors as the wind whipped at their coats.

Inside, Sasha headed for the Starbucks line and urged Connelly to get himself a slice of pizza. The peppy holiday music that piped out from behind the counter was a poor fit for the tired-looking, bored barista who took Sasha's order.

"You said a skinny latte, right?" the girl confirmed.

"Right."

"Whipped cream?"

Sasha stopped herself from asking who would order skim milk and whipped cream. “No thanks,” she said, forcing a smile.

“Happy holidays,” the girl intoned, dead-eyed and expressionless as she handed over the gargantuan drink.

Sasha headed to the tables near the pizza joint and was pleased to see Connelly had taken her advice. He sat, his long legs sprawled out under the small table, with a personal pizza and a steaming black coffee in front of him.

“You didn’t have to wait for me,” she said, eyeing his coffee with no small amount of jealousy.

“I wanted to.”

He smiled, but his eyes were serious.

She slid into the seat across from him and leaned over the table.

“Connelly, what’s wrong?”

“What’s *wrong*?” he echoed, frowning at her.

She hurried to add, “I know this is a serious situation. But, we’re doing everything we can. You have the support of the board to talk to the government. We’ve filed a temporary restraining order against ViraGene. There’s nothing else we can do right now, right?”

The tension didn’t leave his face.

“That’s exactly it,” he said in a voice barely above a whisper. “Somewhere out there, someone’s running around with the deadliest weapon you could imagine, and there's nothing I can do about it."

She stared at him.

"It's not your job to stop him anymore. You're the chief security officer for a pharmaceutical company, not a government agent—or a superhero."

She felt her own stress level rising. They were not going to get involved in saving the world. At least she wasn't. She was going to meet with the task force to explain why the first vaccine order had been shorted and then she was going to wait for the court to grant her emergency temporary restraining order. And that was the extent of it. She sincerely hoped Connelly didn't plan to track down a virus-wielding lunatic.

"I know," he conceded, staring down at his pizza. He lifted his eyes and searched her face. "But, you don't understand. That virus *can't* get out."

Sasha nodded but couldn't speak around the lump in her throat. She took a sip of her sweet coffee drink instead. Over Connelly's shoulder, she spotted a state trooper lounging by the vending machines just inside the entrance. She hadn't noticed him when they rushed inside from the cold. On closer inspection, the casual pose was an act. His hand rested just beside his weapon and his eyes swept the area in a constant, careful arc.

"I thought you said the government hasn't

released the news about the virus?" she said, nodding toward the vigilant trooper stationed by the door.

Connelly nodded. "Trust me, they haven't. They can't risk that level of panic and hysteria. They probably alerted all the state governors to an unspecified, unconfirmed threat and asked them to put boots on the ground to monitor for suspicious activity."

"And the states would just do that? With no real information or meaningful explanation?"

Sasha hoped her voice sounded less judgmental than she felt. Given his current mental state, she wasn't looking to rehash their battles over the Patriot Act.

"Yes, they really would. But, there's only so long before some desk jockey in D.C. blurts out to his wife that she should wear a mask to the grocery store , just in case. Then, she'll tell her mother and best friend that there's something contagious and very bad that the feds are worried about. Twenty minutes later, it'll be all over Facebook and twitter. So, the window to handle this under the radar is closing. Quickly."

Connelly balled up his napkin and tossed it on top of his uneaten pizza.

Sasha plucked the napkin from his plate and pushed the food toward him.

"Please eat. You're the one who always says sleep,

food, and exercise are weapons available for everyone's arsenal; anyone who doesn't take advantage of them is a fool." She smiled to lessen the blow of scolding him with his own stupid maxim.

His mouth curved up at the corners in the smallest of smiles, and he picked up a slice of pizza and started to chew.

That hurdle cleared, Sasha returned to her coffee and ruminated on how to get him to move off the idea that he could swoop in and contain a deadly virus.

They finished their pitiful excuse for dinner in silence and left, nodding goodbye to the trooper before they bent their heads against the howling wind and ran back to the car. In her pocket, Sasha's phone vibrated and rang, but she didn't notice.

19

Gavin paced beside his car and willed Sasha to pick up her ringing phone. Instead, her voicemail message filled his ear.

"Sasha, it's Gavin. Call me as soon as you get this. I found Celia. She's up at this prepper compound out past Firetown, and she's really sick."

He exhaled and dropped his phone back into his pocket. He wished he'd caught her. But he didn't have time to worry about it now. He slid behind the steering wheel and started the engine. Then, he leaned over and racked the passenger seat all the way back so Celia could rest more comfortably while he found a doctor's office or urgent care center for her. He hoped he wouldn't have to drive all the way to the hospital in Springport. She was in bad shape; he needed to find someplace closer.

As he returned to a seated position, the weight from the gun pressed into him. He didn't really need it now. There was no one up there other than him and Celia. He removed the gun and holster and locked them in the glove compartment, then he turned the car around and headed for the gravel drive.

When he reached the metal gate, he exited the car and left the engine running. He bent down to examine the arm. If he could raise it, he could drive the car right up to Celia's cabin. He wasn't concerned about his ability to carry her—she was little more than a limp rag at this point—but he assumed being out in the cold would be bad for her condition.

He crouched and pushed on the rusted metal hinge. Behind him, footsteps crunched across the frozen snow.

"Sir! Turn around slowly, please," a voice barked near his ear.

Gavin rose to his feet and pivoted to face the business end of a twelve-gauge Remington Magnum. Its owner held it steady and pointed it at the center of Gavin's chest.

The woman wore an orange parka with the hood drawn tight around her face. Her eyes were unblinking.

He glanced back at his still-running car, with the loaded gun safely locked away in the glove compartment. *You idiot*, he thought to himself. He raised his hands above his head, nice and slow.

THE WOMAN MARCHED him past the cluster of cabins to a long, low rectangular building.

"Open it," she said when they reached the double doors. Gavin pushed through the doors and stepped into a mostly empty mess hall. A dozen and a half wooden picnic tables flanked by scarred benches on each side formed six rows of three. Three men in fatigues were unloading boxes at the far end of the room.

"This way," she said, aiming the gun toward a doorway off to the right. The arrival of a prisoner at gunpoint either went unnoticed or was unremarkable because no one even glanced up as they walked through the mess room and into a small, dimly-lit hallway.

A single naked bulb dangled from a fixture in the ceiling and a map of the grounds, a reminder about not feeding the wildlife, and a calendar of events—relics from when the campsite had been run by the Department of Natural Resources—-still hung from a corkboard nailed into the log wall. Just past the corkboard, a door was set into the wall. Hanging from the door was a laminated sheet of paper that identified the room as "Captain Bricker's Office."

The woman rapped on the door.

"Come in," a male voice rumbled from the other side.

She nudged Gavin through the doorway with the muzzle of her rifle.

The man who had been sitting behind a metal desk jumped up guiltily. He didn't look like any kind of captain Gavin had ever seen. He was in his late thirties, a little soft around the middle, with shaggy brown hair that touched the collar of his hunting jacket.

"You're Captain Bricker? Are you in charge here?" Gavin asked.

The man's eyes opened wide. "No, sir. I'm George—Sergeant Rollins. Lydia, what's going on?" he turned to the gun-toting woman for an explanation.

"Trespasser, sir. I found him messing with the gate while I was on patrol." She spoke in a clipped, militaristic voice.

Gavin wondered where these people had come from. The compound had been empty. Unless they'd been holed up in the recreation center the entire time. But, then where was their vehicle?

While he asked himself questions he couldn't answer, Rollins watched him. Indecision was plain on the other man's face. Gavin decided to take charge of the encounter.

"Look, I'm sorry," he said, addressing Rollins and studiously ignoring the woman named Lydia. She struck him as the trigger-happy sort.

Rollins nodded, visibly relieved that he was doing the talking.

Gavin continued, "There's been some sort of misunderstanding. I'm looking for one of your members—Celia Gerig?"

Beside him, he heard Lydia's sharp intake of breath. The color drained from Rollins' face.

"What do you want with Celia?" he demanded.

"I'm a family friend. Her mother hasn't heard from her in a while. She's worried. She told me Celia belongs to your, uh, organization, so I came up to see if she was here."

Gavin delivered the half-truth convincingly, judging by the way Rollins relaxed his shoulders.

"I see," Rollins said slowly.

"Celia's sick," the woman snapped.

Gavin turned to her. "In that case, let me take her to get medical care."

"I didn't say she was here," Lydia responded, narrowing her eyes. "Anyway, I'm a nurse. I'm qualified to care for her."

"May I see her?" Gavin asked, careful to be polite and nonthreatening.

Lydia cut her eyes toward Rollins. Whatever his actual status was, the mild-mannered man was clearly her superior in the prepper hierarchy.

"I'm sorry," Rollins said slowly. "You can't. She might be contagious."

Gavin would have plenty of time to regret the next words that came from his mouth.

"Actually, I've already seen her. I found her in that cabin. I just want to talk to her and make sure she's okay staying here. If she says she is, I'll leave—I swear."

A look passed between Lydia and Rollins. A long moment ticked by. Then Rollins sighed.

"Quarantine him," he said.

"We have a problem," a female voice said as soon as Anna picked up the ringing phone.

Anna waited for the woman on the other end of the phone to identify both herself and her problem.

Anna wasn't simply Jeffrey's wife; she was his lieutenant. He was the public face of Preppers PA, and he shielded her from his dealings with outsiders, but she was responsible for the day-to-day operations within the organization. She shielded him from the in-fighting, the minutiae, and the tedious work that any group of individuals, no matter how united around a common cause, created. Jeffrey Bricker had the vision, but Anna made the trains run on time.

"This is Lydia. We have a problem," the woman repeated, her voice shaking.

Lydia Markham. Anna called up a mental picture of the woman. Mid-thirties, medium height, straight brown hair. Pleasant, if unremarkable, in appearance. Physically strong. Single. Had specialized training as a nurse, which made her valuable.

"What's the problem, Lydia?" Anna asked, tucking a stray tendril of hair behind her ear and peering through the kitchen window to make sure the kids were all accounted for and occupied out back while she waited for the nurse to gather her thoughts and tell her story. She watched their night-time snowball battle and wondered if Lydia's romance with her segment leader had soured. Anna had told George not to get involved with a woman under his direct command.

"Well, you know how George—"

"Do you mean Sergeant Rollins?" Anna interrupted, sending a clear message that she didn't want to hear about any relationship troubles.

"Uh, right, Sergeant Rollins. Anyway, you know how Sergeant Rollins was charged with obtaining the *medicine*?"

"Of course," Anna said, too quickly.

She had no idea what Lydia was referencing, but

the odd emphasis the nurse placed on the word 'medicine' made Anna think of the vials rolling around in Jeffrey's duffel bag. Under the existing structure, however, she was the only one who would have given Rollins an assignment of any kind, and she hadn't.

Unless Jeffrey had circumvented her? Her face burned hot, and her mouth went dry at the thought that he hadn't trusted her to carry out a mission—whatever it may have entailed. She forced herself to focus on the nurse's halting voice.

"Right, of course you do. Sorry. So, Celia Gerig was put in place to acquire the items, and she did. She did great. But..." Lydia trailed off.

"But what, Lydia? I don't have time for this," Anna said, adding a hint of steel to her voice to prompt the story along.

"Right, sorry." Lydia said before letting the words spill out as fast as they came. "So, after the leadership meeting, we all vaccinated each other—you know, like a first responder team."

A vaccine. Anna exhaled in relief. The vials were just a vaccine. Jeffrey's failure to involve her in such a routine acquisition was odd, and the fact that there'd been a leadership meeting without her was undeniably troubling, but this was all a non-issue. The vials were just a vaccine.

"It's okay," Anna assured the younger woman.

"No, you don't understand! It's not okay. Celia had a reaction or something. She's dead." Lydia's voice cracked, and she began to sob softly.

"She's dead?" Anna repeated stupidly. Her face went numb, and the window glass looked like it was undulating. The dark shapes of her kids carried on their snowball fight through the waves as her hands started to sweat.

"I don't know what happened," Lydia wailed. "She started to feel shaky and queasy yesterday, about eighteen hours after I inoculated her, so Geo—Sergeant Rollins and I took her up to camp to rest. We figured it was better for her to be out of sight for a while anyway. It wasn't going to take much effort to connect her to the missing vaccines. We took her up Saturday night after the vaccine clinics. We came back up this evening with a couple men from the unit to stock the munitions shed and unload the medical supplies. Sergeant Rollins dropped us off and left to refill the gas tanks. I figured I'd go check on her. She was in really bad shape, which she shouldn't have been. I mean, the textbook reaction to a flu vaccine is a mild fever, maybe some achiness. There was nothing mild about this. She was burning up, dehydrated, and delirious. She could barely stand. She was a ragdoll."

"What did you do for her?" Anna asked.

"There wasn't much I could do. I hooked her up

to a hydration IV and tried to talk to her, but she didn't recognize me. She was babbling about her friend."

"What friend?"

"I thought it was just delirium, you know? But, after I got her settled back in bed, I did a foot patrol, and, sure enough, I found a trespasser who claimed to be looking for Celia."

Anna's head was spinning. Celia was dead, and there was a trespasser on their land looking for her.

"But you said she died?"

"She was in really bad shape, Anna. She was slipping in and out of consciousness. If I had to guess, and this is only a guess, she vomited while she was unconscious and choked on her vomitus."

Anna shuddered. Then she drew herself up and pushed past the image.

"Does this friend know?"

"No. I mean, as far as I know, she was alive when I encountered him. I quarantined him, and then I went to check on her. That's when I found her," Lydia said.

"You quarantined the man?"

"I had to. He said he'd seen her already. He's been exposed to ... whatever she had. Sergeant Rollins was back from getting the propane by then. He instructed me to quarantine the man, so I did," Lydia said matter-of-factly.

Quarantine. Unlawful detention. Kidnapping. There were a lot of ways to describe what Lydia and George had done. Anna closed her eyes briefly and tried to think.

"I need to talk to Jeffrey. Do not engage with this friend, whoever he is, until you hear from one of us," she said finally.

"Yes, ma'am. What about Celia's body?"

"What do you mean?" Anna asked.

"Uh, what should we do with the corpse? I mean, people will start arriving en masse in the next twenty-four hours, don't you think? We can't just leave her lying in the cabin, can we?"

Anna's heart thumped. She lowered herself to the nearest kitchen chair. Jeffrey had put out a call to convene at the camp and hadn't told her? That was unthinkable.

"Anna, are you still there?" Lydia asked.

"I'm here. Bury her, I guess," Anna didn't know what else to do with a possibly infectious corpse. More pressingly, she didn't know what to do about Jeffrey's apparent betrayal.

"Will do," the nurse said, chipper now that she had her marching orders.

Anna ended the call and took a moment to steady herself, gripping the edge of the counter. She waited until her heart had slowed and her breathing was steady, then she walked to the door and stepped out into the backyard.

Like mothers the world over, she pushed down the panic that rose in her throat so her children wouldn't sense danger.

She turned on the floodlights and leaned over the porch railing to shout, "Use your remaining ammo and come on in and get ready for bed!"

A flurry of snowballs and hoots of laughter filled the air as the kids finished their battle. Anna inhaled the cold night air, hoping it would drive out the fear and worry that flooded her body. The little ones tromped up the stairs to the porch, trailed by their older siblings. She brushed snow off faces, helped chubby hands unlace boots, and kissed the crowns of six heads, even those she had to stretch onto her toes to reach.

She stopped Bethany as she passed by and pulled her to the side of the porch. At twelve, she was capable of helping—old enough to handle the responsibility and young enough to find it a novelty, not a burden. The older kids would take care of themselves but would chafe at bathing and dressing the youngest two.

"Bethany, I need to talk to Dad. Can you please get Clara and Lacey into the bath and help them with their pajamas?" she asked, keeping her tone light.

"Sure, Mom," Bethany answered with a serious nod.

"Thanks, sweetheart."

Anna smiled at her daughter. After the back door slammed shut behind Bethany, she turned and stared out into the dark, her eyes sweeping her fallow vegetable garden, the sturdy hen house, and the tall oak tree from which Jeffrey had hung the tire swing.

She could barely make out the dark shapes in the night, but she stood there for a long time, trying to imprint the scene in her mind's eyes. She felt, deep in her bones, that she'd never see her backyard again.

She was still standing like that, scanning the dark yard, when she heard the door ease open and then softly shut behind her.

Jeffrey crossed the porch and came to stand beside her. He stood close, his shoulder touching hers, and said, "Is everything okay?"

She kept her eyes pinned forward and steadied her voice before answering.

"No."

He waited. She steeled herself and turned to face the man she'd followed, without question, for almost two decades.

"Celia Gerig is dead."

His eyes widened, and he inhaled sharply, but his expression gave nothing away.

"That's unfortunate. She seemed like a good woman," he said mildly.

Anna pressed her palms against his chest and stared up at him. "Jeffrey, stop. I know. I know about the stolen flu vaccines. I don't know why you didn't share your plans with me, why you didn't trust me, but we don't have time to get into that discussion now. Lydia Markham called. Celia got very sick and died. She's at the camp, along with some civilian who Lydia and George found prowling around. He claims to have been in contact with Celia, so they've quarantined him against his will."

His face crumpled, and he swallowed hard. "I trust you, Anna. I trust you without reservation. I was trying to save you some worry and to wall you off from the mission. We probably broke some laws. The vaccine acquisition was a critical priority, though. I *am* sorry Celia's dead, but she died in the service of our cause."

Anna considered this for a moment. She could tell he was being truthful, if understated—they definitely broke some laws. She could also tell he was holding back information.

"Are those vials in your duffel bag the vaccines?"

"Yes," he answered instantly.

"Is that all of them?"

"No. There are more doses up at the camp, enough to vaccinate the entire organization. I also have some in reserve to barter with if the currency system collapses. I already traded some to a militia outfit in exchange for silver."

"Why do you need them so badly?"

He took her hands in his and stared into her eyes, "Because we received reports from abroad that the killer flu live virus is on its way to the U.S."

"The Doomsday virus? You mean there's been an outbreak somewhere? Asia?"

He closed his eyes briefly and shook his head.

"No," he said, opening his eyes and meeting her gaze. "Someone stole the virus from a research facility in Europe. The virus is on its way here—if it's not already within the borders."

Anna stared at him and tried to comprehend what she was hearing. Jeffrey's reach was wide and deep, he had eyes and ears everywhere: if he'd heard it, she could assume it was true. But, still, she sensed he wasn't telling her everything.

"The killer flu is here, in a bottle somewhere?"

"Yes."

He looked down at her but didn't say the words that they'd spent fifteen years preparing for. The words she always knew would change their lives, even as she hoped the day would never come.

If he wouldn't say it, she would. "It's time to go."

She went inside and talked to each child, one at a time, and explained it was time to move to the camp.

From little Clara up to Clay, her oldest, each of them looked at her with wide, serious eyes and simply nodded. They'd been preparing for this day for years—and, in the case of the younger ones, their entire lives. They hurried to change out of their pajamas and into warm clothes and choose the special items they wanted to bring along—each child was permitted to pick two treasured belongings. Then they filed downstairs and grabbed their Go Bags.

Anna trailed behind them, turning out lights and pushing in chairs. From behind his closed office door, she could hear the rumble of Jeffrey's commanding bass voice but not his words. She was glad for that. He was likely talking to Rollins and Lydia, giving them instructions for dealing with the quarantined trespasser.

She stopped in the mudroom and unearthed the first aid kit and a pile of old towels from beneath the utility sink. She loaded the towels and the medical supplies into the back of the Suburban, next to the chickens, who clucked at her and scolded her from within their cage.

Jeffrey came out from the house, his eyes hooded and his expression unreadable. He zippered his hunting jacket to the chin and hefted two containers of gasoline from a shelf. She waited at the back of the SUV until he walked around to wedge the containers in the corner.

"Everything set?" she asked.

He nodded yes but didn't meet her eyes. She knew him. He viewed the chain of events that ended with a dead woman and a quarantined prisoner as a personal failure. Although she tended to agree with that assessment, he was her husband, and she loved him. She put a hand on his arm.

"Thank you for protecting us," she said in a low voice.

He turned and gave her a brief smile, and then he said, "We should go."

While he warmed the engine, she went back inside and walked through the dark, silent house one final time. It already felt deserted, like a house that had been abandoned years ago, not like the home they'd built together. She allowed herself one look back and then crossed the threshold, pulling the door shut behind her. The click of the lock engaging was loud in the still night.

She hopped into the passenger seat, buckled her seatbelt, and twisted around to look into the back seat. Clara was already drifting off to sleep, but the others were wide awake and watchful. They stared back at her.

She flashed them a reassuring smile before turning to Jeffrey. They looked at each other for a long moment, and then he shifted the vehicle into gear and pulled away from their home.

20

It was after nine when Connelly pulled the SUV into the garage behind his rented townhouse. Sasha stepped out of the car and stretched, working through a series of quick yoga poses right there in the cold night air, stretching in her bulky wool coat, just to loosen her muscles. Connelly shouldered his bag and, over her protests, took hers, too. She trailed him through the small square of gravel that served as his backyard and blinked into the motion-detecting floodlights that snapped on as they approached his back door.

While Connelly unlocked the door, she pulled out her phone to try one more time to return Gavin's missed call. She'd noticed Gavin's message after she and Connelly had left the service plaza and, concerned by the urgency in his voice, had tried twice to reach him, but got his voicemail both times.

She began unbuttoning her coat while the phone rang. Gavin's voicemail picked up again. She waited for the beep and said, "Gavin, I'm getting worried now. Call me."

She ended the call and tossed the phone on Connelly's spotless kitchen counter.

Connelly was rummaging in the refrigerator. He turned and looked at her over his shoulder.

"Gavin's a competent guy, Sasha. He can take care of himself." Connelly stood and raised two bottles of winter lager. "Beer?"

Sasha nodded. "Thanks. I know Gavin's a big boy, but his message said Celia's really sick and she's at the prepper compound. So, who knows what's going on. Maybe Celia has the killer flu. Maybe Gavin's going to get sick." She stopped herself as the *maybes* piled up in her mind, each one worse than the last.

Connelly pried the caps off the beers and handed her one.

"I know. But, worrying is just wasted energy, Sasha."

She sighed. He was right. She knew he was right.

She took a long swallow of the cold, spiced beer. Then she asked, "Do you think the virus is already out there? In your gut, is that what you think?"

His eyes told her nothing and everything.

Images of pedestrians collapsing in the streets, grocery store shelves bare of food, doctors and nurses wearing masks, and soldiers marching door to door quarantining frightened families as babies cried flashed through her mind. She thought of Naya, of her pregnant sisters-in-law, then the rest of her family. Her throat constricted.

Connelly pulled her into his arms, and she pressed the side of her cheek into his warm, broad chest. The cloth of his shirt felt soft against her skin. He held her tighter.

"I don't know, Sasha. I don't know." He murmured the words into her hair.

21

Monday

Monday morning dawned cold. A nor'easter was tracking its way toward D.C., stalking like a cat through North Carolina. A quick glance out the bedroom window revealed a light dusting of snow, but lines of school and government office closings scrolled across the ticker that ran along the bottom of the Weather Channel feed.

Leo supposed that spate of closings could simply be the metropolitan D.C. area's usual overreaction to the threat of snow, but he had to wonder if someone had made the call to shut down the city because of the more serious threat that lurked somewhere out there, far more deadly than even the worst blizzard.

You're paranoid, he told himself. He turned away from the window and looked down at Sasha, curled into herself like a cat, still sleeping. Even sound asleep, she looked tired.

He tried to recall another time that he'd woken before she did and failed. The fact that she hadn't sprung from bed before the sun was a worry in itself. He watched her heavy, slow breathing. Her wavy hair fell over her face in a partial curtain, but her pale skin peeked out. He smiled at the faint smattering of freckles that sat on her small straight nose and annoyed her in the summer, when the slightest tan served to connect the dots into a dark constellation.

The image of a sun-kissed Sasha faded and, unbidden, a very different Sasha, feverish and delirious, her lips cracking from dehydration, the sheets twisted around her legs, flashed into his mind. His heart squeezed in his chest, and he had to force himself to breathe.

"Hey, wake up, sleepyhead," he said, reaching down to touch her bare arm. The contact with her warm body was an effort to drive the picture from his head as much as to wake her up.

She sat bolt upright the instant his hand touched her arm.

"What time is it?" she asked, pushing her tangle of hair out of her eyes.

"Almost seven thirty," he told her.

"What? That can't be right," she said, shoving the blankets to the bottom of the bed. "I never sleep that late."

"You're tired. It doesn't matter. We have plenty of time. There's not going to be any traffic because everything's closed," he told her, gesturing toward the flat screen television mounted to the wall.

The local weather map showed the approaching storm under a cheerful 'White Christmas' headline, even though Christmas was still weeks away. He handed her a mug of coffee, which she took with a grateful smile.

She leaned back against his headboard and sipped the coffee.

"Mmm. Thank you. Look, the federal government's closed. Is our meeting still on?" She pointed toward the screen.

He didn't bother to look. "Even when the government's closed, it's not really closed. Essential personnel will still report to work, and our meeting will go forward no matter what."

As he said the words, the reason for the meeting cast a black shadow over the room, and their few minutes of quiet peace evaporated.

She looked at him wordlessly for a moment then drained the mug and placed it on his bedside table.

"Guess we'd better get a move on then," she said as she headed for the shower.

He waited until he heard the water running, then opened his closet and pulled a small metal box down from the top shelf. He unlocked the box and removed his Glock. He turned it in his hand and inspected it. He had stripped, cleaned, and lubricated it after his last trip to the shooting range. It was ready to go. He loaded a magazine into the well and then returned it to the lock box. Then, he shoved the box back into the closet and shut the door.

Technically, he could carry it. Despite the District of Columbia's strict gun control laws, he'd managed to negotiate permission from Homeland Security to carry a concealed weapon in all fifty states as part of his separation agreement. Technically, that permission exceeded the federal government's powers, but everyone involved in the decision knew that if Leo Connelly drew his weapon, the situation was sufficiently dire that any overstepping would be forgiven.

But, Sasha's gun ban was somewhat stricter than the District's and, given that they were going to spend the morning surrounded by armed federal agents, he saw no point in picking that particular fight with her just yet.

He just wanted to be ready. For what, he couldn't say, but whatever it was, he knew he'd feel better facing it with a loaded weapon.

He heard the sound of the water shutting off. A minute later, Sasha appeared in the doorway, a towel wrapped around her hair and wearing his thick cotton robe, which was only about a million sizes too big for her. The hem dragged across the floor as she walked toward him, following behind her like a train.

The sight of her swimming in his robe brought a smile to his lips, but the words she spoke wiped it off immediately.

"Hey, I was thinking. Maybe you should carry your gun today. You know, just in case." The forced casualness of her tone was belied by the spark of worry in her green eyes.

He nodded, serious and solemn. "Maybe I should. Just in case."

22

Colton dressed quickly as the morning news exhorted him to stay home and ride out the approaching storm. ViraGene didn't close every time the federal government shut down at the sight of a snowflake. He knew plenty of support staff would call off or work from home because their kids would be home from school, but those who could make it in were expected to show up for work every Monday through Friday, unless it was a paid holiday. Period.

He would arrive later than usual, however, because he had an errand to run. Not just any errand, an errand that had to be undertaken in secrecy, so that it would never trace back to him. He didn't want to risk taking his car. The Metro system was still running, for the time being. Colton decided he'd better get going before some lazy bureaucrat looking for a day off shut that down, too.

He checked his pocket for the vial and buttoned his overcoat.

He stepped out into the hall and locked the door. Behind him, he heard the Brandts' door open. He allowed himself his usual moment of annoyance at the fact that his so-called 'penthouse' apartment shared the top floor of the building with one other four-thousand square foot 'penthouse,' which forced him to deal with neighbors. Then he smoothed his expression into a smile and turned to greet whichever Brandt was intruding on his privacy this time.

It was the wife. Marilyn or Marly or something with an 'M.'

"Good morning, Mrs. Brandt. You're not going out in this weather are you? A little thing like you might blow away," he said in a pleasant, mildly flirtatious voice.

He'd learned that she responded well to flirting. The husband liked to talk about the markets and the Nationals. But the wife just liked attention.

He couldn't see her smile through the fuzzy scarf that covered her lower face, but her eyes crinkled, so he knew she was pleased by the banter.

"Oh, Colton," she said in a scarf-muffled voice, "how many times do I have to tell you to call me Marla? I'm just going to run out to the Whole Foods before the storm hits. We can't get caught without organic grass-fed beef in the fridge, now can we?" She laughed self-consciously—whether at her foolish storm preparations or her yuppie eating habits, it wasn't clear.

"Well, you be careful out there, Marla. I hope there's not a run on beef." He jabbed his key back into the keyhole.

"Are you coming or going? I can hold the elevator." she offered.

"No, no. You go ahead. I just realized I left my cell phone charging. It wouldn't do to be without that on a day like this," he lied.

"Oh, are you sure? I don't mind waiting."

"Please don't. I don't want to be responsible for your getting caught out in the blizzard," he said over his shoulder. He opened the door and went inside, closing it quickly to cut off further conversation.

He leaned against the door and waited long enough for the stupid cow to catch the elevator and leave the building. He detested having to socialize with people not of his own choosing under the best of circumstances. He particularly wanted to avoid it while he was carrying around a vial full of death. He didn't trust himself not to give into the temptation to open it and fill the elevator with the virus just for his own amusement.

Besides, knowing that Marla was gone would give

him an opportunity to take care of another task before he braved the weather to acquire a gift box and plan his little surprise for Serumceutical.

After giving her a sufficient head start, he returned to the hallway and thumbed the elevator call button. During the smooth, quick ride to the lobby, he fished out the mailbox key.

He strode through the marble lobby with his head down to avoid further conversations with idiots. When he reached the twin mailboxes that served the penthouse apartment—set slightly apart from the other, smaller boxes—he stood with his back to the security camera and inserted the key into the box on the left.

A small stack of mail stood neatly in the metal box. He flipped through the utility bills, brokerage firm statements, and junk mail. He was looking for something reasonably important, but not time sensitive, and preferably addressed by hand—a holiday card, a party invitation, or a thank you note.

Finding nothing in the day's mail that met his needs, Colton closed the door and locked the box, leaving the mail inside.

23

Connelly parked in a mostly empty surface lot. He and Sasha crossed the snow-dusted lot toward the attendant's hut, Connelly with his usual quick stride, Sasha cautious, testing the uneven ground for ice with her four-inch heels. Connelly had rolled his eyes at the footwear when she'd gotten dressed. He suggested she wear boots instead.

She'd pointed out that these *were* boots. Black, leather, knee-high boots.

So, now, she assumed he wasn't slowing his pace in a deliberate effort to say *I told you so* without having to utter the words. She trotted to keep up.

Connelly exchanged a twenty for a ticket and told the attendant to stay warm.

"You, too. If the city declares a snow emergency,

they'll tow a bunch of cars here. Just so ya' know. Might get yerself parked in." The attendant said in a bored tone and jammed his hands in his pockets and shrugged down into his jacket.

Connelly shrugged back at him. "We'll have to chance it."

They'd discussed taking the Orange Line to Arlington but had agreed it would be smarter to drive in case they needed to travel somewhere not served by the Metro system or the transit authority interrupted service because of the weather. They left unsaid their true concerns—carrying a loaded weapon on a D.C. Metro car was a questionable decision, at best, and mass transportation was an excellent delivery vehicle for anyone who wanted to release a chemical agent or, say, a deadly virus and have it spread quickly. The risk of being parked in by towed cars paled in comparison to those dangers.

They walked out of the lot and crossed the street. A little more than halfway down the next block, Connelly stopped in front of a squat, nondescript stone building. Sasha pulled up short beside him.

"Why are we stopping here? Do you need to get cash?"

She gestured toward the ATM in the lobby.

Connelly laughed. "This is it."

"This is what?"

"Headquarters for the task force."

Sasha looked up at the building. She'd attended meetings at the Department of Justice's headquarters for clients when she worked at Prescott & Talbott. It was an impressive limestone building that occupied a full city block. The entrances were flanked by pillars, and inscriptions about justice had been chiseled into the stone. Once inside, a visitor stood in a massive two-story entrance with a marble floor and ornate fixtures.

The FBI Headquarters, which she'd also visited on behalf of a Prescott client, although nowhere near as elegant, was equally imposing. It was a massive concrete building set with row after row of small, bronze-tinted windows. It loomed over the street.

She found it hard to believe that an important CIA task force worked out of a generic Arlington, Virginia office building with a bank branch and a deli on the first floor.

"You're not serious," she said.

Connelly leaned close and said, "It's a blank building, Sasha."

"A what?"

"This is a covert, inter-agency task force. They aren't going to advertise its existence. The General Services Administration owns buildings all over D.C., Maryland, and Virginia. When an agency needs space for something it wants to keep under the radar, it'll lease short-term space from the GSA in some anonymous building."

He opened the unadorned glass door and ushered her into an unremarkable lobby that matched the building's facade. A small flagpole flying the American flag jammed in the corner behind the cheap-looking reception desk, and a glass mug filled with candy canes on the desk, were the sole decorations. Snow that had been stamped off dozens of pairs of shoes and boots melted into a puddle of dirty gray water on a rubberized mat inside the door.

An ordinary middle-aged white man—not young, not old—sat behind the desk, tapping on a computer keyboard. If Sasha hadn't known she was in a secret CIA location, she'd have accepted him at face value as a bored, under-motivated desk jockey. But looking closely, she noticed his erect posture, the thick muscles outlined under his sweater vest, and his alert demeanor.

"May I help you?" he said blandly, addressing Connelly.

"We're here to see Mr. White," Connelly responded.

The man's eyes flickered with recognition, but he merely murmured, "I'll call up and let him know you're here. What did you say your name was?"

"Smith. Mr. and Mrs. Smith," Connelly said.

Sasha felt a laugh burbling up in her throat and coughed into her hand. *Mr. White? Mrs. and Mrs. Smith?* They were like little boys playing secret agent. She looked around the lobby, desperate for something to distract her from her impending case of the giggles.

The cough caught the attention of the desk worker. He opened a drawer to his left to reveal a stack of surgical masks sealed in clear plastic.

"Are you feeling okay, Mrs. Smith?" he asked.

Her amusement died in the face of the man's urgent concern.

"Perfectly fine. Just a tickle in my throat. The air in here's dry," Sasha lied.

He peered at her, trying to decide if he believed her.

"Honey, I'm going to run in and get a bottle of water. Do you want anything?" she said, touching Connelly's arm and nodding toward the deli across the lobby. As she did so, she wondered if the deli and the bank were real or if the entire building was like the set of a play.

Connelly shook his head. The man looked up from the phone and lifted a finger in a gesture that said *wait a minute.*

"Yes, sir. I'll send them right up," he said and hung up the phone. He focused on Sasha and said,

"Mr. White is ready for you. I'm sure he'll provide you with water."

She smiled at him. "Great. Thanks."

He turned his attention back to Connelly. "Take the elevator to the third floor. Someone will meet you."

Connelly crossed the lobby toward the elevator. Sasha looked around for a set of stairs but saw none. He jabbed the call button, and they waited in silence. A car arrived and the steel doors opened.

As Sasha followed him into the elevator car, she wished she'd thought to ask if they would be under surveillance at all times, but she assumed the answer was yes. They remained silent for the short ride. Connelly reached over and squeezed her hand.

The elevator thudded to a stop at the third floor, and the doors opened to reveal a young man. His ramrod posture, buzz-cut hair, and serious expression screamed *I'm a G-Man*. He was swarthy, with dark skin and eyes. He looked vaguely Middle Eastern.

He offered his hand to Sasha and Connelly in turn. He had a firm, quick handshake. "Mrs. Smith, Mr. Smith. I'm Mr. White's Assistant, Joey. If you'll just follow me this way."

He turned and led them down the corridor, past three blank doors. At the fourth, he stopped and swiped a card through the wall-mounted reader.

After the soft beep sounded, he pushed the door inward and ushered them into a waiting room.

Three squat chairs lined one wall. A water cooler bubbled in the corner, next to a dusty plant.

"Did you still need water?" Joey asked Sasha.

She turned to him, surprised. How could he know she wanted water? As far as she knew, the man at the front desk hadn't told him. She felt naked. Exposed.

"No, thank you," she answered.

Joey shrugged and said, "In that case, let's go in. Everyone's waiting."

Sasha glanced at Connelly as if to say *who's everyone?* She was off-balance, which was an unfamiliar emotion. She was accustomed to walking into conference rooms with a plan—a deposition outline or a negotiating position. Walking into a room filled with unknown parties and unknown agendas in a secret building was unsettling.

Connelly seemed to be in his element, though. Much more so than he'd been navigating the corporate politics of the boardroom the previous night.

They trailed Joey to another identical blank door, which opened into a large conference room. An elongated oval table of light wood filled most of the space. Black, cloth-covered desk chairs were crammed around the table, their arms touching. Over a dozen of the chairs were occupied. She scanned the assembled suits. The faces that looked back at her had a variety of hues, but they were all male.

Joey stepped forward, about to introduce them, but he didn't get the chance. An older, white-haired African-American man walked around the table and clapped Connelly on the back.

"Leo, good to see you again. What's it been—four years?" he said. His expression was somber but his voice registered genuine pleasure.

Connelly smiled and shook the proffered hand. "Hank, I didn't know you were involved in this effort."

He turned to introduce Sasha. "Sasha, Hank Richardson was the Special Agent-in-Charge of the FBI's office in Minnesota. I worked on an anti-terrorism matter with him that the Marshal Service ran out of the Minneapolis Field Office. Hank, Sasha McCandless is Serumceutical's outside counsel for this matter."

Hank's handshake was warm and firm, but unlike some men, he didn't seem intent on crushing the bones in her hand.

"Pleased to meet you, Agent Richardson."

"Oh, please, call me Hank. Okay if I call you Sasha?"

"Of course."

"And, Leo, you left just before I came over, so you

may not have heard—I'm not with the Bureau any longer. I'm the Senior National Security Liaison at the Division of Homeland Security Investigations. So, basically, all I do these days is run these ad hoc inter-agency efforts."

"I hadn't heard, but you're a good man for the job, Hank," Connelly responded.

Sasha was impressed that neither Connelly's tone nor his expression betrayed the fact that Senior National Security Liaison was the plum assignment he'd been up for just before he was unceremoniously axed for the help he'd given her the previous year.

Richardson smiled his thanks; then he put a hand lightly on the small of Sasha's back and guided her over to a brass coat rack near the window.

"Well, take off your coats and I'll introduce you to the rest of this motley crew. Leo, you may see some more familiar faces. We've assembled quite the cast of characters."

Presumably, Richardson was 'Mr. White.' Inarguably, he was in charge of the meeting. The others stood, as Sasha and Connelly shrugged out of their coats. Connelly took Sasha's and hung it for her.

Richard ushered them to the two closest unoccupied seats. Sasha dropped her pale blue leather bag on the chair and dug out a stack of business cards. She handed one to Richardson, who slipped his hand into his pocket and pulled out one of his.

"You're out of Pittsburgh, eh? Wasn't that where you had your last posting, Leo?" Richardson said, squinting at the card.

Sasha felt her cheeks redden, but she couldn't tell from Richardson's voice if he knew that she and Connelly were involved or if he really was remarking on an apparent coincidence.

"That's right, Hank. Sasha broke my nose then stole my heart," Connelly said.

Richardson nodded approvingly, and Sasha heard a few titters behind her.

Connelly winked at her, and she knew she probably should be dismayed that this roomful of men now primarily viewed her, not as Serumceutical's trusted attorney, but Leo Connelly's travel-sized girlfriend. But, he was looking at her with such affection, that she couldn't help smiling. Besides, being underestimated usually worked in her favor.

Richardson stepped closer and said, "Broke his nose? I'm going have to buy you a drink and hear that story someday, Sasha. But now, we should get started."

He sped through the introductions in a cloud of names and alphabet soup agency designations. Sasha smiled and nodded, exchanging business cards as she went down the line. She would keep the cards in order and draw a seating chart on her legal pad, numbering the seats and writing in each person's name where he sat. Then, she'd use the seat numbers to identify who was speaking when she took notes of the meeting.

It was a trick she'd been using since she defended her first deposition in a multi-party case with more than a dozen attorneys seated around the table. It hadn't failed her yet.

While Connelly chatted with an ATF agent he knew from some training program, Sasha walked to the credenza at the far end of the room, where a pitcher of ice water and a line of plastic cups shared space with a carafe of coffee and a tower of Styrofoam cups. Although she'd just turned down an offer of water, she waffled for a moment then reached for the water pitcher and poured herself a cup. She rarely passed on coffee, but then, she rarely felt as jittery as she had ever since she'd walked through the nondescript doors into the building.

She caught Connelly's eye and motioned toward the drinks. He shook his head no and finished his conversation with the guy from ATFA. As she walked back to her seat, she could feel the government attorneys—who sat together in a cross-agency cluster of legal degrees—watching her, assessing her.

She drained her water and tossed the cup into the wastebasket by the coat rack. She reached the table at the same time as Connelly. Because the chairs were crammed so closely together, he stood back and let her slide into her seat first. Even so, her hip brushed his thigh as she swiveled past him and into the chair.

She felt an electric charge, followed by a wave of embarrassment. It seemed there was no end to the pitfalls involved in representing one's boyfriend's company. She grabbed her legal pad and focused on creating her seating chart and scrawling in the names from the stack of cards she'd collected.

Richardson, who had returned to his spot at the end of the table, leaned back in his chair and said, "Okay, folks, now that everyone's been introduced, let's get started. We have a lot of ground to cover, and I don't need to tell you people the clock is running. For our guests' benefit, I want to make it clear that, while I grew up in the Bureau, when I accepted the transfer to HSI, I did so out of a genuine desire to coordinate investigations such as this one among the agencies. These ad hoc task forces leave no room for pissing matches because they address critical issues —and this one is a doozy."

The room was silent, save for the hiss of the old steam radiator under the window. Richardson looked at Connelly and added, "Many of you know Leo from his time with Homeland Security. I just want to remind this group that his clearances did not survive his separation, and Ms. McCandless has no clearances. They're here because Leo's employer apparently has some information that may prove useful. It's a one-way street, though. I'm sure Leo understands."

The subtext was unmistakable: *you used to be one of us, but you aren't anymore.*

"Of course. I know you're busy, so thanks for taking the time to meet with us. Serumceutical asked me to reach out to the General Accounting Office because of an issue we uncovered with regard to our fulfillment of the killer flu vaccine stockpile. When I called a friend at GAO, he suggested this group would be interested in hearing what I have to say. I'm here with the approval of Serumceutical's Board of Directors," Leo said, slipping into his role as an officer of a private corporation with no outward reaction to Richardson's pronouncement.

"Before you get started, do you mind telling us why you have counsel with you? Are you looking for immunity or cooperation credit?" The question came from within the sea of navy blue suit-wearing men.

Sasha checked her chart. Devin Bardman, attorney with the CIA's Office of General Counsel. He was asking if the company was coming in to self-report a crime in the hopes it would qualify for leniency.

Connelly said, "I think I'll let Ms. McCandless field that one."

Sasha swept her eyes across the knot of attorneys

across the table before settling on Bardman. "Serumceutical does not believe it's broken any law or federal regulation, so, from our perspective, leniency's not at issue. I'm here because the company does have civil claims against a third party arising out of the vaccine contract and there is an issue of performance under the contract. So, that said, when we meet with the GAO to work out the contract issue, we would certainly hope that our meeting with you would be taken into consideration as a show of good faith and an attempt to mitigate any damages. But again, no laws were broken. At least, not by my client."

A few small nods greeted her answer.

"Fair enough," Bardman said. "So, what's the issue? Breach of contract?"

Connelly leaned forward, ready to answer, but Sasha put her hand on his forearm to stop him.

"Yes. We have reason to believe that the first shipment of vaccines to Fort Meade was missing approximately eight hundred doses," Sasha said.

The expectant faces around the table fell, deflated. Apparently they were expecting something juicier.

"You think you shorted the shipment? That's it?" Bardman asked.

"We believe an employee planted by a competitor —ViraGene—stole the vaccines as part of a corporate espionage strategy. We've confirmed that more than seventeen hundred doses were taken from pallets prepared by that employee and awaiting shipment to Fort Meade; we suspect she also took doses from the pallets that already shipped," Sasha said.

Bardman snorted. "You called this meeting over a rounding error?"

Richardson interjected, "Your theory is ViraGene wants to force the government's hand to stockpile the AviEx antiviral, is that it?"

"Yes," Sasha said, ignoring the CIA attorney and turning to address Richardson. "Well, it was our theory, and it still makes sense except that the employee who stole the vaccines is in the wind and..." She trailed off and looked at Connelly, unsure of how much she should say about the preppers.

"The employee appears to be a member of a Pennsylvania-based prepper cell. And, in addition to being missing, we have a report that she is very sick, possibly with a flu-like illness," Connelly said.

That information recharged the group.

"That's serious. How good is your source?" Vince Drummond, the ATF agent, asked.

It was Connelly's turn to look at Sasha. Gavin was her contact, not his. If someone was going to vouch for him, it should be Sasha.

"He's former law enforcement, and he's trustworthy," Sasha said.

"But going to remain anonymous, I take it?" Drummond said.

"For now," she answered.

She could tell they were bursting with unasked questions, desperate to pepper her and Connelly with specific inquiries, but they were waiting for a cue from Richardson. They almost certainly assumed she and Connelly were in the dark as to the theft of the virus and would be hesitant to ask any questions that might hint at the possibility of a coming pandemic.

The Project Shield agent who'd tipped off Connelly had broken several laws by sharing that information, so they couldn't let on that they knew.

As a result, the government agents just stared at them, and Sasha and Connelly stared back. Everyone was unwilling to show their cards.

Finally Richardson spoke. "Leo, although I'm sure the bean counters at GAO will be hopping mad that you all screwed them out of some bottles of vaccine, I can state with authority that we can make that a no-harm, no-foul situation. But, we're gonna need your help identifying these preppers and locating them. Now, I hate to do this, but I have to run your name up the flagpole and see how much I can tell you."

Connelly nodded.

Sasha cleared her throat and said, "While

Serumceutical appreciates the assurance that the shipment isn't going to cause a problem with GAO and, of course, will provide replacement vials, I want to be clear that the Board of Directors instructed me to file a temporary restraining order against ViraGene. This prepper business aside, they have serious concerns about a competitor playing dirty pool."

The attorney contingent nodded in unison, with the sole exception of Bardman, who was scribbling rapidly on his legal pad.

Anthony Washington, whose card identified him as an attorney with the Executive Office of the United States Attorney General's Office, Communications and Law Enforcement Coordination Division, spoke up. "If your client intends to rely on its contract with Congress as an exhibit in any civil litigation, you will, of course, have to file it under seal. Portions of that contract have national security implications."

"Of course. We've actually already filed, and the contract *was* submitted under seal. But I don't think the contract specifics will come into play in any way. ViraGene seems to have placed a mole in the organization; we'd have a viable claim even absent the theft of the vaccines," Sasha assured him.

Maybe, she added silently. *If Celia Gerig even had anything to do with ViraGene, which was becoming less clear as the picture developed.*

Washington must have been thinking along the same lines, because he shot her a skeptical look but merely nodded. Bardman kept scrawling notes.

"You already filed?" Bardman asked without looking up.

"Yes, we filed electronically yesterday in the District of Columbia District Court," she confirmed.

Washington leaned over and whispered in Bardman's ear.

Richardson stood. "I'll be in touch," he said to Leo.

The meeting was adjourned.

24

Colton peered at the Salvadoran's blank face. "You understand?" he repeated.

The man, who claimed to be named Tito, nodded. "Yes, yes. Mr. Leo, he is your friend. You want to surprise him. Put the gift in his top desk drawer tonight when I'm cleaning. I understand."

Tito waved the box to punctuate his understanding. Colton tried not wince at the thought of the box crashing to the ground with the vial inside.

"What else, Tito?" Colton pressed. He wished this idiot would talk faster. It was cold, not to mention unseemly, lurking around the dumpster in an alley behind a restaurant in some godforsaken corner of Northwest D.C. The wind swirled stinging snow in his face.

Tito thought. "Ah, don't open the box?"

"Correct! Do not, under any circumstances open the box," Colton said with an encouraging nod.

He reached into his overcoat pocket and felt around until he located the bills he'd removed from his wallet before entering the Metro station. There was no need to pull out his wallet and get robbed. He pressed the thick wad of green into Tito's gloved hand.

The shorter man thumbed it but didn't count it, then he shoved it into his pants pocket. Colton imagined he wasn't interested in being robbed, either.

"Gracias. Thank you, Mr. Jefferson," he said.

"That's payment in full. I don't want to see you again, ever," Colton told the man.

"Si, si," Tito smiled and pointed toward the back of the dingy concrete block building. "You like huevos? This taqueria has the best huevos. I will buy you breakfast."

Colton refrained from wrinkling his nose in disgust. "No. Thank you. I need to go before the storm comes. You should, too, Tito."

He didn't want to pique the man's curiosity about the beribboned package in his hand, but he also didn't want some oaf to elbow it off a table inside the restaurant and waste a perfectly good vial of the virus on a room full of inconsequential immigrants.

Tito waved a hand, dismissing the threatened blizzard. "A man's gotta eat."

"Suit yourself," Colton said, turning on his heel and bowing his head against the wind.

In the end, it made no real difference to him if Tito and his fellow egg lovers died a miserable, painful death. He had one more vial; if need be, he could find another janitor.

25

The door to the cabin swung open, and Gavin blinked as sunlight flooded his tired eyes. He swung his legs over the side of the too-short bed and pulled his sweater over his head.

Rollins stood in the doorway, his ever-present weapon at his side.

"Good morning, Mr. Russell. How'd you sleep?" Rollins asked in the mild, uninterested manner of a hotel clerk. His voice was muffled by a blue paper surgical mask.

Gavin just grunted at him in response. He'd slept poorly—uncomfortable in his clothes, worried about Celia, not trusting Lydia or some other overzealous prepper to burst into the cabin during the middle of the night in a hail of bullets.

"C'mon. Captain wants to see you," Rollins said.

Gavin bent and slid his feet into the shoes at his bedside. As he knotted the laces, he calculated his odds of taking Rollins down. He could lower his shoulder and run at the armed man, just pretend he was back in high school on the football team. Gavin figured he had forty pounds on Rollins. And he'd have the element of surprise on his side. His chances against Rollins were decent.

But the rifle was a complicating factor. And, assuming he did overpower Rollins and get his firearm—then what? Was he going to shoot his way out of the compound? They'd confiscated his keys, wallet, and cell phone before they'd locked him in the cabin for the night. He wouldn't get far on foot.

Reluctantly, Gavin decided attacking Rollins was suicidal. He straightened and grabbed his coat. "Take me to your leader," he cracked.

Rollins didn't laugh or respond. Instead he slid a mask over Gavin's mouth and snapped the band against his head.

Then he waved Gavin through the open door and, like Lydia had the night before, walked behind him, with the rifle pointed at Gavin's back.

Gavin walked a few feet and then slowed his pace and looked around. Off in the distance a group of kids played in a snowy field. Rollins gave him a little nudge with the muzzle of the rifle.

"Let's go," Rollins said. "We're going to the recreation center. Captain Bricker's office."

As they passed the clearing, Gavin took a closer look at the kids.

A half-dozen boys and girls were playing a game of freeze tag, whooping and hollering as they dashed around. He wasn't great with children's ages, but he guessed the group ranged from three or four to fourteen or fifteen years old. They were siblings or maybe cousins: they all had the same pale skin, straight brown hair, and big, round eyes. The littlest girl still had the round cheeks of a toddler, but the others were all lanky, thin and angular.

Kids. He hadn't expected kids. He was suddenly very aware of the gun pressed into his back.

"Keep moving," Rollins instructed.

Gavin shuffled his feet but kept his head toward the knot of kids, who had stopped mid-game to stare at him and Rollins as they approached.

The tallest of the girls spoke first.

"Are you lost, mister?" she asked as she twisted her long ponytail around a gloved finger. She stared up at him with a mix of curiosity and concern for him. She showed no fear.

Gavin hesitated, unsure whether to answer. Rollins seemed equally unsure. Gavin reasoned Rollins wouldn't shoot him in the back in front of a group of kids, so he opened his mouth to speak.

As he did, the tallest boy ran across the field. He came to an abrupt stop between Gavin and the girl. He took in the masks they wore, and his eyes flashed anger and fear. He clenched his hands into fists.

"This is private property, sir. You need to leave." The boy tried to say the words in a firm tone, but his voice cracked.

Rollins interjected, "It's okay, son. I'm taking the prisoner to see your father. The situation is under control."

Gavin ignored Rollins, looked around Bricker's son, and addressed the girl. "I'm looking for a friend of mine. Maybe you've seen her? Her name is Celia, and she has dark, curly hair about—"

The girl burst into tears.

"Celia's dead," she cried.

The boy jutted his chin forward, "Shh, Bethany. Don't."

Celia was dead? Gavin's mind reeled, and he tried to work through the news.

The boy led Bethany back to their game, with a backward glance at Rollins. The other kids clustered around the crying girl with hugs and soothing pats.

"Celia's dead?" Gavin asked Rollins.

"I'm getting tired of telling you to keep moving, Russell. You can talk about it with Captain Bricker. Now let's go."

This time, Rollins' shove was less gentle. The gun hit Gavin's spine with a thud.

Gavin stepped it up and strode across the frozen path to the recreation center.

Inside, the scene was very different from the previous night. The room bustled with activity, shouted instructions and laughter rang out. Men and women dressed in hunting jackets, ski coats, and an array of various camouflage patterns, ranging from desert to forest to tundra, unpacked boxes, trotted back and forth with pots and bowls, and handed out bedding. In the far back corner of the room, a teenage girl led a group of small children in a game of Simon Says. A cluster of slightly older children camped out at one end of one of the tables with paper and crayons.

Rollins and Gavin started down the hallway to the office where they'd met the night before. From behind, the boy from the field darted past them and rapped on the door.

"Dad," the boy called as he knocked.

"Come in," a baritone voice rumbled from the other side.

With a backward glance at Gavin, the boy rushed through the door.

Rollins and Gavin followed.

A tall, fit man with a salt-and-pepper buzz cut and piercing blue eyes rose from behind a metal desk. He gave Gavin and the Magnum-toting Rollins a short nod, then turned to his son.

"Clay, what's going on?"

"The man with George says he's a friend of Celia's. I thought you might need some help—" the boy began.

Bricker responded in a measured tone. "Clay, this isn't your concern. Go back outside. You shouldn't have left your brothers and sisters alone. If you aren't going to supervise them, they need to come inside."

"Yes, sir," the boy said, clearly disappointed at being dismissed. Gavin half-expected him to argue but he immediately turned and walked out of the office, leaving the door open behind them.

"Sir—" Rollins began.

Bricker cut him off. "That'll be all, Sergeant Rollins. Thank you for escorting Mr. Russell to my office. You're dismissed."

Gavin snuck a glance at him. Rollins' face crumpled, but like Bricker's son, he didn't argue.

"Yes, sir," Rollins said. He shouldered his weapon and headed for the open door.

"Shut that behind you," Bricker ordered.

The door closed with a soft thump.

Bricker stared at Gavin, studying the portion of his face that was visible above the mask. Gavin stared back at him for a long moment.

"So, Mr. Russell, it seems we have a problem," Bricker finally said.

"What are you the captain of?" Gavin said by way of answer.

"Pardon?"

"Your people call you 'Captain Bricker.' What are you the captain of?" he repeated.

Bricker squinted hard at him, measuring his response. After a moment, he jerked his head toward the metal chair in front of Gavin. "Have a seat, Mr. Russell, and I'll tell you a story."

"Don't mind if I do," Gavin said.

He eased himself on the hard, cold chair and stretched out his legs, crossing them at the ankles. Bricker returned to his seat, pushed aside a sheaf of papers, and leaned forward on his elbows.

"In 1999, I was working in the banking industry. My wife, Anna, was home with Clay, our oldest, who was just a baby. She was pregnant with our second child. The bank, of course, was very worried about Y2K. We'd been working on contingency plans for years, trying to prevent any interruptions to our service and making arrangements to deal with snafus if they did happen, but no one knew exactly what would happen when the calendar rolled over. Now, Americans look back on that time as a joke. All the panic and preparation were for nothing. But, as I sat praying with Anna on New Year's Eve, waiting for the clock to strike twelve, I had a vision."

Bricker paused. Gavin assumed it was for dramatic effect.

"A vision, huh?" Gavin asked.

"That's right, Mr. Russell. A vivid vision of a post-disaster America, where the government ceased to function and neighbor turned on neighbor for a sack of flour or a glass of potable water. Where the unprepared and untrained starved or froze to death. An America where the strong survived and the weak were slaughtered. Where the dead rotted in fields and city streets, and orphaned children roamed the countryside. And I saw a new civilization rise up. Built by hearty people in good physical condition, who had prepared for this eventuality. People who could start a fire, raise vegetables, hunt, and sew. People who did for themselves instead of relying on the government to do for them. And this new community needed a leader. It needed me."

Despite himself, Gavin was rapt. Bricker could deliver a sermon like the best of the televangelists.

Bricker continued, his voice ringing stronger. "So on January 1, 2000, Anna and I committed our lives to building a network of like-minded survivors. We began by recruiting neighbors and friends who shared our values. Preppers PA is now several hundred members strong with cells throughout the state and a few select members from out of state. We run workshops and drills to teach self-sufficiency and self-defense. As we've grown, it's become necessary to impose an organizational structure. Many of our members have military backgrounds, so the hierarchy that we chose borrows liberally from the armed forces. To answer your question, then, I'm the captain of a band of Americans committed to preserving our way of life when—not if—a large-scale disaster strikes."

He sat back in his chair and contemplated Gavin for a moment. Then he said, "I've answered your question, now perhaps you can do me the same courtesy. What do you want with Celia Gerig?"

Although Bricker phrased his demand as a question, he spoke with the assurance of someone who expected to be obeyed and respected. In Gavin's experience, a man like Bricker would be thrown off-balance if his authority was questioned.

"That's between me and Celia. Take me to her," Gavin responded.

Bricker clenched his jaw. A muscle twitched in his cheek. Gavin waited.

Finally, Bricker said, "She's unavailable right now."

Although Bricker's daughter had said Celia was dead, Gavin hoped the girl was mistaken. "The last time I saw Celia, she was very ill, Mr. Bricker. I'd like to make sure she's okay."

Bricker closed his eyes briefly then snapped them open. "I'm sorry to have to tell you this, but, sadly, Celia's passed away. As you say, she was quite ill, and she succumbed to her illness."

Gavin's head spun. He swallowed hard, suddenly thirsty. Sweat dripped from his hairline.

Bricker squinted at him. "Mr. Russell, are you okay?"

Gavin gulped and tried to nod. His vision blurred and he felt dizzy, lightheaded. He pushed the mask up to the top of his head and gasped for air.

A remote part of his brain registered surprise that he was having such a strong physical reaction to the news of Celia's death. He struggled to his feet, gripping the edge of Bricker's desk to steady himself. He felt like he was underwater, swimming. The lights were growing dim at the edges of his vision.

Far off, from a great distance, he heard Bricker's voice calling his name.

Gavin swayed, the lights went out, and he crumpled to the floor.

26

Sasha and Connelly were walking into a Tex-Mex restaurant a block away from the task force's building, when Sasha's phone buzzed. Naya's name scrolled across the display.

"Why don't you grab us a table?" she suggested to Connelly. "And order some chips and guacamole. I'll be right in."

Connelly walked over to the hostess station and Sasha huddled in the restaurant's foyer and answered the call.

"How's the weather, Naya?" she said by way of greeting, scanning the menu posted inside the door.

"Snowing like crazy. But, Mac, I'm not calling to chat," Naya said. Her voice was calm but tight.

Sasha abandoned the menu and gave Naya her full attention. "What's up?"

"You're not going to believe this, but the D.C. District Court Clerk's Office just called."

"Did we screw something up with the filing?" Sasha thought that was highly unlikely given their shared attention to detail, but she supposed nobody was perfect.

"No, the papers are fine. The case has been assigned to the emergency hearing judge, Judge Minella."

"Great, maybe we'll get an order soon."

"Oh, we'll get an order soon. The judge scheduled argument for two-thirty," Naya said.

"What day?"

"Today, Sasha. You have to appear in the D.C. District Court in three hours and argue the motion."

Sasha nearly dropped the phone.

"Mac, you there?"

"I'm here. The judge scheduled an argument on an *ex parte* motion? There's no one on the other side."

"I know what *ex parte* means, Mac. I don't know what this guy's thinking; maybe the clerk screwed up. You'll show up and everyone will have a good laugh, then the judge'll sign your order and you'll walk out of there," Naya said.

Right. A federal judge would just good-humoredly laugh off a screw up. More likely, it would end up being her fault somehow.

"But, if he really wants me to argue, I don't have the file. I don't even have a copy of the brief," Sasha said, trying to keep her rising panic out of her voice.

"Listen, you can do this. I explained to the clerk that you're in D.C. today but you don't have access to a printer. He was really nice about it. If you go to the counter in the clerk's office and ask for Lamar, he'll give you a packet that contains copies of everything we filed."

"Lamar. Got it." Sasha exhaled. Maybe she could do this. It was a clear-cut argument.

"Uh, two more things. My new best friend Lamar tells me Judge Minella is ... mercurial."

"A mercurial judge, how rare," Sasha deadpanned.

Naya snorted. "Point taken. And the second thing is I checked the flights. There's a Hemisphere Air flight that I might be able to make. Maybe. If the stars align. And it doesn't get canceled because of the snow. I could be there by two-thirty or close. But I'd have to leave now."

The offer brought a smile to Sasha's face. "I appreciate that more than you know. And, ordinarily, I'd love the moral support, but even if you did make it, you wouldn't get here in time to do anything but watch. Besides, we both know you need to get home this evening and get your chair out before you lose your spot."

Naya lived in Point Breeze, which was typical of Pittsburgh's neighborhoods. Many of the homes sat close to one another on narrow streets with no off-street parking. Finding a spot to park could prove difficult under any circumstances, but when there was a snowstorm, scarce parking became nearly nonexistent. Banks of shoveled snow ate up precious spots along the street. So homeowners would shovel 'their' spots right in front of their homes, and then put out chairs to save those hard-won spots whenever they left again. Having done the work to clear the spot, the theory went, the shoveler was then entitled to park in that spot until the snow melted.

The parking chairs ranged from folding chairs to lawn chairs to kitchen chairs to barstools. On occasion, a recliner that had outlived its useful life as living room furniture appeared along the curb to guard a coveted parking spot. Somehow the system worked: the chairs were respected, never moved or stolen.

Naya laughed. "Come on, now, you know Carl probably already shoveled me a spot and plopped a chair down in it. We've got about six inches so far."

Poor, long-suffering, love-struck Carl had been trying to get Naya to date him as long as Sasha had known her. Naya insisted she didn't have romantic feelings for Carl, but Sasha thought she could detect a warming in Naya's demeanor toward her neighbor.

He'd been at her side constantly over the summer right after her mother had died.

"So, leave at five and go home and thank Carl. I'll call you after the hearing."

"You're sure?"

"I'm sure. Unless you're secretly hoping to see Lamar ..." Sasha teased her.

"Yeah, right. Well, I guess you shouldn't need me. I mean, you'll be arguing unopposed right? Pretty hard to lose that argument," Naya teased her right back.

"Virtually impossible," Sasha agreed.

Leo was impressed by Sasha's calm as she told him that instead of having margaritas and burritos, they were going to race to the federal district courthouse in D.C. to pick up some papers and then camp out while she prepared for an argument in a few short hours.

Despite the fact that his legs were considerably longer than hers and he wasn't wearing four-inch heels, he had to struggle to keep up with her as she strode back to the parking lot.

"You might need to testify," she said over her shoulder.

"Wait, what?"

"You're my fact witness. You verified the motion, so if the judge has questions about the facts, I need to have you ready to address them," she said.

"Oh," he said, his stomach sinking. He'd never testified in court before.

His dismay must have shown on his face, because she met his eyes and smiled. "It'll be okay, Connelly. I'll make sure you're prepped. And, besides, this is an *ex parte* hearing. There won't be anyone there to cross-examine you."

"What does that mean, though?"

Sasha stopped at the passenger side door. "It means this'll be a walk in the park, okay?"

She spoke with such conviction that he decided his concerns were unfounded. "Okay," he agreed.

27

Sasha studiously ignored Connelly's fidgeting. He sat beside her at counsel's table drumming his fingers, jiggling his leg, and clearing his throat—in short, doing everything except reviewing the motion she'd placed in front of him.

She wasn't really concerned about him, though. He already knew the facts, and she knew how to gently lead a witness. She focused on familiarizing herself with the cases she'd cited in her supporting brief, trying to identify any weaknesses or differences between her case and the precedent that might give the judge pause. Truth was, she felt confident. Good, even.

She wondered if she'd finally been practicing long enough that she was losing her jitters. By rights, having a hearing on an emergency motion thrown in her lap on essentially no notice should have left her unsettled and apprehensive. Instead, she was eager to get started—even in front of a temperamental judge.

A popping noise to her right drew her attention. She gave Connelly a sidelong glance. He was cracking his knuckles.

She leaned over to tell him to relax, when the door from the judge's chambers opened. A matronly African-American woman in her late fifties entered the courtroom. Her graying hair was pulled back in a tight bun. She wore a black skirt and cardigan sweater over a white blouse. Her shoes were the very definition of sensible. She looked grandmotherly, but Sasha had learned that, when applied to a judge's deputy clerk, grandmotherly could just as easily translate into stern as sweet. A clerk was responsible for insulating her judge from the world, including, but not limited to, clueless legal interns, wet behind the ears law clerks, confused *pro se* litigants, and angling attorneys. It was the sort of job that could sour a person's disposition pretty quickly. Add to that the fact that federal judges were appointed for life and tended to keep their deputy clerks until one of the pair died or retired, and it wasn't unusual to run into a clerk who'd seen it all and was impressed by none of it.

Sasha straightened in her chair and placed a hand over Connelly's. She smiled brightly, but not too brightly, at the woman.

"Good afternoon," Sasha said.

The woman exhaled and pulled her cardigan closed in front of her.

"You counsel for Serumceutical?" she asked in a weary voice.

"Yes, ma'am," Sasha answered.

The clerk nodded her head toward Connelly. "That your client or your co-counsel?"

"This is Leo Connelly; he's an officer of the company."

"Client, then. Well, come on. Judge Minella wants to do this in chambers."

Sasha nodded. It made sense. There was no need for the formality of the courtroom when she was the only party appearing. She scooped up her files, and she and Connelly stood.

Connelly started to walk toward the deputy clerk, but the woman stopped him before Sasha could.

"This door here is for court personnel only. Follow me," she said in a not-unkind voice, as she walked around the bar and skirted the well. Sasha and Connelly followed her through the gallery and out into the gleaming marble hall.

"I'm sorry, I didn't catch your name, Ms. ...," Sasha began.

"Mrs. Walker," she said.

She kept up a brisk pace, trailed by Sasha and Connelly, for the short walk to the heavy oak door to chambers. She unlocked the door using a key that she wore around her wrist on a springy elastic band.

Inside, bookshelves lined the walls. A bronze statue of a fish sat on a small table just to the left of the door. To the right, two law clerks sat at desks that faced one another, typing away on desktop computers, stacks of Westlaw printouts piled around them.

One of them looked up at Mrs. Walker from under a sweep of brown bangs that had been streaked pink.

"Is this the TRO?" she asked, reaching for a legal pad.

"Mmm-hmm, but Judge said no need to attend, Tallie."

The girl's face fell. Her co-clerk smiled slyly down at his research. A rush of memories flooded Sasha's mind—all the petty competitions that sprang up between law students, summer associates, and junior attorneys, anyone at the bottom of the legal pecking order, desperate to find a purchase to claw his or her way up a rung. Apparently, judicial law clerks were not immune.

Mrs. Walker moved on and stopped in front of the judge's secretary's desk. Sasha and Connelly stood beside her.

The secretary could have passed for Mrs. Walker's sister. She placed a finger in between the pages of her *People* magazine and peered at them over half-moon glasses that were attached to a colorful beaded chain.

"'This the movant?" she asked Mrs. Walker.

"Right. This here is Attorney McCandless. And this gentleman is a client representative," Mrs. Walker said.

"Good afternoon. The judge is ready for you, so you all go ahead in," Mrs. Walker's slightly friendlier sister said with a smile before returning to her magazine.

Mrs. Walker rapped on the door behind the secretary's desk and then eased it open.

The judge's private office was spacious. In addition to an executive desk, the room housed a set of tall bookshelves, a high-backed couch, and a long, highly-polished conference table. Sasha counted ten chairs arranged around the table.

One of the chairs was occupied by a surprisingly youthful-looking jurist. He had a full head of dark hair that matched his robe. His face was unlined, and his brown eyes were alert.

Sasha realized she'd been expecting an elderly judge. But, in retrospect, it made sense that the more junior members of the bench would be tasked with handling emergency motions.

"Judge Minella, this is Ms. McCandless and her client," the clerk said.

"Thank you, Mrs. Walker. Could you check the courtroom and see if Ms. Esposito is waiting in there, by chance?"

"Yes, your honor," she said. She pressed a button on the wall near the bookshelves. A clicking noise indicated the judge's door into the courtroom had unlocked, and she left.

The judge turned his attention to Sasha and Connelly. He half-rose and offered Sasha a hand. "Ms. McCandless," he said.

"It's a pleasure to meet you, your honor," she said, shaking his warm hand.

She gestured toward Connelly. "Your honor, this is Leo Connelly. He's Serumceutical's chief security officer."

The judge and Connelly shook hands and the judge waved them into seats. "Please, sit. I'm glad that the company could send us an officer on such short notice."

"Serumceutical takes this matter very seriously. And the company is grateful that the court has taken it up on such short notice," Sasha said, sliding into one of the large leather chairs

"Don't thank me yet," the judge said as his smile faded.

Connelly took the seat next to Sasha and shot her a look.

She shrugged inwardly but gave no outward reaction. The famous judicial temperament was revealing itself, she figured.

She cleared her throat. "Are we waiting for the court reporter?" she asked the judge.

"No. This isn't going to be on the record," he said in a stern tone that dared her to argue.

Great, Sasha thought. *Nothing better than a hearing in front of a cranky judge with no way to memorialize the argument.* She wanted to ask who Ms. Esposito was, in that case, but she figured it was better not to antagonize him.

Connelly nodded toward a framed photo of the judge, clad in hip boots, standing in a stream and proudly displaying a large fish on a line.

"Are you a fly fisherman?"

Judge Minella's frown morphed into a broad smile. "That's right. That picture was taken on an expedition out in Montana. Great fishing."

"I can imagine. You know, a little closer to home, the Yellow Breeches in Pennsylvania has some excellent fly fishing, too," Connelly offered.

"Oh, yes. There's a little town called Boiling Springs that has a white fly hatch in August," the judge said, his eyes shining.

Sasha knew they were speaking English, but she

would have been hard pressed to join in. She smiled politely and let the discussion of anglers and runs flow over her head.

The outer door opened, and Mrs. Walker returned from her second circuit. A frazzled-looking woman about Sasha's age tripped after her.

"I found her," Mrs. Walker announced needlessly.

"Thank you, Mrs. Walker. Kind of you to join us, Ms. Esposito," the judge said with his frown back in place.

The woman hesitated in the doorway. Her hair was pulled back into a messy knot and her shirt collar was folded under the lapel of her suit jacket. She was slightly out of breath.

"I'm sorry, your honor. I returned from lunch to find this file on my desk. I apologize for my tardiness," she said in a respectful tone that almost hid the slick of bitterness underneath.

Sasha didn't understand why the other woman was here, but she felt an instant kinship with the harassed attorney, although she suspected Ms. Esposito represented ViraGene.

"Well, come in and close the door. Mrs. Walker, we won't need you for this," the judge snapped, first at the hapless Ms. Esposito and then at Mrs. Walker, who'd been pulling up a chair.

Mrs. Walker's gray eyebrows shot up her forehead, but she rose wordlessly and walked toward the door. Before leaving, she turned and gave Sasha a look that seemed to say 'good luck, you're going to need it.'

She pulled the door shut firmly behind her and disappeared into the outer office.

Esposito crossed the room and stopped awkwardly beside Sasha's chair. She smiled and said, "Jill Esposito, Office of General Counsel for the Central Intelligence Agency."

Bardman, that dirty, sandbagging weasel.

Sasha tamped down her dismay and shook the woman's hand.

"Sasha McCandless, counsel for Serumceutical. And this is Leo Connelly, Serumceutical's chief security officer," she said, aware that her irritation was audible in her voice. At the moment, she didn't care.

Leo mumbled a greeting and shook the government lawyer's hand. Sasha could tell from the hint of anger in his eyes that he was piecing the situation together, too.

"Okay, Ms. Esposito, have a seat, so we can get on with this," the judge instructed.

Figuring she had nothing left to lose, Sasha spoke up. "Your honor, Serumceutical would like to formally request the presence of a stenographer to record the proceedings in the event there's an appeal."

"Request denied," the judge snapped without looking at her.

Across the table, Jill Esposito—who was perhaps the only person in the room who didn't know the score—formed a small 'O' of surprise with her lips.

"Now, then," the judge rumbled on, "this is an *ex parte* hearing on a motion for an emergency temporary restraining order that Serumceutical has filed against a competitor called ViraGene. The motion is denied because the court finds that the United States government is an indispensable party to the litigation."

Sasha opened her mouth to speak, but the judge cut her off. "The court does not intend to hear argument, Ms. McCandless."

He turned toward Esposito. "Ms. Esposito, if the government were joined as a defendant, is it your office's position that it would consent to jurisdiction?"

Esposito looked down at her notes for a moment. Then she said, "Your honor, the CIA believes that the subject matter of the contract between Serumceutical and the government raises national security implications and cannot be the subject of civil litigation between private parties."

"That's nice, Ms. Esposito. My favorite color is blue. Ms. McCandless wishes this was on the record. Now that we've each shared some irrelevant information, why don't you try answering my question?" the judge demanded.

Esposito blinked down at her papers.

"Would the government consent to jurisdiction?" Judge Minella repeated, enunciating each word.

"No?" Esposito guessed.

"No. Good answer, Ms. Esposito," the judge said. He turned toward Sasha, "Because this Court finds that the federal government, which is immune from suit, is an indispensable party pursuant to Rule 19 of the Federal Rules of Civil Procedure, and because the government has indicated it will not waive immunity, your request for a temporary restraining order is denied and your motion is dismissed with prejudice."

Sasha swallowed her mounting anger. "Your honor, if I may—"

"No, Ms. McCandless, you may not. We're adjourned."

Sasha saw Connelly's hand curl into a fist, and she placed a cautioning hand on his arm. It didn't matter how big of a dick Judge Minella was, he was a sitting federal judge.

Jill Esposito seemed stunned. She hurriedly tossed her papers into her bag and gave Sasha a weak, apologetic smile. Then she said, "Thank you, your honor," and scurried toward the door before her luck could reverse itself.

The judge shook his head at her departing back and said, "Have a safe trip back to Pennsylvania, Ms. McCandless."

"Thank you, your honor," Sasha managed. She gathered her papers and pushed in her chair.

The judge came around the table and clasped Connelly on the shoulder. "Nice to meet a fellow angler, Mr. Connelly," he said in a warm, friendly tone.

Connelly stared at the judge mutely.

28

Gavin awoke in complete darkness. His dry eyes stung, and the skin at their corners cracked as he strained to see in the blackness. A thudding ache reverberated through his head. His mouth was hot and cotton dry.

"Hello?" he said—or thought he did. But all he heard was a hoarse, cracked moan. It took a moment to realize that was his voice. He ran his tongue over his dry, shredded lips. Tasted dried blood. He tried to work up some saliva but failed.

He couldn't lift his head off the flat pillow it rested on, so he turned his face to the side and stared at nothing. A thin, scratchy blanket covered his torso. He pushed it down to his waist. The movement sent a dull pain through the muscles in his arms, and he shook.

He tried to remember where he was. He tried to remember *anything*. But heavy clouds floated in his brain. He strained. Thought hard. *Celia. Bricker.* An idea rolled past him and his tired, fuzzy mind tried to latch on to it but missed.

He shivered and pulled the blanket up to his chin. He swallowed around a thousand tiny knives that pierced his throat, and his eyes fluttered closed. *Sasha. Celia. A little girl in the snow.* He struggled again to grab hold of a thought as it evaporated. He slept.

BRIGHT, relentless light leaked under his eyelids, and he flinched. He opened his eyes slowly, painfully to the white glow. He didn't know how much time had passed, but he remembered the itchy blanket and the hard pillow. He was in the same place, wherever that was. He squinted up at a face, a woman, with delicate, high cheekbones and big, kind eyes. The lower half of her face was hidden by a blue surgical mask. Behind her, as his eyes focused, he saw rough-hewn logs fitted together to form walls. He was in a cabin.

"Here. Drink this," she said, her gentle voice muffled by the mask.

She leaned over him and raised a straw to his mouth with gloved hands.

He tried to speak—to ask what she was giving

him, who she was, where he was—but all he managed was a croak. He decided he didn't care what was in the glass. He parted his lips and sucked on the straw. Cold, sweet liquid hit the back of his throat.

"It's Gatorade. You're dehydrated, and you need the electrolytes," the woman told him.

He sucked again.

"Take it slow," she warned.

Too late. The liquid splashed down, and his stomach roiled.

She jumped back, and he leaned over the side of the bed and retched. The fruity drink mixed with bile and burned his throat.

"Sorry," he managed. He returned his head to the pillow, out of breath and dizzy.

"It's okay," she said. "We'll get Lydia in here to start you on an IV. You need to rehydrate."

He stared up at her, too weak to ask what was happening to him, but she must have read the question in his eyes.

"You have the flu. You passed out in Captain Bricker's office. Don't worry, we're going to take care of you. I'll turn out the lights when I leave so you can sleep. You need to rest up," she said.

She smoothed his blanket, and he could tell from the way her eyes lifted that she was smiling reassuringly behind her mask.

She walked away, out of his line of vision. The

squeak of a hinge and then the bang of metal sounded as she filled the wood-burning stove and lit it.

Then, as promised, the harsh overhead light disappeared. In the blackness, he heard the creak of the cabin door as it opened, felt a blast of cold air, and then heard the thud of the door as it closed. From the sounds of metal clinking, he could tell she was locking him in from the outside.

Gavin pinned his eyes open and stared sightlessly at the ceiling, desperate to drift back into his fitful, feverish sleep, but determined to keep himself awake long enough to piece together what was happening. He listened to his labored, whistling breathing and remembered the names the woman had said: Captain Bricker and Lydia.

Sasha. Celia. Bricker. Lydia. Rollins. The preppers. Gavin coughed, and the force of the cough racked his body. He waited until his rattling breathing slowed again and the burning pain in his chest subsided, then he continued remembering.

They'd taken his car keys and his cell phone. His gun was locked in the car. He was defenseless, unable to reach the outside world, locked in a cabin, and as sick as he'd ever been. Under the circumstances, he was going to need one helluva plan to get out of this alive.

But, for now, he needed to rest. Just for a minute or two. The stove was already heating the small room, and the warmth made him drowsy. His eyes, so heavy and dry, closed of their own volition.

29

Leo was trying to wrap his mind around the ambush he and Sasha had just experienced in Judge Minella's chambers. As they walked from the courthouse to the parking garage, he asked Sasha a series of questions.

"What just happened?"

Sasha threw him a disgusted look. "We got sandbagged, Connelly. I can't wait to report back to Tate—that should be fun."

"I'll handle Oliver," he told her. "But can you explain this to me? Why would the government get involved in a private lawsuit between two pharmaceutical companies?"

Sasha dug her gloves out of her pockets and pulled them on. "I honestly don't know, Connelly. I explained at the meeting that we weren't going to get into the contract specifics, nobody seemed to have any objections then. But, Judge Minella has the discretion to raise the indispensable party issue *sua sponte*—sorry, that means on his own initiative, without a party raising it. And, when the judge fed Jill Esposito her line, she had the sense to agree that it was the official government position that it would be deemed an indispensable party. So that's that."

"What's it mean to be an indispensable party?"

Sasha considered her answer for a moment.

"Okay, this is a little bit of an oversimplification, but under the Federal Rules of Civil Procedure—Rule 19, to be exact—all parties who have an interest in the outcome of a case have to be included in a case. It's called mandatory joinder, and it's a good rule." She continued, warming to her subject. "The purpose of Rule 19 is to consolidate litigation. Let's say you, Naya, and I start a business together and it falls apart. I can't sue for damages, claiming you ran it into the ground unless Naya is in the case, too. Because resolving my case without also addressing any claims she might have wouldn't dispose of the case. It wouldn't be a good use of judicial resources. Are you with me so far?"

"Sure. It sounds like a reasonable approach," he said.

"It is, except for the fact that Rule 19 has been turned on its head. Instead of being used as a tool to bring people into court to ensure conflicts get resolved in their entirety, it's routinely used to shut down a case entirely."

"How?" he asked.

He took her arm as they crossed a cobblestone alley. The last thing he needed was for her to twist an ankle in her ridiculous boots. He half-expected her to shake his hand off, but instead she covered it with her own gloved hand and smiled up at him before continuing with the civil procedure lesson.

"In a lot of cases, when a governmental entity or foreign sovereign has an interest that would merit mandatory joinder, the case ends up being dismissed because those parties have sovereign immunity. They can't be sued unless they consent to the court's jurisdiction. And dismissal of the whole case could keep the plaintiff out of court for good because there's no other forum that can exercise jurisdiction over the matter. That's *not* what the rule was intended to do."

Sasha shook her head, her green eyes dark with annoyance at the misuse of the rule.

Leo still wasn't following the argument. His antenna, finely tuned to governmental bureaucracy, vibrated: something was off.

"So, even though you told the government lawyers today that the details of our contract to supply the vaccines wouldn't need to come in to court, the CIA is saying it will?"

She spread her hands wide, signaling she was at a loss herself. “Beats me, Connelly. I would expect ViraGene to make the argument, maybe. But, I can’t see a reason for any third party to stand up and say, no, this really does involve us, *especially* when the moving party has explicitly said it doesn’t. And I can’t see what the CIA has to do with a domestic contract anyway. But, honestly, it doesn’t matter. Judge Minella had the discretion to do what he did, even if the CIA hadn’t sent a lawyer. But, he’s not an idiot, he’s a federal judge. I’m sure he reached out to someone in the government who put him in touch with Bardman. Now his ruling is basically appeal-proof, because I doubt the Court of Appeals would find he abused his discretion now that the United States said it’s an indispensable party and it won’t waive its immunity and consent to jurisdiction.”

Leo pondered this development.

“What?” she demanded.

Startled, he met her angry gaze. “What what?”

“You’re ruminating. I can tell you have a theory, Connelly. Spit it out.”

He smiled despite himself. To a person, everyone who knew him called him unreadable. He suspected they’d call him inscrutable if they weren’t afraid it would sound racist. His expressions and gestures never provided a clue as to what he was thinking or feeling to anyone—except Sasha.

"The judge didn't call the CIA. They called him, guaranteed. National security issue override," he said, more to himself than to her.

Although all the participating agencies had assigned experienced employees to the task force, the only decision maker in the room had been Hank. He ran through his memory of the CIA's structure.

Sasha waited.

"Bardman doesn't call the shots. He's the equivalent of some mid-level associate in private practice. After the task force meeting, he reported back to his boss, who probably briefed the General Counsel. That's a Presidential appointment, so he has a lot of authority. But given the specter of a pandemic, I'd guess he's in constant contact right now with the Director, too," Leo explained.

"Are you saying the Director of the Central Intelligence Agency personally intervened to prevent a civil lawsuit between two private entities?"

He kept his tone mild when he answered. "I'm saying it's not unthinkable. And maybe I have it all wrong; maybe ViraGene has its hooks in someone at GAO, and that's where the pressure came from. Or maybe this judge did take the initiative. But, unless the government has changed pretty dramatically in the last few months, the first and most important job right now, across all agencies, will be finding and containing the virus. The second most important job will be disaster planning—having contingency plans in place to respond to and contain an outbreak of the killer flu, with a strong emphasis on preventing panic. And our temporary restraining order probably wouldn't have impacted the first part, but I can see an argument that the news of the vaccine manufacturer suing a competitor for unspecific bad behavior could undermine confidence in the government's abilities to handle any outbreak."

Sasha considered this. "Well, Esposito did lead with a national security argument, but Judge Minella shut her down pretty fast. That was probably to keep us in the dark. And it explains his refusal to put the hearing on the record."

They stopped in front of the parking garage and looked at each other. Leo could read in her face that they were having the same thought: they were in way over their heads. *Again.*

30

Gavin floated in and out of wakefulness. He didn't know what time it was when he heard the voices outside his cabin but he strained to listen, pressing his ear right up against the wall by his bed.

He could make out Bricker's booming voice, and one other voice. He thought he recognized the other man as Rollins. It sounded as though they were right outside the window.

That would make sense. The cabin was set off from the others and, by the window, the group wouldn't be visible from either the recreation center or the perimeter where the sentries patrolled. It seemed to Gavin to be a good spot for conspirators to meet.

He listened hard, trying to keep his wheezing breath quiet so he could hear.

"Tomorrow, we move," Bricker said.

The man who Gavin believed to be Rollins spoke in an uncertain voice. "Sir, I don't understand."

"Which part escapes you, George?" Bricker asked, exasperated.

Gavin nodded to himself. Yep, it was Rollins all right.

"Sir, more than two hundred members have already reported and been vaccinated. We have reports that another fifty to seventy-five are on their way. The organization has responded. We're going to weather any storm that comes. If the virus strikes, we'll survive. But ... if I understand you correctly, you want to attack the government. I'm just not sure I follow," Rollins said in a quick, apologetic voice.

"George, it's not an attack. It's a warning. Yes, we're safe, but what about all the civilians out there who are counting on their leaders to protect them? They're exposed, vulnerable. We need to send a message. A message to the government to take care of its people and a message to the people to learn to take care of themselves." Bricker's voice took on the cadence of a speech from the pulpit.

Gavin suspected that was an effort to distract Rollins from the fact that the words rolling off Bricker's tongue were nonsensical and inconsistent. And it seemed to be working

"Okay. Thank you for explaining, Captain. So, can we go over the plan one more time?"

Bricker snorted. "I'm going to leave tomorrow morning for Pittsburgh. I will release the virus and return here. All you have to do is keep an eye on the prisoner and help Anna maintain order here for several hours. It's not rocket science."

"Yes, sir. But, Mrs. Bricker, she's your second-in-command."

Rollins said it as a statement, but Bricker seemed to understand the question.

"This is delicate, George. Anna can't know about the virus. Not because she can't be trusted. She is, as you note, the second-in-command. But, we need to insulate her. To give her plausible deniability, just in case my mission fails or I'm apprehended. In addition, Anna has been busy helping your girlfriend care for Russell. She'll welcome your assistance in my absence."

"Yes, sir," Rollins said, his voice more confident now.

The voices faded away.

Gavin repeated the pertinent information over and over to sear it into his tired, feverish brain before he drifted back to sleep: Bricker was planning an attack. Lydia was Rollins' girlfriend. The kind-eyed woman was married to Bricker.

He didn't yet know what he was going to do with this information, but he knew he couldn't forget it.

31

While Oliver Tate and his twins swooshed down the black diamond slopes under the bright Wyoming sky, Sasha covered his desk with printouts of cases, legal pads filled with scrawled notes, and cup after cup of coffee. Every few hours, she would stand, stretch, and stare out Tate's window at the snow that continued to fall throughout the day. After the sun set, she could still see the flakes swirling under the security lights that lit the perimeter of the building.

True to his word, Connelly had handled Tate. They'd called and reported the results of the disastrous 'argument' in front of Judge Minella, and Connelly had been adamant that there was nothing Sasha could have done to change the judge's mind.

To Sasha's amusement, he also shared his sincerely held theory that the judge had to have been joking.

Tate took the news better than Sasha had hoped. He asked her to look into filing an appeal. He and she both knew it was a lost cause. With no record, a government agency stating that it was an indispensable party, and the specter of national security lurking in the background, they had less than the proverbial hell-dwelling snowball's chance of success of convincing an appellate court that the judge had abused his discretion.

But, Sasha understood that, to appease the board, Tate needed a thoroughly researched memorandum that laid out the dismal reality in minute detail. She needed the same memorandum for a very different reason—to appease her malpractice insurer. But, in the end, Serumceutical wouldn't file an appeal. It would be an utter waste of money.

She was reading a mind-numbing law review article on the misuse of Rule 19 when Connelly poked his head through the doorway and caught her eye. He tapped the face of his watch. Sasha checked the time. Almost eight o'clock.

She shook her head. "I want to get this memo out to Tate tonight so I can catch an early flight back to Pittsburgh in the morning."

As competent and reliable as Naya was, Sasha

knew it was a strain on her to run the office single-handedly.

She expected Connelly would argue with her, but he reached in his pocket and pulled out his car key. He crossed the room and pressed the ring into her hand.

"I had a feeling you'd say that. I'll catch a ride home with Grace."

Sasha placed the key ring on Tate's desk. "Thanks. I shouldn't be much longer. Maybe two more hours tops."

Connelly kissed the top of her head. "I'll wait for you to eat dinner, then."

Grace appeared outside the door.

"Leo, are you ready?" she asked, buttoning a tawny leather trench coat.

"I'll see you in a bit," Connelly said. Then he turned to Grace, "Let me just grab my coat."

They watched him leave, and then Grace turned to Sasha.

"How's it going?"

"Fine, I guess. Oliver wants to explore all avenues, but we're really just spinning our wheels," Sasha answered honestly.

Grace nodded. She picked up a framed picture of a man and two dark-haired girls standing in front of a cabin, squinting into the sun and smiling, examined it for a moment, and then returned it to its spot on the desk.

"I think he's under a lot of pressure. When we caught that janitor stealing papers, the board instructed him to go hard after ViraGene, and he did. But as soon as the legal bills started rolling in, they lost their stomach for it and pulled back. It's kind of unfair. They took away his weapons, and now they blame him for losing the battle."

Sasha considered the middle-aged man in the photograph. He looked perfectly pleasant—one arm thrown over the shoulder of each of his daughters—but not particularly driven. It could have been the setting. Even a formidable general counsel might not seem imposing while wearing a plaid flannel shirt and standing in front of a log cabin. Unless maybe he was wielding an axe.

Connelly reappeared in the doorway, with his leather bag slung across his chest. Grace slid down from Tate's desk and joined him at the door.

"The roads might be icy," Connelly warned Sasha before following Grace out the door.

"I know how to drive in winter conditions," Sasha told him.

He turned. "I know *you* do, but you're not in Pittsburgh. There'll be a lot of nervous drivers out there. Just be careful, okay?"

"Okay."

She turned back to her research as Connelly and Grace disappeared down the hallway. She worked without pause for another forty-five minutes, her fingers flying over the keys. She summarized both the standard to appeal and the cases that established the effort would almost certainly be futile. She reviewed the memorandum for typos then, satisfied, sent an email message to Tate forwarding the document. She rolled her neck, cracked her back, and shut down her laptop.

She tried to reach Gavin one final time, calling his home, office, and cell phone numbers one after the other. He didn't answer any of the numbers. She left messages on all three of his voicemail systems asking him to call her then tossed her cell phone into her briefcase. She felt the beginnings of a headache developing. She was tired from the long day and worried about Gavin. It was time to go back to Connelly's, curl up on his couch, and rest her head on his warm chest.

She shrugged into her coat. As she picked up her bag, she knocked Tate's desk blotter askew. She lunged to catch it before it shoved a pile of papers to the floor.

As she was returning it to its original spot, a hot pink post-it note caught her eye.

In precise block letters, someone—presumably Tate—had printed "CELIA GERIG. NEW KEN DC. $12.50/HR"

Seeing Celia's name served to heighten her concern about Gavin. She replaced the blotter, covering the sticky note, and wished she could bury her anxiety as easily.

She turned out Tate's office light and pulled the door shut behind her with a soft click.

The corridors were quiet and lit only by the emergency lighting over the stairwells. The sprawling headquarters felt deserted. Sasha walked quickly through the lobby, her boots clicking against the marble. The security desk was unoccupied, although the blue glow of a computer monitor suggested that the guard on duty had just left to use the bathroom or get a drink. She scribbled her name on the visitor log and then hurried through the inner doors.

As she crossed the foyer to exit the building, a Hispanic man on his way into the building jogged to hold the door open for her. He wore a navy blue uniform that identified him as a member of the cleaning crew. A knit cap was pulled down over his brow.

"Thank you," Sasha said as she walked through the door into the howling wind.

"You're welcome. Stay warm," he said in a pleasant, accented voice.

She smiled at him and turned her collar up, before she hustled through the parking lot to Connelly's Lexus.

32

Leo stirred the chicken stew simmering and bubbling in his tall stockpot. The sound of a car engine in the alley caught his attention.

He glanced out the kitchen window and was surprised to see Sasha pulling his SUV into the garage almost a full hour earlier than she said she'd be back. For the first year of their relationship, her estimates of when she'd be finished working had only ever been overly optimistic. The year had been strewn with canceled dinner reservations, missed movies, and vacations cut short.

But she'd been trying to be more realistic and balanced about her working hours in recent months. The turning point had been the night she'd run out to handle a client matter while he was trying to propose to her. All the anger and hurt that Leo'd ignored for months had come to a head, and he'd accused her of valuing her work over her personal relationships.

She'd worked hard since then to break her old patterns, and she'd gotten quite good at leaving work as promised. But, she'd never come home *early* before.

He pulled two beer bottles from the refrigerator and twisted off the caps. He'd miss her tomorrow when she returned to Pittsburgh, so he was grateful for the extra time tonight. The more time they spent together, the more time he wanted to spend with her.

She ran from the garage through the small yard and up the deck stairs to the kitchen door. As she stamped her feet to remove the snow, he pulled the door open to greet her. She rushed in, her cheeks red from the cold, and shivered. She dropped her briefcase on the floor and stretched up to plant an icy kiss on his lips.

"It's getting really cold out," she announced as she pulled off her gloves and unbuttoned her coat.

Leo rested the beers on the counter and helped her out of the coat.

"I think I know how to warm you up," he told her. He tossed her coat over the back of a chair and wrapped his arms around her. He thought he would never cease to be amazed by how tiny she actually was.

She leaned into him and rested her head on his chest.

He was just about to thank her for coming home early when his cell phone rang.

"Don't answer it," she said.

He had to. He didn't want to. What he wanted to do was scoop her up and carry her into the bedroom, but he had to. He was the chief security officer of a company that just learned an employee had stolen over twenty-five hundred doses of a vaccine intended to prevent a horrific virus from decimating the American population. He couldn't just let a phone call roll to voicemail because he wanted to ravish his girlfriend. Even if she did look particularly ravishing at the moment.

The phone continued to ring. Insistent.

"I'm sorry." He gently removed her arms from around his waist and reached for the phone.

She sighed and reached down to unzip her boots. As she stepped out of them, she immediately shrunk four inches.

"Hello?"

"Hi, Leo. It's Hank."

"Hi, Hank. What's up?" Leo asked as Sasha retrieved her beer from the counter and walked over to the stove to peek into the pot of stew.

"I ran your name up the flagpole. You sure burned some bridges on your way out the door," Hank said with a chuckle.

Leo had a different view of his separation from the government, but he didn't particularly feel like getting into it with Hank. He'd rather have dinner with his girlfriend.

"I take it my involvement isn't welcome?" he asked.

He cradled the phone between his ear and shoulder and reached into the cabinet to the left of the stove and pulled down two bowls. Then he took two spoons from the utensil drawer.

"Well, officially, that's the case. But, I have a bit of a situation on my hands and I could use someone with your background and connections to the pharmaceutical industry, so I'm going to noodle on it for a day and see if I can't come up with something," Hank said.

"Suit yourself, Hank. You know, I'm happy to help if I can."

Leo ended the call and turned to see Sasha frowning at him.

"Come on, let's eat while it's hot," he said.

She took the seat across from him and searched his face through the plumes of steam that rose from their bowls.

"What did Hank want?"

"To tell me I'm persona non grata as far as the various governmental agencies are concerned," he said, trying to keep the bitterness out of his voice.

"Good. You're a private citizen. They can save the country without your help," she said.

"Sasha—" he began, but she cut him off.

"Mmm, this is really good," she said around a mouthful of stew.

It *was* good, he had to admit. Nicely seasoned, and the sort of filling comfort food that a cold, snowy night demanded.

"Thanks, but, listen. Hank may still come back to me. He said he's going to see if he could work it out. And, if he does ... I might want to do it."

He waited for her response.

She looked at him for a long moment, then she relaxed her shoulders and took a sip of her beer. "You know what, Connelly, I don't want to argue. You're going to do what you want to do no matter what I say. I'd like to just have a nice dinner with you, since I'm going home tomorrow."

Yes, she was, he realized with a pang.

It had taken some time to adjust to a day-to-day routine that didn't include her. For the first several weeks, he'd awoken in a state of mild panic to find his bed empty. And the four-day stretch since Saturday had been the longest uninterrupted time they'd shared since he'd moved. Notwithstanding the constant threat of near-certain death from contracting a killer flu, it had been a very pleasant four days.

He drained his beer and smiled at her. “In that case, why don’t we call it a night.”

She checked the time. “At nine forty-five?”

He just kept smiling until understanding dawned in her eyes. Her cheeks flushed and her bow mouth curved upward.

“I guess I’m finished here,” she allowed in a soft voice.

33

Tuesday

Tuesday morning dawned gray and cold. Colton pressed the button on the wall beside his headboard. The heavy blackout curtains drew back and inched across the window. From his bed, he could see that the city below was covered in a thick blanket of snow.

He yawned and then rose from the bed. Snow or not, he had to stay on schedule. His carefully placed phone call couldn't come from a number traceable to him. He needed to be at the filthy corner bodega when it opened to buy a prepaid calling card—and a lottery ticket, so he would fit in with the other patrons. Even though he already had his lottery ticket; all that was left to do was cash it in.

He calculated the figures as he walked into the master bathroom and adjusted the water temperature for his shower. If the government purchased the same number of doses of AviEx as it had committed to purchase of Serumceutical's vaccine, ViraGene would gross in excess of two hundred and twenty-five million dollars, just on the contract.

He stepped into the steamy shower and continued his musing. That sum didn't even account for the inevitable skyrocketing stock price.

The twenty-five million dollar bonus that the board had agreed to write into his contract—mainly because the small-minded fools believed he could never attain the profit target to unlock it—was within his grasp.

All he had left to do was make one anonymous phone call to the authorities, reporting the shocking news that Serumceutical's Chief Security Officer had, in his top desk drawer, a deadly biological weapon. Faced with the public relations disaster that the company chosen to provide the vaccines intended to protect the American people from a grim and certain death was harboring the very virus it was supposed to eradicate, the government would have no choice but to approve and then purchase AviEx. The public outcry would demand it in a panic and amid paranoid theories about Serumceutical's true intentions.

As the water pounded against his back, Colton

grinned. And, as if all that weren't enough, the survivalist brigade in Pennsylvania was probably this very moment whipping itself into a frenzy. He'd recognized the true believer fervor in Bricker's eyes. He'd do whatever it took—including releasing the virus himself—to deliver the apocalypse he'd spent over a decade predicting. By the end of the week, the American people would be dropping dead in droves, the survivors would be clamoring for an antiviral medication, and he was the only man who could deliver it.

If he'd been the type, he'd have broken into song right there in the shower.

34

Sasha was humming "Have Yourself A Merry Little Christmas" as she and Leo pulled onto the private road that led to Serumceutical's sprawling campus. She loved new snow, when it was still pristine. After one rush hour, it would be dirty and slushy and uninspiring, but right now, it made her feel like the frozen, crystalline world was full of possibility.

Her almost-perfect mood was marred only by the fact that she was leaving Connelly behind when she returned to Pittsburgh. But she had too much work to do to stay in D.C. an extra day or two. She had discovery deadlines, filing due dates, a mediation to prepare for—the list was long.

Connelly turned to her and said, "Feeling the Christmas spirit already?"

She never got the chance to answer.

They rounded a curve, and Connelly slowed. They were still several hundred yards from the main parking lot, but the road was lined with cars. Irritated-looking people milled around with their hands shoved in their pockets for warmth.

Farther down the road, a wooden sawhorse sat in the center of the road. Behind it a cluster of black sedans, some with dashboard-mounted lights still flashing sat at various angles across the paved road. Three more sedans were strewn across the lawn that edged the road. At the mouth of the parking lot, an ambulance and an SUV marked Fire Chief sat nose to nose. And beyond them, two fire engines flanked the entrance to the main building.

"What the devil?" Sasha murmured.

Connelly braked and the car came to a stop. His face registered no reaction to the scene, but Sasha saw him clench and release his fists.

He pulled his cell phone from his coat pocket and checked the display. "I don't have any missed calls or messages."

Sasha was about to suggest he call Grace, when she saw a willowy blonde in a fitted leather trench coat running past the ambulance and down the drive toward them.

"Here comes Grace," she said, nudging Connelly, who was staring down at his phone.

"Call Oliver," he said as he opened his car door and stepped outside.

She pressed the number for Tate's ski chalet and urged the phone to ring. On the third ring, a female voice answered, formal and pleasant despite the very early hour.

"Tate residence."

"Yes, I need to speak to Oliver. It's urgent."

"I'm sorry, ma'am, Mr. Tate left yesterday evening," the woman said.

"Left?"

"Yes, ma'am. He and the girls decided to cut their trip short."

"Why? Where did they go?"

The woman's tone took on a sharp edge. "I wouldn't know. I take care of the property, not Mr. Tate's social calendar."

"Of course. Sorry," Sasha said, rushing to hang up and dial Tate's cell phone number.

It rang only once and then the call rolled over to his voicemail, which announced in a tinny electronic voice that his mailbox was full before disconnecting her.

She stared down at the phone in impotent frustration for a few seconds. Then she shoved it in her bag and opened the passenger door.

Later, she would remember that the next moments seemed to slow down. From her Krav Maga training she knew this perception was common in a crisis. The brain sped up, became hyper-alert, and analyzed as much information as possible as part of a survival mechanism.

When she replayed the scene in her mind, Grace, Connelly, and the FBI SWAT team in their navy blue jumpsuits with their submachine guns pointed at the car all seemed to be moving with exaggerated slowness. For what seemed to be a very long time, Grace ran toward Connelly, waving her arms and yelling at the SWAT team.

Connelly slowly raised his arms over his head. And a gun-toting FBI agent lowered a shoulder and plowed into Connelly, dropping him to the ground.

Another agent wrapped his arms around Grace's waist, holding her back.

By the time Sasha stood outside the car and closed the passenger door with shaking hands, she was surrounded by three agents.

"Down on your knees, ma'am!" the nearest of the three barked, pointing toward the ground with the muzzle of his weapon.

Sasha dropped to the ground, her hands over her head. Twenty feet away, Connelly was being hauled to his feet, with his hands shackled together behind his back. He twisted his neck to meet her eyes. They maintained the contact until the agent restraining

Grace released her, and she came storming toward Sasha.

"What's wrong with you? She's the company's attorney!" Grace shouted, tugging on the arm of the agent who stood over Sasha, handcuffs out and ready.

A dark-skinned man in a soft tan coat jogged over, stiff-legged with his hands in his pockets. As he approached, Sasha realized it was Anthony Washington, the Justice Department attorney who'd been at the task force meeting.

"Stand down, stand down," he said as he huffed to a stop, out of breath.

"Sir, she was with the target. It's procedure," explained the agent whom Grace had been manhandling.

"I understand, but Mr. Connelly's in custody now. Ms. McCandless doesn't pose a threat," Washington said.

"Sir, we haven't searched her person or the vehicle," the agent protested, flicking his eyes toward the cluster of suits that clumped around the sedans.

"I'm not armed," Sasha offered, rising to her feet slowly just in case anyone was trigger happy. She was pleased to hear that her voice sounded reasonable and calm despite the panicked fluttering of her heart in her chest.

A look passed between Grace and Washington.

"What?" Sasha demanded.

Grace cleared her throat. "They aren't looking for a weapon."

A stocky, prematurely gray-haired man broke off from the pack of supervisors near the cars and headed their way. Sasha recognized him from the meeting, too. He was the attorney with the longest title on his business card: Deputy Counsel with the FBI Office of General Counsel's National Security Law Branch.

"Mr. Hubert," Sasha said, thankful for her seating chart cheat sheet and her fail-proof memory.

Howard Hubert nodded at her. "Ms. McCandless."

Then he turned his attention to the agents. "Gentlemen, a word?"

The trio followed him to a spot about five or six feet away and engaged in furious whispering.

Sasha focused on Washington and Grace.

"Is someone going to tell me what's going on?"

"The FBI received an anonymous call this morning. A male caller claimed there was a vial of the Doomsday virus in the top desk drawer of Serumceutical's chief security officer. He disconnected the call without providing further details," Washington said.

"That's insane! All *this* is over a crank call?" Sasha exploded.

Grace shook her head and said in a quiet voice, "No. There was a vial in his desk."

Sasha looked from Grace to Washington, not sure she understood.

"You found a vial of live virus in Connelly's desk?"

"The contents haven't been tested yet, but, yes, it appears so," Washington said.

"Well, it's obviously a set up!"

"Sasha, believe me, I am with you, okay? I don't for a moment believe Leo did this," Grace said in a tone that was both placating and mournful.

"Are you sure, Grace? You didn't call to let him know what he was walking into," Sasha turned on her.

Washington stepped between Sasha and Grace.

"We wouldn't let her. You seem very sure that Mr. Connelly is being framed. Are you aware no one else has a key card that can access his office?" Washington asked.

Sasha stared at Washington for what felt like a long time. Then she simply said, "He didn't do this."

Hubert returned, flanked by SWAT team agents and trailed by a fresh-faced woman wearing a blue FBI windbreaker.

"Ms. McCandless, this is Agent Nickels. With your consent, she's going to perform a search of your person," Hubert said, gesturing toward the woman, who flashed Sasha a reassuring smile.

Sasha dug into the recesses of her memory for criminal law information that she'd long since relegated to the category of trivia. If the assembled law enforcement officers believed she had a weapon—and she could craft a compelling argument that a deadly virus was a weapon—they were entitled to pat her down over her clothes even if she objected.

"You can pat down my clothing and inspect my bag," Sasha offered, "but you're insane if you think I'm consenting to a strip search."

The agents gave her sidelong glances as if she were a criminal for not merely agreeing to strip naked in a snowy field because they asked politely, but the two government lawyers shrugged. She was within her rights, and they knew it.

Agent Nickels snapped on a pair of rubber gloves and stepped forward.

"You don't have a latex allergy, do you?" she asked.

"No."

"Open your coat, please," she said.

Sasha unbuttoned her coat and gripped the lapels. She stretched out her arms and held it wide open, like she had wings.

Nickels squatted in front of her and ran her hand along Sasha's inner legs. She unzipped Sasha's boots one after the other and felt along the lining, then she re-zippered them quickly. She stood and patted Sasha's stomach and chest, as if maybe Sasha had a bottle of the flu virus stuffed into her bra. She motioned for Sasha to drop the coat, and Sasha let it fall and hang open. Nickles slipped her hands into both pockets.

She turned to Hubert and said, "Ms. McCandless is clean."

Sasha gestured to the car. "Don't you want to check my bag? It's in the car."

The pat down had been cursory, at best. She sensed it had been a compromise between the lawyers and the SWAT team, so that the agents didn't lose face in front of a civilian.

Nickel's response confirmed that theory. As the female agent walked away, she said over her shoulder, "Let the jerkoffs do it. They're itching to tear something apart."

Hubert put his hand up like he was a crossing guard, "I'll look through Ms. McCandless's bag. You gentlemen can get started on the search of the vehicle."

One of the agents trotted to the car and fetched Sasha's pastel blue bag. He thrust it at Hubert wordlessly. The attorney opened it and peered inside. He didn't move anything around or take anything out, just pawed through the papers, opened the zippered compartment that held her quilted change purse and her lipstick, and then handed the bag over to her.

"Look, it's obvious you know I don't have anything to do with the theft of the virus. Please tell me you realize Leo doesn't either," she said.

Washington stamped his dress shoes on the ground like he was trying to warm up his feet. Then he blew into his hands to warm them.

Finally, he said, "Everyone who knows Mr. Connelly from his time at Homeland Security speaks well of him. But, as you know, he left under a cloud and with a bit of a reputation for being a cowboy. We have to run this down. There was a vial of germs in his desk that could wipe out the entire Eastern seaboard from Florida to Maine."

Sasha stared at him for a moment, formulating an argument and then realized it would be a waste of breathe to try to convince the assortment of law enforcement officers to release Connelly.

She turned to Hubert. "I want to talk to him."

HUBERT WANTED to give her two minutes. Washington pushed for five. In the end, Hank Richardson broke away from the group he was directing. He took her by the arm and walked her over to the car where they were holding Connelly, who sat with his head hung down and his eyes fixed on a point on the floor of the car.

"You've got three minutes, okay?" Richardson told her.

"Thank you."

He tapped on Connelly's window, and the agent sitting behind the wheel buzzed it down. Connelly turned his head toward the window. Relief washed over his face when he saw Sasha.

"Are you okay? You aren't hurt, are you?"

"I'm fine, Connelly. But you're not," she said, noting a purple bruise that was spreading across his high cheekbone under his left eye.

Hank sucked in his breath. "Sorry, son. Want some ice?"

Connelly tried to wave his hand, but his wrists were cuffed to a ring that had been mounted into the back of the front passenger seat. He grimaced, embarrassed.

"I don't need any ice, Hank. I need you to let me out of this car," he said in a measured tone.

"Leo, I got you three minutes to talk to your girlfriend. That's all the time you've got. Don't waste it yapping at me. I'm working on getting you out of this mess. Trust me," Hank said.

He turned and walked off.

Sasha reached through the window and stroked Connelly's cheek. "Does it hurt?"

The agent in the driver's seat looked back and said, "Ma'am, please don't touch the subject."

The subject. Sasha could see that the words were like a knife to Connelly.

"I'm fine. I didn't do this," he said.

"Connelly, please, I *know* that."

He attempted a smile that faded into a tight twist of his lips.

"These friendly civil servants inform me that, according to Grace, Tate placed me on immediate unpaid leave pending the outcome of the investigation."

"Forget about Tate. Listen to me, I'm going to call Will Volmer. He used to work for the U.S. Attorney, he'll know someone who knows the best criminal defense attorneys down here. I'm going to find you an attorney you can trust. Just, promise me you won't talk to these idiots without counsel present."

Sasha stared at him, willing him to understand how critical it was that he follow her advice.

"Sasha, I didn't do anything wrong."

"Connelly, do not talk to them. Don't talk to *anyone*. Not even Hank. Promise me," she enunciated each word, slow and firm.

"Okay," he said in apparent defeat.

"Promise me," she repeated.

She felt the agent's eyes drifting back to watch them and ignored the intrusion.

After a pause, Connelly said, "I promise. Now you promise me something."

"What?"

"Promise me you won't get mixed up in this. Go back to Pittsburgh and catch up on your work. Take my car. After I get this cleared up, I'll catch a flight out and meet up with you. I apparently have some unanticipated time off."

He finished with a hurt laugh that made Sasha want to find Tate and kneecap him.

"I'm not leaving until we clear your name," she protested.

"Sasha, please. Someone is obviously out to get me. I do not want you to stick around and make yourself a target. I don't need to worry about you. I'll lawyer up, if you'll go home."

They stared at each other for a moment.

"Fine," she relented.

He smiled, a small smile, but it reached his eyes.

She leaned through the open window and kissed him. She took her time and pretended not to hear the sputtering agent. Connelly's mouth yielded to hers.

"I love you," she said in a low voice.

The agent hit the button to raise the window and Sasha pulled her head back.

She stood there, unwilling to break eye contact with Connelly—the only connection they had now—until Richardson came over and led her away from the car, back to the knot of government attorneys.

While she'd been talking to Connelly, Bardman had joined the group. She scanned their faces—Bardman, Hubert, and Washington—but she wasn't sure which of the attorneys she could trust. So she turned back to Richardson.

"Leo maintains his innocence, which makes sense because he *is* innocent. That said, I've advised him to invoke his Fifth Amendment privilege against self-incrimination and to obtain an attorney. I'm going to make some calls to find counsel for him. I'd like to do it in relative warmth, if that's okay with everyone."

"I'm sorry, Sasha, the building's barricaded until we get a CDC team up here to take away the virus," Richardson explained.

Bardman interjected, "You're free to go, though."

"Did you clear the car?" Sasha asked, addressing the question to Hubert.

"Yes, the car was searched and found to be clean."

"Imagine that," Sasha said.

Washington shot her a look, which she ignored.

"I'm taking the SUV," she announced to no one in particular then waited for the push back. None came.

"The keys are in the ignition," Richardson told her.

Before Sasha left, she scanned the scene for Grace but saw no sign of her.

She adjusted the driver's seat forward as far as it would go, checked her mirrors, and started the engine. Under the watchful eyes of a couple dozen federal agents, she executed a flawless three-point turn and drove away from the campus even though her brain was yelling at her not to leave Connelly and every muscle in her body tensed, yearning to go back to him.

She would keep her promise and could only hope that he kept his.

As soon as she turned onto the main business artery, she looked for a spot to pull over. But the snowplows had been through. The parking lanes were buried under piles of snow.

She zipped across the Beltway and merged onto Interstate 270, grateful for the light traffic, no doubt thanks to all the weather-related cancellations.

Once she had the SUV up to highway speed, she hooked her phone into the vehicle's Bluetooth system and told it to call Will Volmer.

Will had moved from the prosecutor's office to run the white collar criminal practice at Prescott &

Talbott, Sasha's former employer and one of Pittsburgh's most prominent law firms. In the aftermath of the Lady Lawyer Killers case, he'd been asked to take over the management of the firm.

He was a skilled advocate, an ethical and upstanding lawyer, and a genuinely kind person. It was a trifecta of qualities possessed by only a handful of Prescott's eight hundred attorneys.

"Good morning. Mr. Volmer's office," Caroline Masters, Will's capable assistant said in a polished voice.

Sasha hesitated. Despite her warm feelings for Will and Caroline, Sasha'd spent the past two months studiously avoiding everyone and anyone who had even a tenuous connection to the Lady Lawyer Killers case. And Will and Caroline had been deeply enmeshed in the case and the ensuing scandal.

"Hello? You've reached Will Volmer's office, may I help you?" Caroline said.

Sasha took a centering breath and said, "Sorry. Hi, Caroline, it's Sasha."

The older woman's pleasure was immediate and real. "Sasha, it's so good to hear from you. Things are well, I hope?"

Sasha plowed ahead. "Actually, Caroline, I'm in a bit of jam. I need to talk to Will, urgently. I'm not trying to be rude, and I would love to catch up. I know I owe you several phone calls."

"Yes, you do," Caroline chided her. Then, she said, "But, I forgive you. Will's in a meeting, but I know he'll interrupt it for you. Hold the line, and I'll put you through. It may take a few moments for him to clear everyone out of his office, okay?"

"Yes, that's fine. And, thank you so much," Sasha said, suddenly feeling ashamed of herself for having brushed off Caroline's social overtures.

She resolved to invite Caroline to lunch—just as soon as she got her boyfriend sprung from federal custody and tracked down her wayward private investigator, and provided they weren't all casualties of a pandemic.

"Sasha, Caroline tells me you have a problem," Will's deep, thoughtful voice came across the line. "How can I help?"

Sasha glanced at the speedometer. She'd accelerated without realizing it. She was now pushing eighty miles an hour and riding the bumper of a minivan. She signaled to move into the left lane then swung past the minivan, while she tried to gather her thoughts to explain enough to Will to make sure he understood the gravity of Connelly's situation without divulging the information that Connelly had learned confidentially.

"It's a long story, but the high points are that Leo

Connelly's been taken into federal custody as the result of a multi-agency investigation into a classified national security matter. He needs a D.C.-barred attorney, fast. Someone who has some clearances, or the feds are never going to talk to him," Sasha explained.

"Her," Will corrected her. "Colleen Young-Wetzel fits the bill, and she'll take very good care of Leo. She's the best."

"Great. Can I get her number?"

"Let me call her and explain who you and Leo are. I mean, she's probably heard of you from your past exploits, but if I call I can impress upon her just how important you and Leo are to me personally," Will said.

Sasha didn't think she could feel any lower than she had when she'd talked to Caroline, but, as it turned out, she could.

"Thank you," she said simply.

"You're more than welcome," Will replied. "Should Colleen reach you on your cell phone?"

"Please. And, Will?"

"Yes?"

"I'm sorry for brushing you off since October. There's no excuse, I know. I've just been struggling—"

"Sasha, please. No apologies are necessary. You've been through a great deal in the past year. You need to deal with that however you can. It's okay," Will assured her.

Sasha felt hot tears stinging her eyes. She'd been operating under crisis parameters: Focus on getting the help Connelly needed. Move forward. Don't fall apart. But now Will's kindness threatened to topple her.

"Thanks, Will," she said, blinking away the threatened tears.

"I'll have Colleen call right away," he promised before ending the call.

Sasha drove in silence for several minutes. She needed to call and let Naya know about Connelly, and she also needed to track down Gavin, wherever he was. But she wanted to talk to Colleen Young-Wetzel first.

She left the phone charging and just drove. She'd gone about five miles down the uninspiring ribbon of highway that cut through Maryland headed for the Pennsylvania Turnpike when her phone came to life. She hit the button to connect the call through the Bluetooth device.

"Sasha McCandless," she said to the empty interior of the SUV.

A female voice, husky but clipped and businesslike, came through the speakers. "Sasha, this is Colleen Young-Wetzel. May I call you Sasha?"

"Of course. Thanks for reaching out to me so quickly," Sasha said.

Colleen brushed off her gratitude. "Listen, I've known Will Volmer since his sons were in short pants. Will said you need the best criminal representation available in D.C. and you need it now. So, you've got it."

Colleen's voice oozed competence and confidence. Sasha felt her shoulders relax.

"Okay, how much did Will tell you?" Sasha asked, searching the road ahead for a convenient place to pull off the road.

She didn't want to split her attention between the road and this conversation. A green milepost sign informed her that Frederick, Maryland sat at the next exit. She and Connelly had stopped in Frederick once before. There was a diner that served breakfast all day. She had no appetite, but this wasn't the time to let her energy flag. She eased the car into the far right lane.

"Will said that your friend is a former federal air marshal who had been assigned to an internal affairs role within the Department of Homeland Security until October, when he left to take a position as the chief security officer for a pharmaceutical company. As I understand it, this morning, he was taken into custody in conjunction with a coordinated, cross-agency national security investigation. That's what I know." Colleen recited the background in a brisk, dispassionate voice.

"Before we get into the details, would you just confirm that I can tell you this stuff without breaching any government secrets?" Sasha asked, as she slowed and took the exit ramp toward Frederick's business district.

She navigated by memory to the diner, which stood at the foot of a mountain.

Colleen answered, like any good lawyer, with a question of her own. "Your friend has, or had, security clearances, I'm sure, but do you?"

"No."

Sasha brought Connelly's SUV to a stop in a parking space near the diner's door. Judging by all the empty spaces, she'd hit that sweet spot between the breakfast rush and the lunch crowd. She killed the engine.

"Well, in that case, nothing the government told *you* is classified. If, hypothetically, Leo came into possession of classified information, he may have breached security by telling you. Too bad you aren't married."

"Excuse me? Oh, spousal privilege?"

"Right, I mean, it's still a crime to share the information, but you couldn't be compelled to testify against him. But, listen, at this point, that's the least of your worries. We'll proceed as though this is a privileged and confidential conversation between the two of us, okay?" Colleen sounded impatient to cut to the chase.

"Okay. Well, the first bit I know because I am—or, I guess, was—representing Connelly's employer in a civil matter. Serumceutical has a government contract to deliver a killer flu vaccine. An employee who falsified her references disappeared along with more than twenty-five hundred doses that were supposed to be sent to the government stockpile. The company believes a competitor called ViraGene was behind the theft. My primary responsibility was to file a temporary restraining order against ViraGene. But I was also counseling my client to self-report the theft of the vaccines and the breach of the supply contract that resulted from that theft to the government." Sasha paused to give Colleen a chance to ask any questions she might have.

"Go on."

"Over the weekend, Connelly learned that the mutated killer flu virus had been stolen from a French research facility, one of the French researchers had been killed, and our government believed the stolen Doomsday virus was either en route to the U.S. or already within the borders."

Colleen let out a long, low whistle, then she said, "I take it Mr. Connelly learned that information on a confidential basis?"

"Right," Sasha confirmed. "He didn't name his source, and I didn't ask. He did tell the Serumceutical Board of Directors that there was a threat, but he didn't go into any details. We wanted them to agree to let us share information with the ad hoc task force that had been created to deal with the theft of the killer flu."

"There's always a task force," Colleen observed.

"Apparently. Anyway, we met with the task force yesterday morning. We told them about the stolen vaccines and that Serumceutical had filed a TRO against ViraGene. Lawyers from several agencies were present at the meeting, and no one raised any objection to the TRO. After the meeting, though, I got a call from the federal district court, scheduling the hearing for that same day."

"Let me guess. Some government attorney showed up, claimed the feds were an indispensable party, refused to waive immunity, and mentioned national security implications. In response, the judge folded like a cheap suit and kicked your case. Off the record, of course. How'd I do?" Colleen asked in a tone that was at once jaded and outraged.

"Nailed it."

"Okay, so, what happened this morning?"

"We were headed into the Serumceutical campus and ran into a road block. An FBI SWAT team was in position waiting for us. They took Connelly into custody, a female agent patted me down, but it was really cursory, and they searched Connelly's SUV. I am told they received a tip from an anonymous caller that Connelly had a bottle of the stolen H17N10 virus in his desk drawer. They checked it out, and found a vial."

"So, your working theory is Leo was framed?"

"Definitely," Sasha said.

"Do you think it was an inside job?" Colleen asked.

"I honestly don't know. Connelly's office door is locked and can be opened only with his personal key card. I don't know how the virus got there, but I know Connelly didn't put it there."

Colleen was silent.

Sasha waited a moment then said, "And, it's hard to explain, but I got the sense that, despite the display of power, with the SWAT team and everything, that nobody was all that concerned about Connelly. I mean, if they really, truly believed Connelly was responsible, they should have impounded his car, right? And done a more thorough search of my person and my bag? The whole thing felt ... superficial, like they were just going through the motions."

"Hard to say," Colleen cautioned her. "It could be that they didn't want to deal with the maelstrom of grief an attorney could bring down on their heads if they were aggressive with you. Or they may be according Leo some professional courtesy because he's a former Homeland Security agent. Or your instincts are right and the whole scene was just security theater. I'll have a better sense after I talk to someone associated with the task force and see how much they push back about getting me access to Leo. Who are the lawyers involved?"

Sasha thought for a minute then said, "There are a bunch of them, but take a run at Anthony Washington from the Department of Justice. He seemed like the most reasonable."

"Washington, DOJ. Okay. Now, you hold tight. I'll call you later today."

"Thank you, Colleen. Oh, we didn't talk about your fees. You can bill me directly whatever your standard rate is for this sort of work, seeing as how Connelly isn't going to be getting a paycheck until this gets cleared up," Sasha said.

"Don't worry about the fees," Colleen said. "I owe Will a favor, and I understand he owes you one."

"Well, we can work it out later," Sasha said, hesitant to let the woman handle the matter without compensation.

Sasha ended the call and sat looking out over the parking lot. She took several deep, slow breaths.

Colleen had relieved a lot of the tension that had been building in a band behind her eyes. She was still worried about Connelly, but she trusted Will's friend to get a handle on the situation. She would grab a quick bite and get some badly needed coffee, then she would deal with the other man in her life who was contributing to her tension headache—Gavin Russell.

35

Leo rubbed his forehead with one palm. He was tired. He was a little bit sore from being thrown to the frozen ground by an overenthusiastic rookie agent. He was worried that whomever had hidden an ampule of the Doomsday virus in his desk drawer was out there, in the fading winter light, rolling a vial along a Metro car or leaving one casually propped against a display in one of the Smithsonian buildings.

And every minute that he sat here in stony silence staring down an interrogator was just more time the government was wasting not finding the guy who had the virus.

He sighed heavily. But, he had promised Sasha he wouldn't talk. So he continued to clamp his jaw tightly closed and look wearily at Hank Richardson.

"Leo, give me *something*," Hank pleaded.

Leo felt almost worse for Hank than he did for himself.

Hank had made a show of pulling all the strings. Leo's handcuffs were removed, he'd been offered food, drink, and dry clothes, but still he refused to speak.

Leo merely repeated the one sentence he'd said to each of the agents who'd cycled through the interrogation room, "I want a lawyer."

Hank rubbed his own temple, mirroring Leo's movement—whether he did so out of a shared sense of frustration or a deliberate attempt to create the illusion of a bond, Leo couldn't tell. Leo shifted his attention away from Hank to focus on a crack in the corner of the ceiling that was spidering down the side of the wall. It was the extent of the windowless room's decor.

"Son, you may have gone over to the private sector, but you're not fooling me. You're still one of us. You want to catch this nasty piece of work just as badly as I do. That's why you came in to talk to us yesterday. Now's your chance. But, you know the clock's running on this. Help me." Hank finished his speech and leaned forward on the gray metal table, staring at Leo.

Leo *did* want to talk to Hank; he *did* want to help. Not because of Hank's somewhat heavy-handed and cliched appeal. But, because he'd been yearning to jump in and start digging from the minute he heard about the investigation.

But he wasn't going to talk to anyone until they let him speak to the lawyer he knew beyond a shadow of a doubt had to be sitting out in a waiting room somewhere. There was no chance Sasha hadn't gotten an attorney for him within minutes of her leaving the campus.

Delaying—not denying, but delaying—a suspect access to his counsel was a time-honored law enforcement strategy. He knew it. Hank knew it. The task force was in for an awakening, though, if they thought they could out wait him, Leo thought.

Now he mirrored Hank's posture, leaned forward over the table, and said, "Lawyer, Hank. Let me talk to my lawyer."

They locked eyes. After a long moment, Hank shook his head, sadly, almost imperceptibly. "I'll send her in."

He pushed back his metal chair from the table, its legs screeching against the gray-green floor tile. He walked out of the room without a backward glance at Leo.

Leo figured his attorney, who had no doubt been kept waiting with a series of excuses, would walk in the door within three minutes of Hank's departure. He started to count off the seconds in his head, as his watch had been confiscated along with his Glock and his phone.

He made it to a hundred and forty before the door opened. A junior agent ushered a woman through the door. She wore square-rimmed glasses with black frames, which matched her short, neat hair and her black, tailored pantsuit. A large, turquoise-beaded necklace added a splash of color to her otherwise severe image. Then she smiled, a broad, open smile, and the room lit up.

He felt himself exhaling. He didn't know where Sasha had found this woman, but he already felt better.

"Thanks, Agent Tortetta. I'll take it from here," she said in a firm but friendly voice to the agent, who was lurking in the doorway.

He dropped his gaze to the floor and shuffled out into the hallway.

She waited until the door shut with a loud *click*. Then she crossed the room toward Leo, holding up a piece of paper that had been ripped from a legal pad. In large, looping letters, she'd written: *Assume they're listening in.*

Leo nodded. He didn't have to assume. He knew for certain that somewhere deep within the maze of the FBI building a cluster of representatives from various agencies were huddled around a speaker, waiting to hear what he and his attorney said to one another.

"Hi, I'm Colleen Young-Wetzel," the woman said, extending her right hand.

"Leo Connelly," he said. "Are you a friend of Will's?"

"That's right," she said, flashing him another big smile. "And he had wonderful things to say about both you and Sasha."

Despite his surroundings, Leo felt himself smiling back at her.

She held his gaze for a moment then shifted gears.

"Okay," she said in a brisk tone, "this should be the part where I ask you to tell me what happened. Then, I assure you it's going to be okay, while at the same time, I manage your expectations so you don't think I can work magic and get you out of here today."

"But, I guess Sasha already told you what happened?"

"She did, but ordinarily I'd still want to get my client's version. However, your friends out there tell me you're free to go." She cocked her head to the side, in an exaggerated display of confusion.

He blinked at her.

She shrugged her shoulders, palms up, in a big gesture.

He understood that she was trying to tell him something was off, that the FBI was up to something, but she didn't know what.

"Really?" he said slowly.

"Yep. Agent Richardson did ask if you would talk to him briefly before you leave. Says he has a favor to ask you."

Leo's instinct was to hear Richardson out, but he wanted to get his attorney's take on it. "What do you think? Should I talk to him?"

She tapped a manicured finger to her lips. "That depends. You have any interest in getting killed?"

It was Leo's turn to cock his head in confusion.

"What do you mean?"

Colleen spoke in a clear, confident voice, like she was addressing a jury. "I'm fairly certain, Leo, that, if a group made up of FBI, CIA, ATF, DHS, and DOJ needs a favor, then the task is dangerous, ill-advised, illegal, or all of the above."

She smiled again, cat-like and sly, and turned her head to the door. As she did so, Hank, trailed by his CIA and FBI counterparts, hustled into the room.

"Ms. Young-Wetzel, you have a very suspicious view of human nature, don't you think?" Hank chided her.

She raised one shaped brow. "I'm stunned that you were able to hear me from out in the hall, Agent Richardson."

Hank just smiled; Leo knew it wasn't his style to insult her intelligence by claiming they hadn't been monitoring the conversation. Besides, it wasn't as though there was recourse for the eavesdropping, and everyone in the room knew it.

Ed Appleman, the FBI agent, was holding Leo's phone, wallet, watch, and weapon in his hands.

Leo stood and took the gun first, hefting the black plastic polymer in his hand for a moment before sliding the gun into its holster. Then he reached for his cell phone and wallet, both of which he slid into his pocket. Appleman dropped the titanium watch into Leo's palm.

After securing his watch around his wrist, Leo nodded to Hank. "I hear you need a favor."

The CIA agent cleared his throat and cast a meaningful look in Colleen's direction. "We do. But we can't discuss it in front of a civilian."

Colleen twisted her mouth into a wry smile. "Hint taken. Just remember, Leo—dangerous, ill-advised, and illegal. Good luck to you."

"Thanks for everything," Leo said.

She gave a short laugh and headed for the door. "They should all be this easy."

Hank waited until she was gone. Then he turned and met Leo's eyes. "She's got two out of three right. It's dangerous and technically illegal."

36

Gavin licked his cracked lips, encouraged by the fact that he was able to work up enough saliva to wet them. The intravenous fluids that Lydia had started him on must be helping. His fever seemed to rage less, too.

In fact, he felt almost human again. Certainly he felt well enough to come up with a plan.

He rested his head on the pillow and shifted to his side, thinking.

They seemed to be checking on him frequently, perhaps afraid that he, like Celia, would take a sudden turn for the worse. The first woman—the kind-eyed Anna—and Lydia alternated visits. At least, he thought they did. He wasn't positive, as the first several hours had passed in a hot, cloudy haze.

But, if he was right, then Anna should be coming

soon. He had to convince her to let him use her phone. Or overpower her and take it.

One way or the other, he needed to call Sasha. Tell her what was going on. He was lucid enough to know they'd probably kill him if the flu didn't do it for them. He didn't want to die. He especially didn't want to die surrounded by paranoid delusional preppers. If he had to die, he'd like it to be in his own home, in his bed, with at least one more cup of decent coffee in his system. But, he wasn't going to let Bricker get away with his terrorist act. Not if he could stop it.

He rested, conserving his strength, and waited. Finally, he closed his eyes to nap.

The sound of the lock turning on the door startled him awake.

The door opened, the overhead light flickered to life, and the door shut again. He waited for his eyes to adjust to the brightness, and then he turned to look: it was Anna.

She walked quietly, trying not to disturb him. He turned his face toward her.

"Hi," he croaked.

"Oh, you're awake. How are you feeling?" she asked through her mask.

"Better."

"That's good. Let's take your temperature."

She removed a digital thermometer from her

pocket, slipped it into a plastic protective sleeve, and stood over him. He opened his mouth, and she inserted the probe.

While she waited for it to beep, she checked the level on his fluid bag.

"Do you feel the need to urinate?" she asked him.

He nodded. He didn't, not yet. But, it would be an excuse to get out of bed. He shifted his gaze to her jacket pocket. He could see a flat metal rectangle encased in pink rubber peeking out of the corner. An iPhone.

"I'll bring you a bedpan. I don't think you're up for the walk to the latrine just yet."

The thermometer beeped, and he opened his mouth. She removed it and read the display.

"Ninety-nine. You're on the mend, Mr. Russell."

He cleared his throat. "Great. I guess I won't be your prisoner much longer, then."

She frowned. "You aren't being held captive. You're quarantined. There's a difference."

He pushed himself up on his elbows. He was breathing heavily from the effort.

"Is there? I'm locked in this room. You—or someone—confiscated my car keys, my phone, and my gun. It sure feels like I'm being held captive."

She considered this while opening a fresh Gatorade for him. She slid a straw into the bottle and handed it to him.

"I can see how you could feel that way. But that's for your own safety. And our safety, too. You should bear in mind that you're a trespasser here. We would have been within our rights to treat you harshly and, make no mistake, some of us wanted to. Jeffrey—Captain Bricker—insisted we tend to your medical needs in a humane fashion."

Gavin took a long drink of the cold, sweet liquid.

"Captain Bricker's your husband, right?"

She hesitated for a moment then said, "That's right."

"You have kids?"

"Six." Her clipped response was suspicious.

He pressed on. "And it doesn't bother you? All the innocent people—children, too—who might die?"

She looked at him, puzzled. "Of course it bothers me. I wish everyone would heed Jeffrey's warnings and develop a preparedness plan, learn to be self-reliant. But we can't force people to listen, Mr. Russell. When the pandemic comes, I'll mourn the deaths of the unprepared, but I can't prevent them."

He barked out a laugh, which turned into a coughing fit. After he regained his breath, he leaned back, his eyes watering from the hacking.

"You really don't know, do you?"

She just stared at him.

"Your husband is going to unleash the virus. He's

going to *cause* the global pandemic you all fear," Gavin told her, his voice hoarse with effort.

She shook her head. "No, you're confused. We don't have the virus, we have the vaccine. Celia—and you—didn't get sick because you were exposed to the Doomsday virus. Lydia says Celia developed a similar strain of the flu as a side effect of being vaccinated. It's rare, but it happens. You just caught that flu." She spoke to him in a soothing voice.

"No. I heard your husband and Rollins talking. He has the virus, too. And he plans to go to Pittsburgh tomorrow to infect the population. Your husband's a killer. And if you don't do something to stop him, so are you."

Her eyes flashed above the mask. "That's a lie."

"Ask him."

"I don't need to," she snapped.

She turned away from the bed.

"Wait. Please."

She looked back over her shoulder at him.

Gavin swallowed painfully. "Listen, please, just ask him."

She looked at him with sad eyes for what seemed like an interminable amount of time but was probably less than twenty seconds. Then she turned and left without answering.

37

Sasha had passed Hagerstown and was crossing the border from Maryland into Pennsylvania when her cell phone rang.

"Sasha McCandless," she answered through Connelly's Bluetooth connection.

"Hi, Sasha, it's Colleen Young-Wetzel."

"Hi, Colleen," Sasha said, mildly surprised to be hearing from the attorney again so soon.

"So, that was easy," Colleen said.

"You met with Connelly already?" Sasha asked, checking her rear view mirror. The roads had become icy as the temperature had dropped and she'd climbed into the mountains. The last thing she needed was for someone to rear end her.

"Yeah, I spent more time cooling my heels while

the FBI played their usual games than I did talking to Leo."

"How is he?"

"He seemed fine. To his credit, he didn't talk to anyone until I arrived, but, as it turns out, they didn't really want to talk to him anyway," Colleen said in a voice that didn't quite manage to hide her irritation.

"What?"

"When they finally decided to give me access to my client, Hank Richardson intercepted me on my way into the holding room. He said the government attorneys had decided they didn't have enough to hold Leo, but that the task force was hoping he would do them a favor," Colleen explained.

"A favor? Wait—back up. They found a vial of a killer virus locked inside an office that only Connelly can access. That's not probable cause?" Sasha asked, perplexed and relieved at the same time.

"Of course it's probable cause. Given the current political atmosphere, they could have disappeared him to Gitmo!" Colleen exploded.

"Oh. Okay."

Colleen exhaled loudly. "I'm sorry. I'm not frustrated with you. I'm mad at myself, and worried about Leo."

"Hang on, I'm going to pull over so I can focus on this conversation. Give me a second."

Sasha wasn't sure what was going on, but she felt

that she needed to concentrate on what Colleen was saying. She flicked her right turn signal, indicating her intention, and crunched over the gravel shoulder covered with crusty snow. She put the SUV in park and turned on her emergency flashers. "Go ahead."

"I should have known the feds weren't serious about Leo as a suspect. You told me it was mostly Kabuki theater at the scene this morning. They barely checked your bag, for Pete's sake."

Sasha found herself nodding. She should have realized it, too. At the time, it seemed odd, but she'd been so relieved, she'd just accepted it as good fortune.

"Colleen, are you saying the entire thing was staged?"

The other woman hesitated before answering. "Not the entire thing. I think they really did get an anonymous tip and responded as they would to any threat like that. But, once they realized Leo was involved, then, yeah, I think they were just running through it like a training exercise. I think they know he didn't steal the virus *and* I think they know who did."

"Who?"

"Oh, I don't know. But, once they released Leo, they sent me on my way and spoke to him privately. Based on everything I know about the agencies involved in this—in particular, the OGA—I'm sure they told him they had a suspect and asked him to help them in an unofficial capacity," she explained.

"OGA? You mean GAO—General Accounting Office?" Sasha asked.

"No, OGA. Other Governmental Agency. It's shorthand for the CIA. You know, they're supposed to limit their activities to foreign intelligence and counterintelligence activities. But, somehow, they always seem to have a hand in everything. Anytime an FBI, DHS, or ATF agent mutters under his breath about the OGA, you can be sure the CIA is sniffing around. Because of the nature of the threat—the virus came here from France, they've been involved in this since the outset. If the CIA had information about the suspect, I absolutely can see them demanding to participate in the take down. But, they couldn't use one of their own agents to do it."

"And you think the CIA would ask a private citizen like Connelly to take part in a covert action? That's insane."

"That would be insane," Colleen agreed. "But your friend isn't just a private citizen. He's a former special agent with the Department of Homeland Security who's already neck-deep in this mess. It's a no-brainer. For the CIA, I mean—not Leo. Leo should tell them to pound salt."

Sasha's stomach dropped. She knew to a certainty that if Connelly was asked to help, he would help. "Why would it be such a bad decision? I mean, hypothetically, if they asked him to do something, and he did it?"

Colleen's laugh lacked any humor. "Because they want to use him so they have their precious plausible deniability. If something goes wrong, no one's going to admit that Leo was working under the supervision of our federal government. He'll be on his own."

Sasha didn't know what to say. As a lawyer, she had to agree with Colleen: Connelly shouldn't get involved in any covert actions to help a government agency that would hang him out to dry if it needed to. As Connelly's girlfriend, she knew it would be nearly impossible to talk him out of it.

"So, what do we do now?" Sasha asked.

"Now, you wait. And pray to whatever god you pray to that nothing goes wrong."

SASHA DECIDED to turn around and drive back to D.C.

She knew she really shouldn't—she had far too much work to do. But she wanted to see Connelly and, if she could, talk him out of whatever Hank was trying to talk him into. Besides, she told herself, she should return his vehicle. The rationale rang weak even to her own ears.

Before she reached an exit, though, Connelly called.

"Hey," she answered the ringing phone.

"Hey, yourself. Thanks for finding me a lawyer. She was great."

"It was no problem. Colleen said she didn't really do anything—they decided they didn't have enough to hold you."

She was careful not to ask any questions, but he must have heard the inquiry in her voice, because he said, "Yeah. They want a favor in return, though."

"Are they getting it?"

Connelly took his time answering. Finally, he said, "I'm not sure. Right now, I'm not available to help them. I'm packing."

"Packing?"

"Tate called me about a half hour ago to let me know Serumceutical no longer needs my services."

"He fired you?"

"We mutually agreed that, although the company appreciated my service, the optics of the situation could detrimentally affect the stock price. So, I have a nice, fat separation payment, and Grace has a nice, fat new job." He mimicked Tate's lawyerly, dispassionate delivery.

"I'm so sorry," she said.

"Don't be. Grace is much better suited to surviving in that viper pit than I am."

"Still."

There was silence on the other end.

A mile marker flashed by on the roadside. Her chance to turn around and return to D.C. was just ahead.

"Listen, I'm turning around. I'll be there in two hours, tops."

Connelly chuckled. "Don't do that. I told you—I'm packing."

She ignored the sting she felt from his response and said, "Oh. Where are you going?"

"Pittsburgh. Someone very special to me lives there."

A smile made its way across Sasha's face. "Oh?"

"Yep. Will you pick me up at the airport at four o'clock?"

"With bells on, Connelly."

"Skip the bells—that's just more to take off."

38

Anna knew Russell was wrong. She told herself there was no reason to bother Jeffrey about the accusation. But as she followed the path from the quarantined cabin back to the recreation center—which Jeffrey had rechristened the command center—she could feel an uneasy weight settling in her heart.

She'd been Jeffrey's wife her entire adult life. She'd given him six children. She should have known beyond any doubt that he would never attack the country they both loved. And yet she found herself walking slower and slower—putting off what should have been an easy conversation.

You're being ridiculous, she told herself and quickened her pace.

She pushed open the door and hurried through

the mess hall. Three women were wiping down the tables after lunch. From the distant kitchen, she could hear laughter and banging metal, as another group washed and dried dishes. She kept her head down and avoided eye contact.

Now that she'd resolved to talk to Jeffrey, she wanted to get it over with.

She rapped on his office door then pushed it inward without waiting for an invitation.

George Rollins and Bud Newton were leaning over Jeffrey's shoulders staring down at some documents—possibly a map—with their brows furrowed in twin ruts of concentration. Jeffrey casually turned the papers upside down and smiled up at her.

"Do you need something?" His tone was kind but it carried an undercurrent, a suggestion that he was busy with important matters and she was interrupting him.

She plowed ahead. "Yes, I do."

She looked first at George and then at Bud with a steady, unblinking gaze.

Bud got the message faster.

"Uh," he said, clearing his throat, "George and I can come back in a bit."

George nodded his agreement, and both men saluted Jeffrey, then scurried past her into the hallway.

As George pulled the door closed behind him,

Jeffrey stood and walked around the desk. He took Anna in his arms and hugged her close briefly. She had just snuggled into his chest when he pulled back and held her at arm's length, peering into her face.

"It's good to see you. These past two days, we've been so busy getting the troops organized, I feel as though I've hardly spent any time with you." He smiled down at her—not his broad, public smile but a private, quiet smile she knew well.

She smiled back at him but then steeled herself.

"It feels like we've been distant even longer than that," she said.

He frowned. "What do you mean?"

"Preppers PA has always been *ours*, almost like one of the kids. A shared responsibility and joy," she began.

His eyes softened. She'd been watching him reel in skeptics, critics, and fence-sitters for years. Step one was always to establish common ground.

"That's still true."

She shook her head. "No. You're keeping secrets from me."

He began to deny it, but she fixed him with a look that stopped him cold.

He looked briefly, then he raised his head and met her gaze. "I have. I'm sorry."

She reached for his hand. "But, why?"

"I want to protect you," he said.

Despite the teachings of their church and their own conservative values, they'd always been true partners in all of their endeavors, including rolling up their sleeves and breathing life into the prepper organization. It was true that Jeffrey would, on occasion, tell her about certain projects that were of questionable legality only after the fact. But, this vaccine business was taking that to a new level—he'd been actively avoiding telling her anything unless she pressed him.

So, press she would.

"Come on, Jeffrey. This is me you're talking to."

"Anna, honestly, there are just too many moving parts to preparing for the pandemic. Hundreds of people are counting on us. I've had to bring George and some of the others in on the planning. It's no reflection on your abilities—or my love—I need you to focus on the family. Our family and the other families. Tending the hearth fires is noble and important work, too."

She laughed bitterly at the blatant flattery. Her eyes fell on the map sitting face down on his desk.

"Don't lie to me, Jeffrey. If nothing else, you owe me the truth."

The anger that welled up in her chest masked the fear that was also clawing its way to the surface: maybe Russell was right.

He reversed course and nodded somberly. "You're

right. I do. I owe you the truth and much, much more, Anna. Forgive me. It's just difficult to explain our next steps."

Anna appraised her husband. Despite his serious expression, she recognized the excitement building within him—his eagerness to appease her and get on with his mission.

"Are you planning a terrorist attack?" she asked.

Just like that. The words rang in her ears, and a dizzy heat flooded her body, but she stared coolly at him until he answered.

"I take issue with the phrase 'terrorist attack.' That implies there's a legitimate government that's been targeted," he finally said.

It was true.

Anna forced herself to breathe. "Jeffrey, you can't attack the United States government—a legitimate, functioning sovereign—just because we have some vaccines and have amassed a few hundred followers. That's madness."

He shook his head, rejecting her words.

"The government *has* broken down, it just doesn't know it yet," he insisted. His eyes shone.

Anna shivered at the zealotry in his voice but persisted. "Listen to yourself. You're playing word games, not addressing the issue. What do you have planned?"

"I didn't mention this to you, because I didn't

want to worry you, but I was able to get a small sample of the Doomsday virus."

He rocked back on his heels and watched her face as she processed what he'd just said.

She blurted out a flurry of questions. "You have the virus? Where is it? Did you bring it into our home? What in God's name do you plan to do with it?"

He raised a hand and made a *slow down* motion.

"I know it's a lot to take in. The French network contacted me and told me an American had been sniffing around certain parties, looking to hire someone for wet work."

She looked at him blankly.

"Murder, Anna. The American had found a source who could obtain the virus, but he wanted to kill him afterward—to remove the risk he would talk. Claude put him in touch with ... someone capable of doing the task. And then Claude put me in touch with the American after he had the virus."

Even with notions of murder and deadly viruses crowding out rational thought, the chain of events made sense to Anna so far. Claude—Claude Pierre Bonet—was the former Clyde Peter Bonner from Jim Thorpe, Pennsylvania. Jeffrey had known Clyde since high school—Clyde was a survivalist before being a survivalist was a thing. It wasn't terribly surprising that he'd be in the middle of theft, murder, and conspiracy—he was often mixed up in unsavory business. In fact, the circumstances of his move abroad were clouded by some legal issues that Jeffrey had never fully explained to her.

"But, why?"

"Originally, as an insurance policy of sorts. Knowing that the virus was going to be out there somewhere, in private hands, it seemed prudent to have the same weapon. Mutually assured destruction has always been an effective defense."

She just stared at him, taking in the fevered gleam in his eyes.

"Once I met Mr. X, I realized he didn't plan to release the virus. But, it's important that the American public understand the danger they live in. The only way to do that is to bring it into their homes. When their children get sick, and there's no medicine, no drinkable water, no fresh food, and no help, then they'll grasp their situation."

The way he said it, so determined and committed to his own narrative, frightened her. He was making decisions out of ideological fervor now. Having decided the possibility of a pandemic was a real and present danger and having rallied his followers, he couldn't back away and admit that, at least for now, the government was in control of the situation.

"People are going to die."

"Not our people. Most of our followers have

already been vaccinated and will have full immunity by the time the virus starts spreading. They've left their homes, their jobs in anticipation of the pandemic. It's too late to stand down."

"No, it isn't. The organization did its job—we got everyone to a safe place. If the threat's over, we can return to our regular lives."

"Don't you see, Anna? Our safety is an illusion. We need to send the government a message to prepare itself."

"What kind of message?" Anna asked. She was afraid of the answer, afraid of her husband, afraid of the emptiness she felt looking at him.

"Late tonight—well, actually, just after midnight—so early tomorrow morning, Bud and I are going to drive to Pittsburgh. He'll stay in the vehicle while I take the virus to Steel Plaza and release it at the crèche display. Then, we'll return here. We should be back for morning exercises, but George is standing ready to help you in case we are delayed. Or apprehended."

"You're going to infect people who come to view the nativity scene?" Anna asked. Her tongue felt thick, and the words sounded slow and slurred to her own ears.

"It's a very effective plan. There will be school choirs singing. And children and the elderly have weakened immune systems. It should spread rapidly." He gave her a satisfied look.

Her stomach turned.

"That's murder."

"You may think so—" he began.

"I do think so. And the government will think so, too."

He waved a hand at the idea.

"Jeffrey, you're going to kill innocent children."

She watched to see if that reality sunk in, but nothing seemed to penetrate his madness.

"Not me, Anna. Society will be responsible for their deaths."

She shifted gears and tried a new tack. "You'll go to jail. We both will. What about *our* kids?"

He shot her a disgusted look. "First of all, you're not going to jail—that's exactly why I kept you out of this. Second, I'm not going to jail. An illegitimate government will never be able to seize me, not alive, at any rate. And third, the kids will be fine. We've raised them to be self-sufficient."

"Clara is three years old!"

"I know how old my daughter is. The community we've built will help. Surely you aren't ready to abandon all the people who count on us?" Bricker asked.

"They count on us? I thought we were teaching them to count on themselves?" Anna countered.

"They still need leaders. Everyone does. It's the natural order."

He was blind to the inconsistency—his followers needed leaders, but his three-year-old daughter didn't need parents? There was no reasoning with him.

But she tried anyway. "I'm not saying we should abandon anything or anyone. But, I have no interest in martyring myself or our family. You can't be serious."

Anna searched her husband's face for almost a full minute and saw no trace of the man she knew—the man she'd built a life with. Her chest tightened with sorrow.

She walked out of the office, blinking away hot tears.

39

Colton waved to the federal agent slouching against the lamppost across the street from his penthouse and turned away from the window. The man ducked his head and pretended to check his watch.

Idiots. As if by following him around they were going to stumble onto a hidden cache of the virus or find a cancelled check made out to Michel Joubert.

Did they suppose he'd gotten as far as he had in business and life by being incompetent and careless? He nearly laughed, but then his eyes fell on the Trader Joe's tote bag sitting under his desk.

He had to get rid of the silver. It wasn't contraband, of course, but when—not if—law enforcement officers came knocking on his door, he would prefer not to have to explain away a bag full of silver ingots.

He supposed he could store it in his personal safe or in his safety deposit box, but both of those plans had flaws. A search warrant, presumably, would be worded in such a way as to include the contents of his safe; and a safety deposit box wouldn't be immediately accessible if he did, in fact, ever need to flee to avoid prosecution—although given the clumsy surveillance techniques on display down on Connecticut Avenue, he assumed he'd have ample warning if the feds were closing a net around him.

All the same, he decided, the silver was best stored off the premises but where he could get his hands on it as needed. He'd put it with the remaining vial.

He reached into the middle drawer on the right side of his desk and removed a thin stack of mail. He took the top envelope and slid the rest back into the drawer. Clutching the pastel pink envelope, with its glittery sticker over the envelope flap and the looping, childish script that addressed it to "Aunt Marla," he left the apartment and crossed the hall to the Brandts' door.

He raised the knocker and let it fall against the door then straightened the knot in his tie with his free hand as he rehearsed the conversation about misdirected mail that he'd have to suffer through if one of the Brandts happened to be home.

No footsteps sounded on the other side of the

door. He knocked again, louder this time, and waited another minute. No one came to the door, so he returned to his apartment.

After returning the envelope to its drawer in the desk, he crouched on his heels and lifted the heavy cloth bag filled with silver. Then he stood and carried it into his master closet.

When Colton had remodeled the walk-in closet shortly after he'd moved in, his carpenter had called him in a mild panic. As he'd been installing the cedar, the man had accidentally broken through the wall.

That was how Colton had discovered that, in their efforts to carve out two separate three thousand square foot penthouse suites, the building management had backed his closet up to the Brandts' identical closet, which met his in a U-shaped space blocked off from the main concourse. Colton had resisted his initial impulse to complain to the condo board and assured his carpenter he'd take care of the damage with the neighbors across the hall.

Instead, he'd spent a weekend chatting with the helpful employees of a suburban hardware store and creating two false panels.

He dropped the bag to the cherry hardwood floor with a *thud* then crouched and ran his hands along the cedar wall near the baseboard. When his fingers touched the small notch in the wall, he pried the panel off and set it aside.

He quickly located the identical notch in the panel he'd affixed to the Brandts' side of the closet. He eased off the length of wood and placed it on the floor of his closet alongside its mate.

Then he poked his head through the opening to survey the inside of the Brandts' closet. The light that filtered through the gap from his own closet was sufficient to confirm that the small box holding his virus ampule sat undisturbed behind Marla Brandt's boot collection. He turtled back into the hole and grabbed the heavy bag. He heaved it two-handed through the opening and lowered it as quietly as he could to the floor beside the virus. Several pashmina shawls hanging from a bar swung gently as he brushed them with his forearm.

The space between the closets was narrow and best suited for hiding papers and drugs—perhaps a firearm, if Colton had been a gun enthusiast. The bag fit in the cache, but just barely. He folded the bag's excess cloth down tightly over the bricks of silver and gently slid the panel over the items to hide them from view on the Brandt's side of the closet. He crawled backward through the gap to his own side and replaced his panel.

Then he stood and brushed his hands on his slacks, satisfied and unaware that just days earlier the Brandts had mounted a discreet security camera high on the opposite wall of their closet. The small camera was aimed directly at the large jewelry armoire that sat beside the boot racks. Its electronic eye blinked red and recorded Colton's every movement.

40

Leo spotted Sasha waiting at the security gate when he arrived in the middle of a wave of chattering travelers. She stretched up on her toes, smiled her megawatt smile, and waved at him over the crowd.

He nodded to the vaguely familiar TSA agent who sat perched on a stool near the entrance to the security lines and hurried toward her. His bag bumped out a rhythm against his thigh with each stride.

"Long time, no see," she said, as he swung her into his arms and inhaled the familiar, faint, spicy scent of her body lotion.

They walked hand-in-hand through the short-term parking garage to her car.

"Have you heard from Gavin?" he asked. He'd

forgotten about Gavin's efforts to locate the missing Serumceutical worker in all the chaos surrounding his arrest.

She shook her head. "No, not since he left that message Sunday night. I'm getting worried, Connelly."

So was he.

"I'll talk to Hank. Maybe he can reach out to local law enforcement and have them send a car out to the preppers' campsite, just to check it out."

She popped the trunk of her Passat so he could toss his bag inside.

"I don't know if you should be asking Hank for any favors," she said uncertainly, "but, we have to do something. It's not like Gavin to go dark."

Her green eyes met his, and he could tell that grim scenes were unfolding in her imagination.

"Hey, we'll track him down."

As she pulled out of the compact parking spot and circled past the airport, he reached across the console and turned on the car radio.

"Do you mind if we listen to the news? 'All Things Considered' should be starting," he said.

She pressed the pre-set button for the NPR station and they listened in silence to a report about the impact the storm was having on the Eastern seaboard.

Leo looked out his window as she merged onto

the highway. Judging by the piles of snow stacked along the roadside, Pittsburgh had gotten at least half a foot. But the roads had been cleared and salted. It was a stark contrast to the slushy mess his cab driver had navigated through D.C. on the way to Reagan National.

Sasha kept her eyes on the van in front of them, which was weaving in and out of its lane. "My dad called. The kids are all sledding at the park near my folks' house, so my mom's got a few pans of lasagna in the oven, if you're up for dinner with the clan tonight," she said without looking away from the road.

Leo was the only child of a single mother whose job required them to move around. Sasha seemed to think that his background meant that he found her noisy, extended family overwhelming when, in reality, he loved the laughter, the squabbling, the frenetic energy of the kids, and the meals shared crowded around her parents' too-small dining room table.

"Sounds like fun," he said.

She glanced over and smiled at him. "Good. But, you'll call Hank first, right?"

He nodded.

Sasha dutifully slowed the car, as the van in front of them braked and decelerated. They were nearing the mouth of the tunnel that led to downtown. For reasons Leo had not yet grasped, all Pittsburgh drivers seemed to slow to a crawl before entering tunnels, as if a road with a roof posed some threat to their safety.

After inching their way through the tunnel, they emerged and crossed the bridge to town. Leo turned his attention to the pop-up book skyline. He loved this approach to the city. As he gazed out the window at the gray, frozen river, he realized with a jolt that he felt like he was home.

He'd moved around so much as a boy, going from place to place for his mother's job as a traveling nurse, that he'd never considered *anywhere* home. It was a routine that he'd continued after college, moving from one government assignment to the next, always willing to relocate.

How had Pittsburgh crept into his blood and made itself his home?

The answer to that question shifted in her seat beside him. "Listen," she said, turning up the volume on the radio.

A French correspondent was reporting that research that could be misused with disastrous consequences was reportedly missing from a Level Four laboratory at the Pasteur Institute. Neither the Institute nor the French government had returned calls for comment. The reporter cautioned that the report was unsubstantiated.

The report didn't mention the Doomsday virus

by name. Leo was impressed by how effectively the task force seemed to have suppressed the details of the theft. The host tied the story back to an ongoing series about the ethical issues surrounding "dual-use" research into deadly pathogens and then moved on to the next news item.

Sasha weaved through the early rush hour traffic with a furrowed brow but said nothing.

It was time to call Hank, Leo thought to himself.

He pulled out his phone to make the call, but Sasha's phone rang before he had the chance.

"Could you get that?" she asked, chewing on her lip and inching past a PAT bus that was picking up passengers who had to navigate a mountain of snow to board.

"SASHA McCANDLESS'S PHONE," a male voice answered.

Gavin couldn't be sure, because the voice was distorted by the tinny speakerphone, but it sounded like Leo.

He glanced away from the iPhone and met Anna's troubled gaze. "It's okay," he stage whispered, "It's her boyfriend."

Anna nodded and made a frantic motion with her hand to indicate he should hurry up.

She'd said hardly anything since she'd returned to the cabin. He could tell from her red, puffy eyes that she'd been crying. But, she hadn't confided in him—she'd just thrust the phone at him and said, "Make the call."

Gavin cleared his sore throat. "Leo, it's Gavin Russell. I really need to talk to Sasha."

"Hang on, I'm going to put you on speaker. She's driving."

A moment later, Sasha's clear but distant voice came through the speaker.

"Gavin? Are you okay? I've been worried about you."

"Sasha, I don't have much time. Just listen carefully: Celia is dead, I'm sick with the flu and being held in quarantine by the preppers. They're planning to attack Pittsburgh."

He waited a moment for her to process the information.

Sasha pelted him with questions. "What kind of attack? When? Do you know the precise location?"

"I don't, but Anna might. She's married to the head guy."

"Can we trust her?"

Gavin looked at Anna, whose eyes kept darting to the closed cabin door.

"I don't know. But I don't have any other choice," he said, his voice hoarse.

Anna met his gaze and swallowed hard.

"This is Anna Bricker. Jeffrey—my husband—somehow gained possession of a vial of the Doomsday virus. He's planning to release it sometime after midnight at the big nativity display in downtown Pittsburgh." She spoke in a stilted, formal voice.

"The crèche in Steel Plaza?" Sasha asked.

"I guess. He said some school group will be singing there in the morning," Anna responded.

Gavin could hear murmured voices as Sasha consulted with Leo. Sasha's was soft and urgent. Leo's deeper voice rumbled calmly.

"Gavin," Leo said louder, "are you and Ms. Bricker in a safe location?"

"Negative. We're at the compound. I'm being held in a locked room against my will. Anna is one of the preppers tending to me medically, but if they find out she's helping me—" Gavin answered.

Anna shook her head at him, rejecting what he'd left unsaid. But Gavin knew he was right. He'd seen his share of men like Bricker posture and rail in front of Judge Paulson. Strip away the delusions of grandeur and the ideological bullcrap, and Bricker was no different from the meth-heads who beat their wives because the kids were crying.

"Can you get out of there?" Sasha asked.

"Not without Anna's help. I've turned a corner, but I'm still pretty weak," Gavin admitted.

Anna kept her eyes fixed on the floor and said, "I can't put my children in danger by trying to leave. Just ... get someone up here, fast. Please."

41

The call came in to the Dogwood Station. But after the caller clarified the location, the operator determined the area in question was served by the Elk Run Station and transferred the call, where it was answered by Tanner Royerson. He was fresh out of the Marines and had returned home to Clear Brook County to get some civil law enforcement experience while he put in his applications with the various federal government agencies.

The caller gave her name as Sasha McCandless and reported a man being held against his will at the old Department of Natural Resources camp up by the state game lands. Tanner dropped his half-eaten energy bar on his desk and started pecking out notes on his ancient computer.

He made it a habit to surf the government websites for bulletins and alerts every day at the start of his shift. The veteran troopers got a big kick out of it because they claimed nothing that interesting ever happened way out where they were. But, Tanner was undeterred. He figured it was like the advice his girlfriend Melanie always followed: Dress for the job you want, not the job you have. If he kept acting like he was on the front lines of homeland security, maybe, eventually, he would be.

So the location at the campsite set off a bell for Tanner, and when the woman on the phone mentioned the Preppers PA group, the alarm in his head rang louder.

He listened intently to the information the caller imparted, even though it was hard to hear her over the drumbeat of his heart. She spoke in a measured voice, managing to convey urgency without resorting to hysteria. He figured her for a doctor or maybe an EMT, not because she said anything that led him to believe she had any medical training, but for the simple reason that she wasn't freaking out.

She explained there was a sick man—possibly infected with a deadly, contagious virus—being quarantined by the preppers. She also said some of the other individuals at the site might not be there completely voluntarily.

He asked how many other individuals were on

site, and she hesitated. She said she couldn't estimate with any accuracy but there could be dozens, if not hundreds, of preppers, including women and children and that most of the adults of both sexes would likely be armed.

He typed quickly and inaccurately. His fingers shook from all the adrenaline coursing through his body. He thanked her, hung up the phone, and rocked his metal desk chair back on two legs.

He pulled up his browser history. There it was—an alert flashing across the top of the Department of Homeland Security's page: Possible kidnapping/hostage situation at Pennsylvania campsite. Militia group involved. Contact Hank Richardson directly with information.

"Hot damn!" he said to no one in particular. Then he brought his chair back down on all four legs with a bang, and fumbled around with the phone until he managed to punch in the mobile number that appeared beside Hank Richardson's name on the website.

42

Sasha's joy at seeing Connelly was severely dampened by the call with Gavin and Anna. A weight was settling between her shoulder blades.

She changed out of her sheath and jacket and rolled her shoulders while she surveyed the contents of her closet. Jeans and a sweater seemed like the logical choice for the post-sledding get-together at her parents' place. Instead, she reached for black wool running tights, a dark gray shirt, and a black fleece jacket.

She walked into her bedroom to see that Connelly had traded his suit and tie for black athletic pants and a black hooded sweatshirt.

It was almost as if they had chosen clothes suitable for skulking around in the woods in the dead of winter rather than a family dinner. They exchanged knowing looks, but Connelly didn't mention the cat burglar attire, so neither did she.

Connelly's phone rang and vibrated on the window sill. He palmed it and checked the display.

"It's Hank."

He answered the call and activated the speakerphone.

"Leo, I got your message. I also had a call with a Trooper Royerson, who tells me your girlfriend called to report a hostage situation at that prepper camp," Hank said, skipping the small talk.

"That's right, Hank. I'm in Pittsburgh with Sasha now. You're on the speakerphone," Connelly told him.

Sasha heard an irritated cluck and pictured Hank sucking air in between his teeth on the other end of the phone, not sure whether to be candid now that he knew she was listening.

"Hank, let me just put your mind at ease—in light of Leo's recent detention, he's asked me to advise him as to his legal rights and obligations. So, I'm present in my capacity as his counsel and am bound by attorney-client privilege not to divulge the substance of any conversation the three of us may have," she said.

Connelly shot her a curious look, which she

interpreted as asking whether any of what she had just said was even remotely true.

She raised both hands and shrugged. She didn't have the faintest idea. People seemed to keep forgetting she was a civil litigator who specialized in complex commercial disputes.

"Hmm. It's not like I'm calling in my official capacity, anyway," Hank reasoned.

"You're not?" Connelly asked.

"No. This conversation isn't happening."

Connelly gave her a puzzled look that she suspected mirrored her own and said, "Understood. You said Trooper Royerson called you? Now, why would he do that? Sasha reported a hostage situation. That doesn't fall under your purview."

"Ordinarily it wouldn't, but the rookie who caught Sasha's call is one Trooper Tanner Royerson, recently honorably discharged from the Marine Corps, home in Clear Brook County, and dreaming of bigger things. He has enough ambition to troll the alerts on the website and he saw my alert regarding Ms. Gerig."

Gerig? Sasha mouthed.

"Did you say Gerig?" Connelly asked.

"Sure, your missing employee. After you and Sasha met with the task force and shared what you knew, I did some digging. We'd been looking at Vira-

Gene very closely for the theft of the Doomsday virus, and Celia Gerig's name hadn't popped. So, I was pretty sure you were barking up the wrong tree with the theory that ViraGene was behind the stolen vaccines."

"Gee, thanks for letting me know," Connelly deadpanned.

"Now you know that's not how things work. I couldn't tell you without compromising an existing bioterrorism investigation. Frankly, I'm surprised you two didn't put it together when that Judge Minella deep-sixed your temporary restraining order. We think ViraGene's good for the stolen virus, not the stolen vaccines. In fact, that was the mission I wanted you to help out with—we're sitting on ViraGene's CEO, but you decided to run off to Pittsburgh instead."

Connelly opened his mouth, but Sasha spoke over him.

"So, your alert is for Celia, not Gavin Russell?" she asked.

"We learned that Gerig had last been seen on Saturday, in the company of two known preppers, buying gasoline at a station en route to that campground they maintain. It seemed prudent to treat her as a victim until we found her. Most people who disappear voluntarily tell someone they're leaving. Who in blue blazes is Russell?" Hank said.

"Gavin Russell is a private investigator in Springport and a former sheriff's deputy. Sasha and I know him—knew him—from that whole fracking scandal. It turns out he also went to high school with Celia Gerig. He agreed to try to locate her. And, he did. He found her at the compound, alone, and apparently very sick. Now, she's dead, and he's sick, being held in what the preppers are calling quarantine."

"Gerig's dead?"

"Yes. We believe from natural causes," Leo confirmed.

"I told Royerson to drive out to the compound and watch it from the road. He's to sit there until we get a team up there. It's going to take a while. The campsite is about four hours north of the closest trained SWAT unit. If we get lucky, we should be able to extract your friend."

"You're going to want to have that team on the ground here," Sasha said.

"There? You mean, in Pittsburgh?"

"Right. A man by the name of Jeffrey Bricker is the head of the prepper organization. According to Bricker's wife and Gavin, Bricker obtained a vial of the virus and plans to release it sometime between midnight and tomorrow morning at a Christmas display in Downtown Pittsburgh," Connelly said in a low, serious voice.

"It's called the Pittsburgh Crèche. It's a big

display at Steel Plaza in front of the USX Tower," Sasha added.

Hank was silent.

"Hank?" Connelly prompted after a moment. He dragged his hand through his hair.

"I'm here. I'm trying to figure out how to deploy my resources. The SWAT unit assigned to the Pittsburgh field office is already mobilizing—I was planning to send them to the compound. But if there's an imminent attack planned for their backyard, I can't send them four hours away. I'll need them at that crèche. How far away is Philly? Or Baltimore? Buffalo? I could activate one of those teams. I can't send the Washington team, they have to protect high-value targets located there."

"Too far, Hank. There's no time. You'll have to loop in the State Police," Connelly told him.

"I don't think Dogwood Station has the specialized tactical response team I'm going to want up there, son. And, more to the point, I need to keep this situation out of the media for as long as possible. I can't risk adding law enforcement officers outside my control if it means I'm going to see the governor on television reassuring his constituents that he's got the planned terrorist attack under control," Hank said.

"You have Royerson up there," Connelly reminded him.

"Royerson falls to sleep every night fantasizing

about working for someone like me, Leo. I told him to keep it quiet; there's no way that kid's breathing a word to anyone and messing up his big break. His job is to sit. Nothing else."

Sasha watched the muscles twitch in Connelly's right cheek as he tried to decide what to say.

But she already knew what they would do—it was what they'd both secretly known they would do all along. She started down the stairs to the kitchen.

From above, she heard Connelly say, "You should ask a freelancer to check out the camp."

She tossed a handful of energy bars and apples into a sack. She added two sports bottles filled with water and eyed the coffee maker. Once Connelly hung up, she'd grind beans to make half a pot for the road.

"You know anybody?" Hank asked, as Sasha returned to the loft bedroom.

"As it happens, Sasha and I were planning to take a drive through the countryside tonight. I guess we could stop and check it out," Connelly answered.

"That'd be a help," Hank said, his casual tone matching Connelly's.

Sasha tilted her head and tried to make sense of the words she was hearing. The government didn't work this way. It had branches, and agencies, and departments, and divisions, and task forces. There was a chain of command for everything. Every project has its own little organizational chart of boxes and lines leading to more boxes. There were no freelancers.

"We're leaving now," Connelly said.

"I'll call Royerson and let him know you'll be in the area, but you're not to approach the preppers, understand? Just keep an eye. Maybe relieve Royerson so he can take a whiz and get some food. As soon as we've secured the target area and apprehended Bricker, I'll send a team up to handle the scene. You do not engage. Are we clear?" Hank said.

"Crystal," Connelly answered.

Connelly ended the call and zippered his black, down-filled vest.

"You ready?" he asked as he started down the stairs and toward the front door.

"I guess so," Sasha said, casting a yearning backward glance at the coffee maker.

WHEN THEY WERE about a hundred miles north of the city, the looming oil derricks and scarred patches of earth began to rise from the snowy hillsides along the highway. The fracking industry's relentless march through Pennsylvania had continued unabated. Just six months earlier, they'd have had to have driven another forty-five to fifty minutes before seeing the first signs of gas fracking.

Sasha checked the time and dialed Anna Bricker's number for their pre-arranged status call.

"Hello," the woman answered in a whisper that echoed through the Bluetooth connected to the SUV's radio.

"Anna? Are you with Gavin?" Sasha asked.

"Yes, but I can't stay long. It's Lydia's turn to check on him, she'll be here soon."

"Has there been any change?" Connelly said without looking away from the road.

Gavin answered.

"No, Anna says they're sticking to their plan to leave after midnight. But ..." he trailed off.

"What?" Sasha demanded. Her stomach clenched and she prepared herself to receive news of another setback.

Beside her Connelly urged the SUV forward. The constant thrum of roadway passing under the tires grew faster.

"We need to get her kids out of here," Gavin said. "The littlest one is only three. If something goes down—"

He didn't finish the thought; he didn't need to.

Sasha's pulse exploded in her ear. Beside her, Connelly made a fist with his right hand and pounded the steering wheel softly.

"Do you have a plan?" she asked.

"Sort of. A half-baked plan, you might say," Gavin laughed.

"Care to share it?" Connelly asked.

"My oldest son has his learner's permit, and I know where Jeffrey's keeping the keys to Gavin's car. It's dinner time now, there's a lot of people coming and going. I think they can slip away. I'm not sure how far they'll get, especially if the roads are icy, but they can't stay here," Anna said in a voice that quavered with unshed tears.

"Why can't you go with them? Just leave," Connelly said.

"I've tried to convince her. But she's part of their screwy command structure—her absence will be noticed right away. Without her, the kids have a shot at getting a decent head start before anyone realizes they're gone," Gavin said.

"Can't you all get out of there?" Sasha said. "If you're together, you stand a chance, even if Bricker sends someone after you."

"Gavin's too weak. And, to be honest, I think if Jeffrey notices the kids are gone, he won't say anything. He *is* still their father. But, if he learned I've betrayed him ..." Anna left the rest unsaid.

"Are there other kids there?" Sasha asked.

"A few. Three or four—no six, the twins arrived late last night," Anna said.

Sasha closed her eyes at that piece of information and tried to ward off the image of children caught in cross-fire.

"Anna, listen, there's a state trooper watching the entrance. He shouldn't be too far down the road. Tell the boy to drive straight for him. We'll try to get a message to him so he knows what's going on. He can get the kids to safety. Meanwhile, we're on our way. You two hang tight," Connelly said.

He checked his mirrors and accelerated. The speedometer hovered between eighty-five and ninety.

Sasha was grateful that PennDOT's road crews had been working around the clock since before the first flakes had hit the ground, keeping the major arteries salted and cleared.

"Understood. Hey, Sasha?" Gavin said.

"Yes?"

"I'd love an Americano. With an extra shot. The coffee here is total crap."

Despite herself, Sasha smiled.

"You got it."

43

Tanner hunched over the steering wheel and stared unblinkingly down the road at the access drive leading to the camp. A car was parked in the grass about one-third of the way up the drive, but he hadn't seen anyone approach the vehicle. He hadn't seen anyone, period.

If he was being honest with himself, he'd admit he was relieved. He'd left the station riding a wave of adrenaline that had somehow transformed, first, into nervous excitement and, finally, a sense of dread that nibbled at his stomach.

As he sat, his patrol unit angled across the road, and waited, he decided the best outcome would be if he secured the scene, ensured that no one fled, and handed over control to the feds when they showed up. Then he could bow out gracefully and return to the safety of the station having at least gotten his name in front of some federal agents. That could prove helpful down the line.

He hoped Richardson would send some reinforcements soon. His back was getting stiff from sitting and he needed to take a leak. He passed a few moments ignoring his increasing need to relieve himself but finally surrendered, casting a baleful gaze at the empty Super Big Gulp in his cup holder. No man could withstand the urgent call of forty ounces of Mountain Dew needing to exit his body, he reasoned.

He left the ignition running, stepped out of the Expedition, and trotted over to the nearest tree. As he jiggled himself dry and zipped up, keeping his eyes trained on the camp down the road the entire time, bright lights flared on the drive and a car engine roared to life.

He raced back to the truck, his shoes sliding on the icy road, and skidded to a stop as he careened off his open driver's side door. The car backed down the gravel road while he fumbled with his cell phone.

"Richardson, it's Trooper Royerson, sir. I'm sitting on the location as instructed," he shouted, breathless from running, "and a vehicle is leaving the compound."

"Good," Richardson answered in a voice that held no hint of panic or excitement.

"Sir?"

Richardson continued, "I just received a report that a group of six unarmed minors is attempting to leave the camp. They're gonna be scared. And the driver is unlicensed, so he may be driving erratically. They've been told to stop when they see you. Tell them their mom is going to be okay and then get them the hell out of the area."

"Roger that. But, sir?"

"What?"

"What about watching the camp?"

"I have a team on its way. You worry about the kids."

"Yes, sir."

Tanner jammed the vehicle into gear and jerked it to the right side of the road to enable the driver to maneuver around him. He wanted to give him plenty of room. Although the main roads were clear, the side roads were still messy. An inexperienced driver and icy conditions didn't make for the best combination.

The car fishtailed as it bounced off the access drive and onto the road. Tanner squinted. He figured the kid had to drive about a mile and a half.

"C'mon, kid," he whispered.

He threw the switch to turn on the light bar on the truck's roof. Six kids. He was glad he'd signed out the Expedition instead of taking one of the Crown Vic's from the pool.

Eight long minutes later, the car came to a jerky stop in front of him.

He walked over to the vehicle and shined his flashlight into the car. The boy behind the wheel sat pale-faced and shaking. Beside him a girl held a squirming toddler in her lap. Three more tear-streaked faces looked up at him from the backseat.

"It's going to be okay," he said loudly, so they could hear him through the window. He hoped he was right.

44

When Leo called Anna to report that her children were enjoying hot chocolate and smiley cookies at the Eat'n Park in Deerton, she burst into relieved tears.

Gavin patted her arm awkwardly.

"Thank you," she said, wiping her eyes. "Thank you for helping me get them out of here."

"You're welcome. Now, let's go see about getting my gun."

She'd told him Lydia had confiscated it from his car, but she'd searched her husband's office and had found no sign of it. The only other place it was likely to be, according to her, was the munitions shed.

If he had a weapon, he figured he might stand a chance, despite the fact that his leg muscles quivered every time he stood. He figured the munitions stores would serve his purposes whether he located his own gun or stole one of theirs.

He pushed himself up off the bed and coughed.

The room tilted, with the floor rising to meet the walls at an angle, and he threw out an arm to brace himself against the log wall. He tried to control his breathing.

Anna examined his face.

"You're not going anywhere," she told him.

He tried to protest, but she gave him a gentle push and he landed on the bed with a thud.

"I'll check the shed," she said.

He struggled to a semi-upright position.

"Anna?"

She turned back and looked at him while she zippered her jacket. "Yeah?"

"Bring me a gun. Any gun."

He fell back against the pillow and tried to catch his breath.

Anna nodded and pulled the door open.

Bricker, Rollins, and Lydia stood just outside the cabin. Rollins and Lydia had their rifles drawn and aimed at Anna's gut.

"Going somewhere, honey?" Bricker said in an unnatural high, strangled voice.

Anna said nothing.

Gavin sat up, ignoring the spinning room.

Bricker stood just inside the doorway and smiled at him, wild-eyed.

This is going to end badly, Gavin thought. Then he collapsed.

He regained consciousness to find that his hands were cuffed together. He turned his head. Anna sat on the ground near the bed, her hands also cuffed.

"Where are they?" he said.

She looked up at him, and he winced.

Her lip was split and swollen. One eye was also puffy—a faint purple bruise already forming around the socket.

"Jeffrey's trying us in absentia. He has my phone, with the log of the calls we made. And he knows we helped the kids leave. The group is going to vote on the punishment for my treason and your aggression against the movement, but there's only one choice," she said in a defeated, flat voice.

"What's the choice?"

"Firing squad."

45

Leo and Sasha sat in the SUV, drinking gas station coffee in silence. They'd taken up the vigil in the spot that the state trooper had recently vacated, judging by the tire tracks in the snow.

It was a good location, Leo decided. Slightly elevated, with a clear sight line to the camp. He was confident they would see lights or moving vehicles, but they were far enough away to avoid being discovered by foot patrols on the campgrounds, thanks to the elevation.

When he'd called to tell Anna that her children were safe, he'd asked her to check in with them in an hour. They had another twenty minutes to wait.

He glanced over at Sasha. She was staring

intently at the tan swirl patterned on her Styrofoam cup.

"You okay?" he asked.

She flicked her eyes away from the cup and met his gaze.

"Just thinking?"

"About?"

"About the mess I got Gavin into. That you lost your job. The end of civilized society. My pregnant sisters-in-law wandering around a city that's been targeted for a biochemical attack."

"Cheery. You forgot to add that Celia Gerig is dead," he said.

He saw the hint of a smile start to spread across her mouth and leaned over to cover it with a kiss, but she jolted upright.

"That's it!"

"What?" He pulled back and watched her face.

She nodded her head, and he could see her marshaling her argument, checking off the points to make.

"Tate's involved with the preppers."

"Oliver Tate?" He nearly snorted in derision.

"Hear me out. Last night, when I was working in his office, I knocked his desk blotter off the desk. Underneath it, there was a sticky note with Celia Gerig's name written on it," she said.

"You were snooping in Oliver's desk?

He was surprised at the sneakiness—Sasha's style was usually straightforward to a fault—but he didn't really care that she'd done it. After all, the man had just fired him for the sake of appearance. But, the notion that Oliver was mixed up with the preppers was ludicrous.

"No. I told you, I bumped the blotter." She shot him an offended look and then continued, "I didn't think anything of the note last night. My mind was on the appeal, I guess. But, I realized today that he was already in Wyoming when Grace learned about Celia Gerig. He had to have written the note beforehand."

"What are you suggesting?" Leo asked. Suspicion pricked at his nerves. If she was right about the note; something was definitely off.

"I think if Grace interviews the human resources people, she'll learn that somehow—either directly or indirectly—Tate got Celia that job."

Sasha stared across the car at him with placid, serious eyes.

He nodded. "Maybe. I'll call her—"

"That's not all," Sasha interrupted. "When I tried to call him this morning, his housekeeper or property manager or whoever answered the phone said that he and the girls left Wyoming last night."

"No, that's wrong. When he called to terminate me, he said he was between ski runs."

"I don't care what he said. He cut his trip short. So where is he?"

Leo stared at her. "I don't know. Where do you think he is?"

She jerked her chin forward, toward the distant campground. "There. With his daughters."

Anna's words—*the twins arrived late last night*—echoed in his mind.

"Tate's a prepper?" he asked.

She shrugged. "Yes. I mean, I don't know him at all. But if I'm right, it explains how Celia got the job and why she used her real social—he would have known that Human Resources would check that right away. Just say he believes a pandemic is coming and civilization is going to collapse—and, working at the company, I'm sure he's heard about nothing but the killer flu day after day. So he starts to believe it. He's a smart guy, but he knows he doesn't have the skill set to survive in a post-apocalyptic world. He decided to find a way to make himself indispensable to Bricker's merry band of lunatics. He used the resource he had: access to the vaccine."

She said it so matter-of-factly that it sounded almost rational.

"So, you think when Bricker put out the call for

the preppers to bug out, Tate hightailed it here from Wyoming?"

"Maybe. Or maybe he bugged out when Judge Minella denied our temporary restraining order—that was a sure sign something bigger was going on. It could have spooked him. All I'm saying is you should prepare yourself in case I'm right, and your former general counsel is holed up in the woods purifying water or skinning a rabbit."

Or loading a rifle, Leo thought, trying to imagine Oliver shooting a gun. His imagination failed him.

Flickering light caught his eye. He straightened and leaned forward, peering through the windshield.

"Do you see that?" he asked Sasha, pointing toward the campground.

She squinted. "It looks like fire."

"What the devil are they doing down there?"

"Connelly, are those *torches*?"

He blinked, clearing his vision, and then two shapes materialized in the darkness: shady figures holding the burning torches aloft.

Sasha sat the coffee in the cup holder and reached to open her door.

"What are you doing?" he said.

"Getting a better look."

He grabbed her hand to stop her.

"No, the interior lights will come on if you open the door. They'll see us."

She released the door with a sheepish look.

He removed his Glock from the center console. Then he loaded rounds into the magazine, one after another, until it was full, then he slid it into the shaft. The catch engaged, and he pulled the slide back until it sprung forward.

Sasha watched him but didn't speak.

They had to leave the SUV at some point if they wanted to see what was going on. He considered their options: open the doors and risk the figures below noticing the flash of light or start the car and move it to the large brush off to their right and risk them hearing the engine.

Sound didn't travel nearly as far as most people thought. But it was a quiet night.

Mind made up, he jabbed the key into the ignition and turned it to the 'Accessory' position. Then he pressed the button to lower the passenger window.

"Go."

Sasha clambered through the open window and dropped silently to the ground. He followed, less gracefully he was sure, but noiselessly.

They crept around to the front of the vehicle and stared down at the field. The flames danced wildly in the darkness.

A *crack* sounded and then echoed off the mountainside. Only one thing in the world made that sound—the sharp report of a rifle being fired.

A faint scream rose from below—a woman's scream.

Sasha scrambled down the hillside with Leo on her heels.

46

Sasha stumbled over the rocks and frozen ground, the wind stinging her eyes, and came to a copse of trees about a hundred yards short of the clearing.

Connelly came up behind her a few seconds later and leaned against a young pine tree.

They peered over the top of a row of sparse shrubs. Sasha gasped involuntarily and pressed her hand against her mouth.

The field was lit by the two torches, which were still burning and had been placed in two metal holders that stood twenty feet apart from one another. Between the posts, a young tree rose from the earth, straight and tall. The lower branches had been sawed off. A man's body was tied to the narrow trunk, his head slumped forward.

The flames flickered over his face, casting part of it in shadows, but even so, Sasha recognized Gavin. Dark liquid pooled in the snow at his feet, pouring from his forehead. He'd been shot between the eyes. Executed.

Across from his corpse stood a man and a woman, each holding a rifle, and, between them, a taller, older man. Sasha could tell by his bearing it was Bricker. He had the authoritative air of a military leader.

Bricker was not holding a firearm. Instead, he was holding a heaving, handcuffed woman. The woman had her head twisted to the side to avoid looking at Gavin's dead body. Bricker put a hand on her neck and wrenched her forward to face Gavin.

"Do you see what happens to those who cross us, Anna?" he said in a low, rough voice that carried on the wind.

She sobbed.

"I asked you a question."

"Yes, Jeffrey. I see," she said in a defeated voice. She slumped against him and said, "Just get it over with."

"You heard her, Lydia. Are you ready to see if you can match George's marksmanship?" Bricker said to the woman to his right.

"Yes, sir."

Bricker thrust his wife toward the man. "Cut him

down and line up the prisoner."

The man slid his rifle into a black nylon sling, slung it over his left shoulder, and began to drag Anna toward the tree between the torches.

Sasha heaved. She kept her hand clamped over her mouth in case she vomited.

Connelly leaned forward and whispered, "Once they're clear of us, I'm going to shoot the woman. I need you to disarm and take down the guy who has Anna. He's going to be distracted; it shouldn't be too hard. Okay?"

Sure. Piece of cake. In fact, she'd just taken a continuing legal education class on disarming murderous survivalists without harming their hostages. No problem.

She realized Connelly was waiting for an answer, his breath hot against her ear.

"Okay."

"Go when I say."

Anna and her captor passed in front of the shrubs. She was walking slowly and awkwardly, tripping over her feet. He dragged her forward, toward Gavin's inert body.

Sasha's throat tightened, and adrenaline flooded her system.

"Go!" Connelly said, giving her a small nudge.

She tucked her chin into her chest and ran. Her mind clicked through her options to overpower a right-handed man who had his hands full.

She settled on a tackle takedown. It was one of her least preferred moves because size and strength mattered when tackling.

But she didn't have time to engage him. Connelly was probably pulling the trigger already. So she ran hard and fast at the man, aiming her lowered shoulder at his head. As she neared them, Anna gasped.

The man turned toward Sasha and his eyes widened. He dropped Anna and groped over his shoulder for his gun.

Sasha sank down, gathering her power and momentum from her hips and legs, and exploded toward him, pushing up from the ground and encircling his knees with both arms as she crashed into him.

Behind her, she heard the report of Connelly's gun. Loud and close. Then an agonized yelp from the woman who was waiting to execute Anna.

The man tumbled backward and she held on. They landed with a thud on the hard earth. As they made impact, she scrambled to smash her right knee into his groin. As fast as she could, she crawled up and straddled his chest.

He reared up at her, but he was out of shape and clumsy.

She locked eyes with him, grabbed his hair with both hands, and snapped her neck back. She brought the crown of her head down hard on the bridge of his nose and heard the crunching of cartilage and bone. She released his hair and let his head bang down onto the ground.

She stayed on his chest until she was sure he was going to remain motionless, then she climbed off him and joined Connelly and Anna.

Lydia sat on the ground, one leg folded under her, the other extended. She cradled her shattered kneecap between her hands and rocked in pain.

Connelly held the Glock in front of him, aimed at Bricker's center mass, as he neared the man.

"This magazine was fully loaded," Connelly told him. "In case math's not your strong suit, that means I have sixteen rounds left."

Bricker glared at him.

"Where are your troops, Bricker? Cowering in their cabins?"

He didn't respond to Connelly. It was a question Sasha wanted to have answered, though. If they were about to be rushed by a mob of armed preppers, they were going to need more than sixteen rounds.

Lydia retorted, "We aren't cowards. Everyone's just used to the sound of shots being fired. We abut state game lands."

Connelly turned his attention to her.

"Slide your weapon away from your body."

She released her knee cap and did as he ordered.

She used both hands to push the rifle forward on the ground. It skidded to a stop about ten feet from Sasha.

"Cover your boy with that, Sasha." Connelly jerked his head toward the long-gun.

"He's not going anywhere. Trust me."

"Sasha, please," Connelly said.

She huffed out a breath and bent to retrieve the rifle. The wood felt cold even through her gloves.

She aimed it in the general vicinity of the prone man, who rolled from side to side, moaning. Air whistled through his busted nose.

She turned her head to see that Anna had taken the fallen man's rifle and was stalking across the field toward her husband.

"Connelly," Sasha said, her voice sharp with warning.

He looked back.

"Anna, don't," he said in a calm, low-key voice.

His words didn't seem to register. She just kept walking, the gun in front of her, straight at Bricker.

"Anna," he said in a firmer voice.

"He killed Gavin. He was going to kill me. My *husband* was going to execute me so I wouldn't interfere with his plan to infect hundreds of thousands of people with a deadly virus," she said, her voice shaking with anger and emotion.

Bricker stared at her. A slow smile spread across

his face.

"You won't do it, Anna. You don't have it in you," he said.

He wants his wife to shoot him, Sasha thought.

Anna raised the rifle, pointing it at his head.

"Anna, wait," Sasha said.

The armed woman didn't turn to look at her, but Sasha kept talking. "Look at him smiling. He wants you to do it. Why do you think that is?"

Anna didn't respond immediately, but Sasha thought her shoulders relaxed.

"The kids. If I kill him, I'll go to prison and won't be able to be with my babies. He wants me to lose the kids," she said after a long pause.

"That's right," Connelly agreed.

Anna stepped closer to her husband.

Sasha held her breath and waited for the gun to fire.

Instead, Anna spat. Her saliva dribbled down his face.

She dropped the gun to the ground.

Sasha took her by the arm and guided her away from her husband, the battered preppers, and Gavin's corpse.

Anna buried her head in Sasha's shoulder and cried—great gulping sobs.

"I'm so sorry about your friend," Anna wailed.

Sasha closed her eyes. So was she.

47

By the time the SWAT team arrived at the compound the pre-dawn sky was a light gray.

Anna had left hours ago. With Hank's blessing, Trooper Royerson had returned and picked her up to take her to a Comfort Inn to be reunited with her children. She'd be subjected to a series of long and unpleasant interviews in the coming days, but first she'd have a chance to hug her kids and try to explain how their lives had fallen apart.

Lydia and the other prepper, who identified himself as George Rollins, were the next to leave the scene. The first FBI agents to reach the camp had assessed their injuries, taken them into custody, and then bundled them into the back of an ambulance for the long trip to Clear Brook County General Hospital.

Next, they'd hustled Bricker into the back of their car to be interrogated.

Sasha and Connelly just stood in the field and kept vigil over Gavin's body.

Most of the remaining preppers stayed inside their cabins. The few who emerged did so with their hands up, looked around, and then ducked back inside. There was no uprising, no call to resist. They just waited to be told what to do.

At some point, someone had thrown a light green wool blanket over Sasha's shoulders and pressed a thermos of hot coffee into her hands. She was grateful for both.

She was more grateful for Connelly, who smoothed her hair back from the large swollen lump on her forehead and told her Gavin's death wasn't her fault.

Finally, the coroner arrived for Gavin.

"Wait," Sasha said.

She bent and folded the blanket over his body.

"You're right," she whispered, "this coffee is crap."

Then, she turned so she wouldn't have to watch the waiting medic zipper him into the black body bag.

Connelly put a hand on her shoulder, touching it

lightly, as if he knew how tender it was from plowing into Rollins.

They stood in silence and watched as Gavin was loaded into the coroner's wagon. When the door closed with a loud, final bang, they turned away in unison.

One of the agents stood a respectful distance away and cleared his throat.

Connelly turned to him.

"Sorry to interrupt, but we do need to interview you and Ms. McCandless about the shooting and, uh, scuffle. Separately. Just as a formality," he said.

"Sure."

"We're about ready to send the guys cabin to cabin rousting these losers. You want to wait or do it now?"

"Now is fine with me. Sasha?" Connelly said.

She was staring at the first cabin on the far left. Off to the side of it was a fire pit ringed with white stone. She recognized that fire pit. And the cabin.

"No one's come out of that cabin, right?" she asked Connelly, pointing at it.

"I don't think so."

She turned to face him. "Tate's in there."

Connelly looked at her for a long moment, then he said to the agent, "Actually, let's do the interview later. Come with me."

Sasha watched them approach the cabin, guns

drawn. Connelly was talking to the agent in a low voice.

"FBI!" the agent shouted as he banged on the door.

After a moment, the door opened and Oliver Tate's face, paler and considerably less cheerful than it had been in the photograph, flashed into view. Behind him, two teenage girls huddled together.

Connelly and the agent stepped through the doorway and closed the door.

Sasha wandered away to watch the hazmat-suited CDC workers trundling in and out of the cabin where Gavin had been quarantined. She stood just outside the hot zone they'd cordoned off.

The workers bagged and removed every piece of furniture and every stitch of bedding from the cabin, making trips back and forth like ants carrying away a fallen sandwich bit by bit.

On one of his return trips, one of the workers made his way toward her, his arms extended and his legs stiff in an awkward spaceman walk.

"Ma'am," he said, through his helmet, "is it true you broke a guy's nose with your forehead?"

She gave him a faint smile in answer.

The spaceman flushed but pressed on, "If you don't mind my saying so, that's badass, ma'am."

He raised his arm in an awkward salute and then turned to head back into the cabin.

Behind her, she heard Connelly's laugh.

She turned and he pressed his lips to her forehead and said, "Let's go home, badass."

And in that moment, she *was* home. It didn't matter if the mailing address was in Pittsburgh or D.C. or someplace else entirely, being home meant being with Connelly. The realization hit her like a wave, knocking her a little sideways.

"What about the interviews?" she managed.

"You were right about Oliver. Right now, they're more interested in talking to him than us, since he's good for federal charges. Of course, he's lawyering up, but the arresting agent will still get to cover himself in glory," he said with a wry grin.

"So, we can go?"

"We can go. They know where to find us."

"What about Tate's daughters?" Sasha asked.

"Mom's on her way and she's *pissed*. If I were Tate, I might be more worried about her than the FBI right now," Connelly laughed.

Sasha smiled up at him. "Let's get out of here."

48

They didn't go home.

Instead, Connelly drove to the lake house. Away from the news reports of the murder at the prepper camp and the belated, reactionary panic to the news that the Doomsday virus had been stolen and then recovered. Away from everything and everyone else.

By the time the adrenaline had drained from their bodies, replaced by sheer exhaustion, it was mid-morning. Connelly built a fire in the hearth. They wrapped themselves in blankets and stared at it, too tired to sleep.

After the noon news shows aired, their cell phones started to ring.

Naya. Hank. Her parents. Grace. Her brothers.

They let the calls go to voicemail, not yet ready to talk to anyone else.

Sasha sent out a text message that said they were okay and would be in touch soon, and then she closed her eyes and rested her head against Connelly's shoulder.

She thought she might actually sleep.

Then her phone buzzed and a number with a 202 area code popped up on the display. She knew she should recognize it, but through the cloud of fatigue, she couldn't place it.

"Who was that?" Connelly said.

"I'm not sure," she answered, returning her head to its spot on his shoulder.

His phone trilled to life. The same 202 number.

"Take it," Sasha said.

He picked up the call through his speakerphone.

"Hello?"

"Leo?" a husky female voice said.

Sasha placed the voice immediately—it was Colleen, the criminal defense attorney.

"What can I do for you, Colleen?" Leo asked in a cold, formal voice.

"Listen, I won't keep you long, I know you must need time to decompress, but, trust me, you want to hear this news," Colleen said in a sunny, amused voice. "Hey, is Sasha with you?"

"Hi, Colleen," Sasha said, mildly curious.

"Okay. I was at a breakfast meeting today with a friend who practices real estate litigation. Mainly he represents rich homeowners in front of the Historical Review Board when they want to appeal the denial of their permit to replace the windows that were on the house when John Adams slept there or whatever."

"This story needs to get much better very quickly," Connelly said.

"Patience, grasshopper. Anyway, he mentioned this sexy new trespass case he got in this morning. And, I must have rolled my eyes a little too hard, because he started dishing details."

"Colleen—" Sasha began.

"Fine. You two are no fun. So, some high society couple came into his office in an outrage, toting a nanny cam. The missus thought the maid was stealing her jewels, so they rigged up this camera in their closet, where she kept her jewelry armoire. They play back the tape, expecting to see Luisa shoving pearls into her pockets and what do they see instead?" Colleen paused for effect.

Sasha didn't know where Colleen's tale was headed, but she had to admit the criminal lawyer was a good storyteller.

"I don't know. What?" Connelly asked, intrigued.

Colleen burst into staccato laughter. "They saw their penthouse neighbor across the hall—one

Colton Anders Maxwell, Chief Executive Officer of ViraGene—sidling through a false panel that he'd apparently installed between the apartments' closets."

"Maxwell was stealing his neighbor's jewelry?" Connelly asked in disbelief.

"No, better. He was using the drop space between their closet and his as storage for his illicit goodies."

"Like what?" Sasha asked.

"Like five hundred thousand dollars' worth of silver ingots and an ampule of H17N10."

Sasha and Connelly sat in stunned silence.

Colleen hurried to explain. "Don't worry. The virus has been secured. The neighbors had the sense to call the police immediately, and I'm told your boy Bardman swooped in and took control of the scene."

"Oh, good," Sasha said, breathing out in relief.

"Yep. And Anna Bricker has given a statement that ties her husband to the silver, which he traded for a vial of the virus. Maxwell is dead in the water," Colleen cackled.

"Good," Sasha said.

"And, I also heard that Serumceutical's new security officer has already gotten the human resources director to admit that the Gerig woman had been a referral from Oliver Tate himself."

Good for Grace, Sasha thought. She'd get off on

the right foot with the board of directors if her investigation was both swift and thorough.

"How do you know all this?" Connelly asked.

"I don't reveal my sources," Colleen said. "But, I thought you might be interested in the news."

"Thanks for the call," Connelly said.

"No problem. You two take good care of each other," she said and hung up.

Sasha looked at Connelly and smiled. "Let's do that."

"Do what?"

"Take good care of each other," she answered, snuggling into his side.

49

Several weeks later

On Christmas Eve, they had dinner with the entire McCandless clan—plus Naya and Carl.

Everyone crowded around Sasha's parents' dining room table, ate too much food, and drank too much wine, shouting to be heard over the excited squeals of Sasha's nieces and nephews.

After a dessert of cookies and truffles, Naya and Carl peeled off to attend the pageant that Naya worked so hard on. The McCandlesses waved goodbye to them and then walked en mass to the neighborhood Catholic church, where Sasha had made her First Communion, and took up two full pews during the candlelit midnight mass.

From there, Connelly and Sasha each carried a heavy, sleeping child back to her parents' house, as her brothers helped their hugely pregnant wives navigate the snow-dusted sidewalks.

"Are you sure you don't want to stay here tonight?" Sasha's dad asked her, as she hugged him goodbye.

She shook her head. "We'll be back tomorrow afternoon, Dad."

"Merry Christmas, baby," he said.

"Merry Christmas."

Then she rescued Connelly from her mother, who had trapped him on the porch and was regaling him with her secrets for a juicy turkey.

"He'll taste it tomorrow, Mom," she said, giving her mother a kiss on her perfume-scented forehead.

"Okay, okay, you lovebirds go. Drive carefully, please," her mother said, waving them off the porch.

Sasha leaned back against the headrest of Connelly's SUV and closed her eyes. "I'm beat, let's go home and get some sleep."

She'd been tired for weeks. The aftermath of yet another near-disaster had been an exhausting gauntlet of interviews with the FBI, inquiries from the press, calls from concerned friends and former coworkers, and the increase in new clients who were inexplicably drawn to a commercial attorney with a penchant for highly publicized trouble.

Connelly didn't answer.

He started the car and pulled out from the parking spot wordlessly.

Half-asleep, Sasha hummed "What Child Is This" and wriggled her toes out of her high heels.

She was getting accustomed to having Connelly around again, she thought to herself drowsily. He'd had several job offers from around the country as a result of their notoriety—including an invitation to return to Serumceutical, which he turned down immediately. He said he was staying in Pittsburgh, beyond that, he had no plans. That suited her fine.

The SUV came to an abrupt stop far too soon for them to be home.

She opened her eyes to see if there had been an accident in front of them. There hadn't. Connelly was parked illegally in front of the USX Tower.

He took the keys from the ignition and smiled at her. "Come on."

She slipped the shoes back on and joined him outside the SUV.

They crossed the brick plaza and skirted the fountain to stand in front of the nativity scene.

She stared up at the stable and thought about the destruction that Bricker would have created if he'd released the Doomsday virus. She shivered.

"Are you cold?"

"No."

He tilted his head and studied her face.

"Merry Christmas, Sasha."

"Merry Christmas, Leo."

His eyebrow shot up his forehead. "*Leo?* Did you just call me *Leo*? That's twice this month. What's the occasion?"

"Christmas, you idiot."

ALSO BY MELISSA F. MILLER

Want to know when I release a new book?

Go to www.melissafmiller.com to sign up for my email newsletter.

Prefer text alerts? Text BOOKS to 636-303-1088 to receive new release alerts and updates.

The Sasha McCandless Legal Thriller Series

Irreparable Harm

Inadvertent Disclosure

Irretrievably Broken

Indispensable Party

Lovers and Madmen (Novella)

Improper Influence

A Marriage of True Minds (Novella)

Irrevocable Trust

Irrefutable Evidence

A Mingled Yarn (Novella)

Informed Consent

International Incident

Imminent Peril

The Humble Salve (Novella)

Intentional Acts

In Absentia

Inevitable Discovery

Full Fathom Five (Novella)

The Aroostine Higgins Novels

Critical Vulnerability

Chilling Effect

Calculated Risk

Called Home

Crossfire Creek

Clingmans Dome

The Bodhi King Novels

Dark Path

Lonely Path

Hidden Path

Twisted Path

Cold Path

The We Sisters Three Romantic Comedic Mysteries

Rosemary's Gravy

Sage of Innocence

Thyme to Live

Lost and Gowned

Wedding Bells & Hoodoo Spells

Wanted Wed or Alive

ABOUT THE AUTHOR

USA Today bestselling author Melissa F. Miller was born in Pittsburgh, Pennsylvania. Although life and love led her to Philadelphia, Baltimore, Washington, D.C., and, ultimately, South Central Pennsylvania, she secretly still considers Pittsburgh home.

In college, she majored in English literature with concentrations in creative writing poetry and medieval literature and was stunned, upon graduation, to learn that there's not exactly a job market for such a degree. After working as an editor for several years, she returned to school to earn a law degree. She was that annoying girl who loved class and always raised her hand. She practiced law for fifteen years, including a stint as a clerk for a federal judge, nearly a decade as an attorney at major international law firms, and several years running a two-person law firm with her lawyer husband.

Now, powered by coffee, she writes legal thrillers and homeschools her three children. When she's not writing, and sometimes when she is, Melissa travels around the country in an RV with her husband, her kids, and her cat.

Connect with me:

wwwmelissafmiller.com

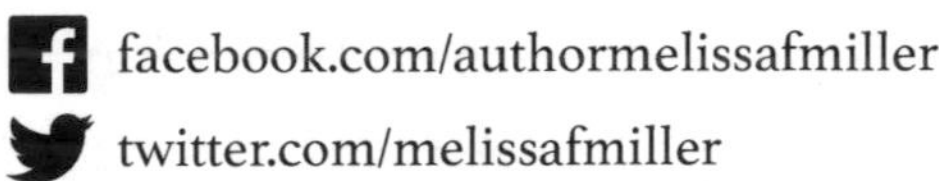

ACKNOWLEDGMENTS

Sincere thanks and appreciation to my editing and proofreading team, especially Curt Akin and Louis Maconi. Any mistakes or errors that remain are mine and mine alone. Thanks also to Colleen Young-Wetzel, whose generous contribution to the Amelia Givin Library earned her a role in this story. Finally, and always, my love and thanks to my understanding husband and children for their support.